Pie in the Sky

and
Other Illusions We Live With

Short Stories, Poems,
a Novella, and a Play

by
R. Luce

ISBN: 979-8-9922202-6-1 (Hardback)
ISBN: 979-8-9922202-7-8 (Paperback)
ISBN: 979-8-9922202-8-5 (Digital)

———

An earlier version of "Jimmy Valens" was published in the *Chiron Review* 123: 53-60 (Fall 2021).

An earlier version of "Thunder and Ice" was published in *Should This Book Be Banned? An Anthology*. Brienne Daugherty and Travis Ray, eds. Ohio Writers' Association, 2025, pp. 88-96.

———

Cover design and layout by the author. Microsoft 365 stock image (apple pie), photographer unknown.

Acknowledgments

I am indebted to Donald Weise
for his insights related to an earlier version
of this book
and to John Cunningham always.

You'll get pie in the sky when you die.
(That's a lie!)

Joe Hill, from the song, "The Preacher and the Slave"

Contents

INTRODUCTION, 1

ALL ABOUT LIGHT, a poem, 5

CHIAROSCURO, a short story, 7

THUNDER AND ICE, a short story, 15

DEAD RISING, a poem, 25

DAS VIERTE REICH, a poem, 29

JIMMY VALENS, a short story, 31

APPALACHIAN REQUIEM, a poem, 41

BLACK DIAMONDS, a novella, 43

ELAINE, a short story, 129

ABDICATION, a short story, 141

LABYRINTH AND MINOTAUR, a short story, 149

MY FATHER'S EYES, a poem, 163

BACKSTAGE, a short story, 165

GRAYSON FAMILY GATHERING, a play, 177

JAR IN THE RAIN, a poem, 249

NOTES FROM A LIFE NOW FLEETING, 253

ENDNOTES, 269

Introduction

I once thought that by the time I was an old man, I would have figured out life's meaning. Sometimes, I kind of, maybe, sort of, think I've got a handle on what my own life has been about, but as for the rest of humanity I'm still pretty much lost—particularly right now as I try to understand the intense hatred, selfishness, and lust for power and control on the part of so many people in my country and elsewhere in the world. At no other point in my life have I been so keenly aware of the beliefs I have lived with all my life about truth, justice, and the American way [ala Superman], the power of "We the People," and the declaration that "all men [human beings] are created equal" and have unalienable rights ... these, it would seem—as exemplified by our current leaders—are not what guide our decisions and define our worth on this planet after all.

I had already become disillusioned long ago by the messages we have absorbed through the culture as "the way things are": when all else fails, family is what you can count on; anybody can be successful if she or he works hard; we live in the greatest country in the world; we will be rewarded in heaven; etc. The clichés pile up. In reality, most of them constitute "pie in the sky"—ideals that may or may not be true in some, many, or even most cases, and certainly not for everyone. In fact, for many of us, they are flat-out lies, dreams we wish life was about.

This is a book about the many illusions we live with, their consequences, and the realities of day-to-day survival. As I have gone through the process of making the words that follow, many people who identify with Trumpism and the MAGA movement are demonstrating clearly that they cannot and will not accept a concept of themselves as co-equals in the shared space of the United States living alongside people who may have different skin colors, backgrounds, beliefs, customs, and opinions. Collectively, they are railing against diversity of thought and perspective and seem to gain much of their self-esteem through the hatred and oppression of others and a desire to destroy the concept of democracy and constitutional government. They don't like the term *fascism*, but it is what they espouse. They are obsessed with power and control exclusively determined by wealthy white men free from all negative consequences for their actions: oligarchy and autocracy. Donald Trump, their champion, is busily assuming the role of Fuhrer/Il Duce. Trump's sycophants and the MAGAs (a minority within the US) are becoming ever more vicious and violent toward people who challenge their views of what person-hood means. They are working to determine what is and is not acceptable in American life in general, in scientific inquiry, in teaching within our schools and universities, in our legal system, and elsewhere. They behave lawlessly, believing they are immune from any and all consequences because the rules are whatever they declare them to be. Unless their lawlessness is checked, our freedom to read and write what we wish and our ability to access the broad spectrum of the arts in general will be controlled by the state. Any illusions we may have had about what America was prior to 2025 are dissipating. Oppression grows on a daily basis.

Pie in the Sky is likely to join those works already being censored. The short stories, novella, poems, and play in this book deal with the human struggle to survive within the confines of our culture. It touches upon illusions we have about such things as what living meaningfully actually means; what it means to love self, others, and ideas/ideals; what we accept about others who are unlike ourselves—people sometimes living at the fringe of mainstream cultural expectations. It is also a book about disappointment: my disappointment in those who have chosen to hate, to impose upon others, to give little and take much, and to willfully create pain, hardship, and suffering for their fellow human beings in order to satisfy their own lust for power and wealth.

The title, *Pie in the Sky*, comes from a line in the Joe Hill song, "The Preacher and the Slave"[1] (1910), an anti-Capitalist protest song specifically targeting the Salvation Army and its preaching about accepting poverty and suffering in this world to gain assurance of a rich afterlife: Pie in the sky! The lyrics challenge the dishonesty coming from what Joe Hill referred to as the "Starvation Army" and its religious leaders. It also takes potshots at the Capitalist system's leaders ... each taking advantage of the working poor ("work slaves") to line their own pockets. I can't help but think about how the title is a metaphor for the way many Americans live their lives: clinging to a myth that if they try harder, work more feverishly and save their pennies, they or their children or grandchildren, will "make it," (whatever that might mean to them). Others cling to the notion that they just have to accept what life throws at them—"it is what it is"— and suffering will buy them a ticket to heaven when they die: their vision (illusion?) of finding meaning in life by dying.

At times, the book deals with issues that may be uncomfortable for some readers. I believe that all art must challenge readers in one way or another, or it is merely decoration. However, everything in the work is intended to suggest that even in our current state of crisis, we are not without hope. The human condition can be better than it is, but we may have to come to terms with the past: the vision of America as it grew, what we did right, and what we didn't do so well or didn't do at all to become the country we might still be. Like William Faulkner, I believe, "The past is never dead. It's not even past" (*Requiem for a Nun*, Act 1, Scene 3, spoken by Gavin Stevens). Of course, Faulkner is not talking about the minute details of our individual lives that can easily disappear; he is referring to human nature, the impact of culture to carry beliefs and values from one generation to the next, and the notion that the past (our basic instincts, combinations of cultures and our individual, familial and collective histories) shapes who we are and what we do as individuals and as members of our various communities for good or ill. Some of the stories and poems in this collection are set in times long gone. However, the issues dealt with are as relevant to today as they were within the timeframes of the stories, particularly as they refer to humankind trying to make sense of unanswerable questions about the meaning of meaning.

An Aside

All creative writing reflects the author's interests and knowledge. However works of fiction can be deceptive. Authors take on personas to tell their stories. They stretch truth, make it fit their purpose; and yet good writers always seek to tell a truth greater than the individual works of fiction they create. That is what I have tried to accomplish in each piece. All of the works in this book are works of fiction with the exception of "Notes from a Life Now Fleeting," the book's final entry. That piece provides samples (actual experiences) of my life that pertain to the theme of the book as a whole. I have written as honestly as I can what I remember, what it meant to me to grow up poor believing in the illusions I had of fitting into the larger culture, myths, and realities of America and what the cost of "making it" has been. It is personal, nonfiction, and was painful to write, but necessary.

All About Light

ONE

The Impressionists knew it:
Everything changes in light—
its "on,"
its flickers (fluctuations, if you will)
and its "off."

I like to say,
so much depends
not merely "upon a red wheelbarrow,"
but where the wheelbarrow sits,
when it's seen
and how it's used

and upon whimsy of clouds and shudders of air
what a thing is called, by whom,
and why

and the mind's eyes'
capacity to perceive
unstoppable alterations:
their resulting points
and counterpoints ...
and shadows defining what we think
we see, those
we lay upon the earth
ourselves and those laid within
our blood and bones
by others dead or dying."

TWO

Today I saw a photograph"—

"black and white" people call it,
despite its many shades of gray—

a print an old friend dropped into
a Facebook box:

"New Year's Eve 1959," a memory:
a parental resurrection.

A man and woman, husband and wife,
on yellowing emulsion that is eating the image
of a "classic beauty" and a drunk.

Both are dead the poet said, the son
who had told his father to his face
he had failed
and loved him anyway.

It is an image not unlike the few
fading pictures of children
who were my parents
and not unlike those who were
parents of my friends:

drunken fathers,
ineffectual mothers—

Moonlit rooms of our youth
closing in upon us like coffin lids
to hold the last space of our bodies.

Chiaroscuro

M ark LaZar, lying on his bed, stared at the space above him. He told himself that he wished his ability to sleep worked like a light switch: on and off by command. There. Not there. But it didn't. Darkness did not mean sleep. It meant only the absence of light and the distractions that come with it. It meant thoughts and images, fragments of meaning, and being alone.

Frustrated, he rolled over onto his side, used his hand to find the nightstand and let his fingers stumble across the myriad things strewn over it—cigarette wrappers, Faulkner's *Absalom, Absalom!*, a heavy glass ashtray, 1972's pocket calendar that had lain there ten months beyond any value, and miscellaneous slips of paper on which he'd written reminders of things he had forgotten or would still forget to do.

"Goddamn it," he said out loud as he waved his arm back and forth over the debris trying to find the postmodern lamp's bowed body. When he found it, he felt his way to the click-stub that brought light back into the room. He sat up against the headboard and then picked up the cigarette pack and lighter that had eluded him. He watched his blue-gray smoke drift toward the ceiling and dissipate. The thought came to him that a writer without something to write is a danger to himself and others. The words weren't original or clever, and he wasn't sure of what he had meant—various renditions of the theme arose until he was sick of them and rubbed the hot end of his cigarette against the ashtray to kill it.

He flung his legs over the side of the bed, leaned over and picked up his notepad and pen, looked back at the few pages he had not yet torn from the binder and thrown across the room. After a moment, he drew big Xs across them, called them "shit" before ripping the ink-stained papers from the bound edge, tearing them in half and then half again before pitching them into the space in front of him. There was nothing poetic like "autumn leaves floating on the breeze" about their dead clump drops to the cheap vinyl floor. He stared at the now wordless pad, felt it staring monstrously back at him, threatening him, yelling at him, "Don't waste your time. Find something else to do with your life!"

He picked up his pen, jabbed it like a knife into the heart of the pad with the intensity of a jilted lover killing the woman he loved rather than let another man have her. He sent pad and pen flying to where the day's earlier versions of crumpled paper balls had accumulated around a trash can. The tantrum ended with him wishing he were capable of weeping or somehow removing the emptiness that only an artist knows when he can't create; and even worse, when he is creating but what he's creating is beneath him, beneath his desire to test his limits, beneath what he sees and hears in his head but can't translate through his fingers onto the page.

"I've got to get out of here, think about something else!" he said out loud through clenched teeth. With that, he pulled on his clothes, picked up his keys and wallet, and walked out, closing the door with a slam worthy of a lover's fight.

As he walked along the dark peopleless street trying to free himself of his frustration, he looked up at the silhouettes of treetops against the October sky, thought about the crescent moon as a scythe slicing them into brush piles, thought of the wads of paper that lay in his room and in the back of his mind, thought of Rilke's metaphor of locked rooms and Whitman's lilacs and the gravity of Faulkner, and then, his own weak attempts to write anything worthy of such comparisons. He imagined himself melodramatically standing over his heaps of ink-covered paper scraps, yelling at them as Michaelangelo might have done with his sculptures: "Breathe, damn you! Breathe!" He imagined a sledgehammer in his hands beating a misshapen block of marble into dust.

Red's Place was a neighborhood bar that he liked. As he turned the corner from Third onto Walnut, he saw the yellow lights shining over the bar's entrance door. Approaching the building, he could see through the large glass windowpanes a sparse collection of people, mostly what he imagined were male/female couples sitting at tables—lonely in their togetherness—like those in an Edward Hopper painting. When he grasped the knob and stepped beyond the heavy oak door, he nodded to a couple who had looked up from their table. Red, busily working at the bar, stopped long enough to give him a crooked smile.

"Red" Barker, was a chunky, middle-aged woman with pasty skin and dyed neon-red hair— her trademark. As usual, she was wearing a white, too-tight T-shirt that accentuated her sagging breasts in her overwhelmed bra. When she finished with the drinks she had been making, handed them to the customer and collected his money, she asked Mark, "What can I get you, Doc?"

As he waited for the Warsteiner to be brought out of the back room, he waved acknowledgment to another couple that had looked up at him as he turned his back to the bar to sweep the room with his eyes for people he might know. In a darkened corner were Glen Isherwood and Kelly Matlin, both employees of the university who liked to believe that people would keep their mouths shut about seeing them there holding hands, flirting, talking intimately with one another several nights a week, their spouses either oblivious or powerless. Other "usuals" sat at their usual spots talking with their usual acquaintances, drinking their usual drinks. He didn't recognize the two men who sat on stools at one end of the bar talking quietly and seriously to one another as if discussing a caper on the eve of its execution. As he turned to his right, he saw Carl Angler who sat at the dark end of the bar looking at him, waiting for acknowledgment, raising his glass, and motioning for Mark to join him.

"Anything else I can get you, Doc?" Red pushed the bottle and frosted glass at him after he acknowledged Carl's invitation.

Mark smiled at her as he watched her over-painted lips crack into that misshapen smile made by the loss of teeth on one side of her mouth. "Get me the talent of an artist, and kill the 'professor,' Red." She laughed at him like she understood, but both she and he knew she didn't.

"Wish I could do it for you, Doc. Got no magic tonight. Three bucks, my friend."

Though he knew it was pointless to say it, he said it anyway, "There's no magic anywhere tonight, Red," and he laid four ones in her hand.

He carried his beer to the space beside Angler, shook his hand, and sat on the tall stool. "What's happening, *Professor* LaZar?" Angler asked, emphasizing the word professor like it was an obligatory title owed to someone with a PhD no matter how informal the meeting. Mark responded in kind, over-emphasizing the word professor to fulfill his part in the cliché of uncomfortable human interaction. They were not friends. Mark knew Angler only because the theater and English departments were in the same building, and they interacted occasionally in the hallways, the mail room, and when they shared the one elevator that existed in the building.

"What brings you out tonight?" As Mark asked the question, he looked at Carl's reddened face, noticed the glassy look of his eyes, the tiny drooping of the lip, the tightening of the skin on his forehead. The signs suggested he'd had several drinks—maybe one too many already, and he ordered another shortly after Mark joined him.

"Just having a few. Tired of reading student papers."

"I hear that one." The line fell out of Mark's mouth like the meaningless "good morning," "afternoon" or "evening" spoken in response to a store clerk trained to greet anybody coming through the front door. He wondered why men, himself included, had such difficulty getting a conversation going that moves beyond some superficial topic related to work or sports. He toyed with what would happen if he blurted out, "I've lost confidence in myself, can't find the motivations to write anything I care about, can't find a way to fill the emptiness in my life or fill the hole in my heart. And I am afraid." He wondered how Carl—or any other man—would react if someone said those words instead of asking, "What line of work are you in?" "What got you into that line of work," or "What did you think about that game last night?" as if every male watches all sports all of the time and likes what the other watches and likes and as if a man's ability to rehash a game or demonstrate status in the work world is the true measure of his existence and worth as a human being.

"Mostly, I don't like hanging out in an empty house," Carl said. "Glad to have someone to talk to." He had shattered the vulnerability zone so carefully protected by most men, expressing a bit of his history (experiences of not being in an empty house) and his loneliness and desire for interaction with another person (anyone was better than no one). Men most often danced around talk of feelings except in their loose-lipped utterances under the spell of alcohol or drugs, and on the following day claim "it-was-the-alcohol/drug-talking" cliché to deny what had been said.

Listening to the slight slur in Carl's voice, Mark wondered if Carl might be more drunk than he had originally thought, but then he seemed to be thinking well enough. "I don't mind being alone when I'm writing well," Mark said.

"Are you writing well?"

"No. Not happening. It eats at me. Can't sleep. I thought a beer might help."

"Yeah! Sleep! Still haven't worked that one out. Did theater a lot of years. Theater people rarely go to bed before 4 a.m. or get up before noon ... or, at least, those were the preferences. Makes life hell now that I'm teaching. Never have gotten into the rhythm of going to bed early and teaching at eight or nine a.m."

Carl continued talking about his life as an actor, but Mark's thoughts drifted from the words. He wondered what Carl might have looked like in his prime when the skin around his eyes was tighter and his good looks had the diamond-fire light of youth behind them. Carl's strong chin was a classic, a Kirk Douglas chin. In a different era, he probably could have made a career on his chin alone. He was still good looking for a middle-aged man when you could push aside the sadness that lay upon him like face powder after "lights out." He caught the gist of Carl's last few words, and asked, "Do you miss it, Carl? The theater?"

"Yeah. Sometimes. Lots of times, actually. Don't miss the starving side of it. Loved the people ... well, except the prima dons and donnas ... pains in the ass."

Mark gave a half-hearted laugh, swallowed some beer, looked around the room at the diminishing number of people. For a brief moment, he held an amorphous image in his head of people leaving the bar to return to their something or nothing lives, depending upon their points of view, their dreams and aspirations alive or dead, their hopes or hopelessness. He looked at Carl, thought about when he'd encountered him on campus. He liked the way Carl carried himself like the cocky lead actor in a play written for a younger man, and for his strong, articulate voice that carried a hint of tenderness beneath the male bravado. From somewhere deep within himself, Mark found himself wanting to touch this guy, just make some contact, feel human skin against his fingers. He found himself reaching out but pulled his hand back to his pant leg as Carl's words broke through to his conscious mind: "Seriously, though, I do miss it. The feeling of doing good work. There is nothing like it. The connection to the audience. Knowing you've got them by the balls. Classroom doesn't give me anything like that feeling."

"I'm surprised," Mark responded. "Feels like a performance to me ... trying to keep them engaged, wanting to come back for more. I'm exhausted after every class."

"People keep telling me that. I wish I could feel more excitement for it."

Carl continued to talk, but Mark's mind had begun drifting beyond the words and their meaning once again. He looked into the mirror over the bar, looked at his own face, the writer's face with its age settling upon him like dust. He thought about his own frustrations like the disreputable stubble that formed on his cheeks on a Monday morning after an unmanicured weekend, a weekend of anger at his lukewarm words that lay like water stains on paper, the best he had been able to create for weeks. Suddenly, he didn't want to be here in this bar any longer listening to Carl's woes and tales of glory days. He didn't want to be anywhere. He didn't want to be. Yet, he tossed in "uh huhs" and "sounds great," and "Really?" where they fit like a robot doing a task at a pre-programmed prompt. After a short period of time, he drank the remainder of his beer to get it down and done with and made some poor excuse for leaving, something about preparing for a class, recognized that whatever it was, it was lame and supposed Carl knew it.

Carl's lower lip quivered as the two men stood up behind their stools. When Carl attempted a smile, he couldn't quite find it for the nervousness taking command of his face. Instead, he put his hand on Mark's arm and said quietly, "We don't have to be alone tonight." Their eyes locked momentarily as Mark pondered what he was hearing, the potential for a story. Then, he put out his right hand, grasped Carl's and shook it, felt the moisture of their hands mingling, and said, "I'm sorry. I can't ... I'm sorry."

Carl's gaze dropped to the floor like a spilled drink as he said, "I understand."

Mark turned and walked away, closing the saloon door behind himself, wondering momentarily if he had said all the required things about enjoying the conversation and "let's talk again sometime," or "maybe another time." Tried to believe that he really didn't care.

He was outside the door and began breathing in the night's sweet breath, breathing it in deeply and expelling it in steady, wind-like streams as if cleansing his lungs of smoke from a house fire. He took a few more steps and turned back to look at the closed door of the bar. He thought of locked rooms and Rilke. He spoke, pointing his words at the heart of the door, "No! You don't understand, Carl!" Then he headed home under the streetlights, knowing soon he would enter the lightless portion of the street and walk gently into that blackness. Until then, he would think of how different lamps on different poles cast his shadows from two different directions at once upon the uncaring street. "How fitting," he heard himself say out loud to the deaf ears of the night.

Thunder and Ice

Will Beesom woke up long after morning had been chewed, swallowed, and fully digested. But for all he knew, it could have been almost any time of day. He only knew that there was enough light coming through the dirty window to reject the concept of nighttime. He had no watch to look at, no cell phone, and there were no clocks on the walls. Time and place were concepts that other people built their lives around; he did not. He had been awakened by February's cold accumulating on his skin, sinking into his bones, and agitating his brain to do something about the shaking of his body. Though he had tried to swat it away like a bothersome fly that chooses a spot of bare skin to crawl upon, the effort hadn't worked. The cold was a masterful dodger and would not be flicked away, could not be flattened by a hand crash, and would not leave unless all skin could be pulled beneath blankets or heavy clothing that Will didn't have.

When he sat up, his brain whirled in the after-effects of the drugs and alcohol. He tried to remember the previous day and night, what he had done, where he had been. The best he could conjure were shadows and flickering gray images like the snow and noise of an old TV absent an antenna. His head hurt; his stomach threatened to make him wretch. He raised his hands to catch his face as it fell forward into them. After a minute or two, he raised his head again and started taking in the space where he found himself. He was on a stained sofa—some shade of brown—that reeked of embedded sweat and cigarette smoke. Everything he could see looked like it hadn't been cleaned for years. Mold accumulated on the walls around the windows. No warmth from a furnace or from loving care had been here for a long time. There were other people in the room: two couples lying on the floor—each of the pairs pressed against one another for warmth—and a man sitting low in a ragged chair smoking a cigarette and tapping ashes onto the floor as he stared at Will.

"Spare a cigarette?" Will asked. The man said nothing and held out the pack. Will stepped unsteadily over the bodies between them and took a stick from the half-empty pack. The man reached into his pants pocket for a lighter, plunged the gas and turned the flint wheel to spark a flame.

"Where the hell are we?"

The man stared back at him, took a drag on his cigarette then responded, "You just said it, man: Hell."

"Where's the goddamn heat? It's freezing in here."

The man looked at Will, and spoke in a flat voice, "Ain't nobody paying for heat here."

"Where the hell am I? For real."

"John's place." Seeing the confusion on Will's face, he added, "Canaanville, man. Where did you think you were?"

Will thought about asking who the hell John was and how he ended up someplace called Canaanville but realized he didn't care. "How far are we from Columbus?" he asked.

"Maybe sixty, seventy miles," the man said before turning his head away and staring out through the smoke-dulled window.

"Where's Bobby?"

"No idea, man. Don't know no Bobby." It was said to the window.

"He was with me."

"Don't know how to help you, man."

Will finished his cigarette, crushed the hot ash against the sole of his shoe, and tucked the butt into his pocket as he stood up and began looking carefully at each of the bodies lying on the floor, their faces pressed against the worn carpet or into the bodies of the people beside them.

Bobby wasn't among them. "Bobby!" he yelled. "Bobby, where are you?"

"What the fuck?" a man's voice from down the narrow cattle shoot of the trailer's hall shouted threateningly. "Quiet down!"

"Jesus, man!" the guy sitting in the corner chair said.

Unfazed, Will went down the pathway toward the three doors beyond the destruction of a bathroom. When he opened the first of the three, a man lying on the floor beside two others told him to get out. Will said he was looking for Bobby.

"Ain't no fucking Bobby in here. Get out!"

The next door opened to a tiny room that would have been overcrowded with a single bed and a small dresser had they been there. Bobby was lying on the floor in the fetal position shaking violently and making puppy-like sounds of suffering. When Will spoke, Bobby raised his head, his eyes the eyes of a rabid dog. Slobber rolled down his chin. His fists were clenched.

Will spoke to him again, "It's me, man: Will! It's me, Bobby. You're safe."

Bobby struggled to study the face in front of him, confirm the reality of him and finally mush-mouthed the words, "Didn't know where you were. They're gonna kill us."

"Ain't nobody gonna hurt you. I won't let 'em." Will kneeled, lifted Bobby's upper body, and wrapped his arms around him. He held him close for a long while trying to warm him up, lay his hand on Bobby's face, and made small circular motions with his fingers against the soft whiskers and the whiskerless skin behind the ears. When he could feel the heat being passed back and forth between them, Will whispered, "Let's go home," kissed the side of Bobby's face and lifted the skinny bag of bones Bobby had become to a standing position.

"I'm scared, Will."

"I've got you, Bobby. I'll take care of you." He took the zipper ends of Bobby's thin, black nylon coat, connected them, and slid the tongue up to the top of the zipper teeth, holding him by one arm as they walked. When they reached the entrance door, he looked at the man in the low-slung chair and asked, "Hey, Buddy, which way to Columbus?" The man, no longer looking at him, mostly staring into space, turned toward the window, and lifted his left hand and index finger, aiming right. Will pulled Bobby through the door and closed it behind them.

With each vehicle sound coming up behind them, Will turned and gave the universal hitchhiker's thumb. After a couple miles of stumble-walking and being shunned by drivers in dozens of cars, an old, red Ford pickup truck with rusted fenders and numerous dents and scrapes, pulled off the road and waited for them to come up to the side of the truck. Knowing that putting Bobby beside a stranger was likely to freak him out, Will opened the door, thanked the old woman at the wheel, took hold of the front of Bobby's jacket, and climbed in, pulling Bobby up into the cab behind him. Will told Bobby to shut the door. Robot-like, Bobby tried to obey but almost fell out. Will caught him, pulled him into place, and then lay across Bobby's legs to reach the door and pull it hard against the frame.

Feeling like he owed some kind of explanation, Will—through his chattering teeth—told the woman he was sorry for the fuss. Bobby just wasn't feeling well. He thanked her again for the ride.

"You boys looked awfully cold out there. Where you headin' to?" The woman's voice was gentle on Will's ear.

"Columbus," Will replied as he tried to control the shaking of his body.

"That's just where I'm headin' to.

"Seriously? That's great."

You from around here?"

"No. Columbus," Will said.

"What's got you boys way out here on such a cold day?"

"It's a long story," Will said as Bobby pulled his knees up high, planted his feet on the seat, and wrapped his arms around his knees as he shivered against the door and the window glass. "Just as soon not bore you with it." He hoped she'd drop the subject so he didn't have to make something up to explain when he had no idea whatsoever.

There was a brief silence before the woman said, "I'm Elma Worthing. You got a name?"

"I'm Will; my buddy here is Bobby ... like I said, he's not feeling too good today."

He and Bobby rarely got rides from women, probably for fear people have of picking up drug addicts, rapists, murderers, or all three for the price of one. This one didn't seem the least bit concerned about any of those things. She seemed to want to talk like he was a real person, as though she knew him, like he wasn't just a hophead hanging out with a tweaker. He told himself she sounded kind of like a grandmother he sometimes imagined—not his own, but one of those good grandmothers you see on TV around the holidays. He tried to look at her as much as one could while sitting side-by-side in the confines of a too-narrow seat in a rattling metal box bouncing along the pavement at sixty miles an hour, even when the speed limit was seventy. She was bundled up in a coat unbuttoned at the top, scarf, hat, and boots; it was difficult to make much judgment about her other than she had a kindly face of sagging skin, wisps of gray hair hanging out from under her toboggan hat, a hint of gloss on her lips. Her wrists, or at least what little of them he could see above her gloves, were thin and wrinkled. Her voice was old-woman thin—a voice that presides not because of strength but because of self-respect and respect of others. She engendered a vision of an extended network of friends and a Hallmark-card-like family that always comes home for the holidays: hearth fire, candles, the smell of fresh-baked, made-from-scratch pies.

The warmth coming from the truck's heating system felt good on Will's feet and legs, slowly making its way up his body and allowing him to unzip his coat. He asked Bobby how he was doing and if he was getting warmed up. Bobby shook his head up and down, breaking the side-to-side motion that had been going on for the past several minutes. "Why don't you unzip your jacket, Bobby, so you don't get too hot."

With trembling hands, Bobby tried to obey and fumbled for the zipper. Seeing him struggling, Will took over, found the zipper tongue, and pulled it down, releasing both flaps of the jacket. Bobby was fidgeting more extensively than he had been even moments before, sometimes it seemed as if he wanted to bounce in his seat, and he was mumbling to himself. Will put his right hand on the inside of Bobby's left thigh and whispered to him, "It's okay, man. It's okay."

Will felt himself twitching now and then too. He worried about the woman and feared her stopping and putting them out. He worried about how she might be feeling with him wedged up against her so tightly that he could feel the contents of her coat pocket against his hip, wondering if she felt him shaking as his body fought the drugs and a desire for more. For a long time, she made no comments that suggested she was aware of anything other than getting down the road and helping Bobby and him get out of the cold. She made small talk about hitchhiking, the weather, and what the world was coming to. Will tried to reply politely when she asked a question, tried to remember to express some kind of interest in whatever she talked about ... to, at least, say "no kiddin'" in the pauses, but when she stopped talking and gave him room to contribute, he could think of little to say; he wished she would just deliver Bobby and him home without words, but words would be the price he paid for the ride.

After fifteen or twenty minutes of travel and Will's attempts to make small talk, she shifted the topic gently, "Looks like you guys have had a bit of a rough time, if you don't mind me saying so," the woman said.

Fear raced up Will's backbone: fear that she might get something out of him that would cause her to pull over and put him and Bobby out on the road again, "Yeah. Guess so," Will said warily. "Shows, huh? Sorry if we don't smell too good. Didn't get a shower this morning."

"The old smeller doesn't work that well anymore," the woman said. After a pause, she leaned forward trying to look around Will to Bobby, and asked, "How you doin' over there, Mr. Bobby?"

Will looked at her profile as she turned to focus on the road and watched her give an occasional glance toward Bobby to see if he was going to answer. Talking to himself more than to her, Bobby said,

"They're watching ... gonna kill us." He gripped Will's arm.

"I'm right here, Bobby. Come on, man. Relax. Alma's okay."

"Sounds like he's not doing too well," she said to Will, as though Bobby was out of hearing range.

"He'll be okay."

"Meth?" she asked in a matter-of-fact way. Will turned to her, wondering how in the hell someone like her could have a clue what meth is, let alone how it fucks with a user's head.

"That stuff's nasty shit, Will," she said, surprising him again.

"No shit!" Will responded, mimicking her use of the word and enjoying the interplay. "How's a nice lady like you know about stuff like that?"

"What? Because I'm old, I don't know anything, don't read, don't learn anything beyond my own generation? I've been around the block once or twice ... know about it because I was an ER nurse for a long time. Just retired two years ago. Seen a lot of that stuff come through the doors." She poked him with her elbow and smiled through the statement, "You boys look like you would be pretty good-looking young men if you got off the drugs."

"So, you're saying we're not good-looking?" he joked with her, though he felt the sting of remembering Bobby and himself growing up best friends, thinking themselves "hot" and believing that women would fall at their feet and other men would envy them ... a long time ago and a world away from this one.

"I'm saying that stuff isn't doing you any favors. That's all." She paused for a moment, and then added, "Sorry. Didn't mean to preach at you."

Will said, "No problem. I appreciate the ride."

"No problem," she repeated back to him as she rolled her eyes to the right like a parent to a teenager. Then she went silent, stared ahead at the highway except for the occasional glance in the rear-view mirror, and turned on the radio. Country music. Will kept his mouth shut about how much he hated it. He tried to shut it out, wished he could think of something to say to get the old woman talking again so she would turn it off, but he could think of nothing that might interest her. After a few miles of twanging guitars and mournful voices, he felt himself drifting toward sleep. He fought to hold his eyelids open as they rode for miles without talking, just listening to songs about crying at a bar over a lost love, driving 18-wheelers, cheating hearts, and old dogs. At one point, he felt Bobby's body turning toward him. Sensing that Bobby was not going to be able to control falling into him, he put his arm around him, pulled him to his chest, and held him as the lover he had been when they needed money and discovered the porn brokers would pay. It was nothing—just a job, no big deal—at least that's what they told themselves for a while. Then came the day when they lay together for themselves, not for money, but because they wanted to, and Will said he loved Bobby, always had, and Bobby said, "Me too." When he awoke to some man's gravelly voice singing about having honky tonk blues while a steel guitar screeched in the background, he wiped his eyes on his coat sleeve, and said to the woman, "Sorry. I nodded off there."

"You weren't out long. Don't worry about it. If you'd been bothering my driving, I'd have hit you with my elbow." She turned his direction briefly and smiled, winking her eye mischievously.

About five miles outside Columbus, Elma turned off the radio and spoke again. The abrupt stop in the monotony of the music and her words broke the hum of the motor and the clattering of the untethered tin of the beaten truck body, broke his fall off the razor-thin wire where reality and fantasy converged.

"Can I say just one more thing to you about the drug thing, Will, before we get you into town?" When he told her she could, she said, "If I asked you this question: 'Do you like your life and your future,' what would you say? You don't have to answer. Just think about it. And if you don't like the life you're living, I just want you to know that you don't have to keep living it this way. I don't know you. Don't know what's gone on in your life. It's none of my business. But if you want help, there are people who would help you and Bobby make some changes."

"Thanks, Elma. I'll think about it." He said it knowing he had thought about it many times, told himself he hated what he was doing with his life, and there were times he thought maybe he could do it—quit, that is—maybe tomorrow, or soon, maybe. He thought about waking up in a clean room under clean sheets and getting ready to go to work doing something that mattered, having money that he earned and had not stolen or sold his body to get... but then there was Bobby to think about.

As Elma pulled up to the curb on the corner of Fourth and Spring as Will had asked her to do, she said, "OK, boys! This is the end of the line." Will reached across Bobby to open the door and pushed him to move. "No, not here!" Bobby started yelling. "They're over there," he said pointing in the direction of the adjacent corner where people stood waiting for the light so they could cross.

"It's OK, Bobby. I know those people," he lied. "They're the good guys. I've got your back, man. Come on. Let's let Elma get on her way." Then they were standing outside the truck looking back through the open door, "You're a good person, Elma! Thank you for the ride and the conversation," Will said, and he meant it. When Elma wished them well, he closed the rusty, screeching door and waved goodbye. For a moment, he watched the beaten old Ford shimmy down the street until it was swallowed in the traffic and blocked from view by a bus. He told Bobby he had liked the woman, then turned and started walking.

They made their way down Fourth Street for a short distance, turned right onto McKee Alley, and went another four blocks beyond Grant Avenue. All the while Bobby was carrying on about the *theys* and *thems* and the cameras until he hit upon the question: "We gonna see the man, Will?"

Will put his hand in his left pocket, pulled out a wallet, took seventy dollars in cash and a credit card, and stuffed the loot into his pocket. "Got us covered, Bobby." He looked at Elma's picture on the license, stared at it, and rubbed his fingers over it. "I liked her," he reminded himself as he folded the leather casing, carried it like a spent cigarette butt to the trash bin near Faith Mission, leaving the library card, AAA and ACLU membership cards and license belonging to Elma Worthing caressed in the folds of old leather. He hesitated briefly, looked up at the sky, then dropped the wallet atop the heap of life debris dropped from the hands of many strangers.

Dead Rising

ONE

Books upon books,
petrol drenched.
Flames flash
upward to Nazis' delight:
Aktion wider den undeutschen Geist.[2]

High above the hate-thick tongues
embers rise,
their edges tinged yellow-orange
until beyond the heat in night's cold air
dissipation and death. . .
or so ignorant mobs suppose.

From behind their curtains, people watch,
feel themselves being burned alive,
stifle the screams of their own searing flesh.

Yet, the fascists stand sieg-heiling,
drunk with the absinthe of power
and oblivious to minute ashes falling back—
as prophetic code hate cannot decipher:
"time waits
like old bones laying in the streets for
pyrophytes to be unleashed."

TWO

Mealworms compete
amidst excremental heaps of rich men's waste
eating the fruit remains of old dreams . . .
dreams carved into tombstones here and there
where words weather and wear to unreadable indentations
on soft stones too soon wasting.

Past and future dine daily on excreta of the
children of children of humanity crawling
over their ancestors' bones
within the stench of power.
They know no past,
imagine no future,
despise "I am."
Just are.

I fear it will take dreams themselves
rising of their own accord
in the latent genes of generations hence
that like radon gas rising in a poor man's house,
tell a dumb device to make an unignorable
and odious noise.

THREE

Roads once led to necessary somewheres
and brought us back again
until Panzer divisions of anti-intellect
were unleashed upon us.

Now, those paths are once again
cratered by propaganda, deception,
fallen upon the topography of the world,
its flood plains of derision
its mountains of postcard
images in old keepsake books.

FOUR

I wait in the twilight
writing to I know not whom
waiting, hoping I survive through time
when I might teach my grandson to read
the earth and how
to listen intently
for first sprouts of hope
exploding into existence.

Das Vierte Reich³

Auschwitz,
Buchenwald
Treblinka, and Sobibor ...
their names come easily to mind
even now in twenty twenty-five.

Majdanek⁴, Kulmhof and Belzec
⁵take more time.

Now, there is Tecoluca, Matsapha,
and somewhere-Rwanda,
and prisons yet unnamed
and God-knows-where
chosen by men in suits of black and blue,
white shirts instead of brown,
and Windsor-knotted, Trump-red ties.

Those same men looking down
into the streets today, pissants
shouting and waving above their heads
vulgar declarations—now clichés—
"Fuck Trump!" "No King! No Tyranny!"
and "Save Our Democracy!"
doubtlessly demanding once again
return of freedoms filched
and fenced for pennies on the dollar.
Annoyed by yet another of these daily dins,
a reichman gazing upon this madding crowd

declares the obvious ... perhaps,
to reassure himself, or
perhaps, others in the room:

> "Bald werden solche Leute stumm gemacht.[6]
> They must ... they will ... be silenced ... soon."

But, his words fall unremarked
like dust in listless air the open window breathes
into this room of preening men
busily scrubbing their hands of humanity, scraping
barnacles of decency from their shells, brushing
blood from their fangs at well-maintained
and glistening
white,
men's
room
sinks.

Jimmy Valens

He was what most people would call "handsome" as only nineteen-year-old men can be. He wore innocence in the face above the muscular body made from the heavy lifting, tugging, pulling, and pounding that comes with farm work. He still had the young man's narrow hips, long, muscular legs, all the physical features a parent could wish for a child. And Jimmy had the eyes! Deep brown, dark eyes, set just deeply enough to be enticing, their moist surfaces catching and reflecting light in ways that would have been difficult for women to resist. However all of the structure clashed with the rumpled clothing he wore, his unkempt hair, lack of shoes, and the dingy, barren brick-walled room in which he sat—a room with nothing but a well-worn rectangular oak table and four chairs placed one to a side, each of which had long-since given up most of its varnish to the backsides of too many suspects and prisoners. Beneath the table and chairs was the gray-darkened, scraped, and scratched plank floor that had caught the sweat and drool of the guilty, the accused, and the too-drunk-to-figure-out. The bright June sun of 1873 lay itself on the floor, the table, and the young man's back in the shapes of barred windows.

What seemed most notable to Sheriff Travis as he came into the room was that Valens was absolutely still. None of the normal signs of nervousness about being put in jail, being questioned, perhaps facing retribution seemed to have settled into his appearance. Nothing about Valens showed guilt, shame, or fear—he simply looked tired, maybe bored with the fuss that kept him from sleeping. The officer who had been waiting with the prisoner got up from the chair opposite the prisoner that Travis would take. With his back to the prisoner, the deputy rolled his own eyes as if to say, "He's all yours, but he's not worth your time." Travis ignored the message, carefully watching Valens, who didn't shift his gaze from the wall as sheriff disturbed the scene by his entrance. Travis gestured to the deputy that he should take the spot at the end of the table where he was to sit and take notes during the interview.

John Travis had been a sheriff in Lanning County, Ohio, for ten years. He'd dealt with murderers and accused murderers, and had caught would-be murderers in the act during his tenure; they came in all shapes, sizes, and ages, and almost all of them showed some kind of fear, and almost all of them lied. They all outraged the community—that brutal taskmaster that wants instantaneous justice that no law-abiding sheriff was going to be able to provide. This case would be particularly scrutinized by an impatient populace. The public had been whipped into a frenzy by the morning paper's special edition which determined Jimmy was a guilty murderer of three people—though they had no specific evidence to support their claim. It was an election year. Like anyone running for office, the sheriff thought about how his opponent would make much of anything he said or did or didn't say or do in this case that had people already talking about lynching. He liked being sheriff; he did not like being a politician.

When Travis got up from his bed that morning, he looked in the bathroom's mirror and said to himself, "Just do your job; let the other stuff fall wherever it falls." At forty-one, he was still a good-looking man, had all his hair, kept himself physically fit. He was naturally tall and thin, deceivingly slight in comparison to the barrel-chested, fat-bellied sheriffs of surrounding counties. He had a countenance about him that muffled any apparent threat that other sheriffs projected with ease. He spoke softly, thoughtfully. He didn't argue. Had he not been wearing a badge, he could have been mistaken for a teacher, a preacher or a bank clerk. He liked it that he didn't give the impression of being intimidating, that people felt comfortable with him. It gave him the opportunity to talk people through difficult times and potentially explosive situations, but he had to admit that it was sometimes not to his advantage.

There were some who learned the hard way that Travis's appearance did not mean that he wasn't capable of doing his job or defending himself. Mike Laggars, a much larger man than Travis, found that out when Travis came into a saloon to remove him for causing a ruckus. When Laggers saw the sheriff, he looked him up and down and said, "You think you're taking me in. It's going to take you and three fat-assed deputies to get me out of here." Travis responded calmly, "Mike, I'd like you to come with me without a fight. We don't need to have it go down that way." Laggers laughed derisively, made an aggressive move toward Travis, "You son of a ..." When Laggers came to, he was in the back of a wagon with his hands behind his back in cuffs, his feet bound together with rope, and Travis sitting on the wagon seat beside the driver.

Over the next few days, the various local newspapers carried the story that Laggars couldn't finish his phrase before Travis had used a hard left-handed punch to his belly to pull the huge drunken man's arms downward in reaction to the punch. Then Travis landed a powerful right followed by a hammering left in quick succession to Laggars' jaw. Laggars made one attempt to respond with what looked like a wide looping right-handed punch swooping from his side like he was reaching around a tree to land it. Travis easily ducked it, then landed another body blow, and two more punches to the jaw, the blows seemingly intending to reach through the massive head to the back wall of his skull. The big man crumbled without ever landing a punch. Though reporters got numerous blow-by-blow eyewitness accounts of the fight, when they tried to get Travis's perspective on the story, all he would say was, "I did my job. That's what you pay me for." The papers often ended any accounts of the sheriff's activities with something to the effect of, "Best not to mess with John Travis, boys!"

Travis preferred low-key approaches to dealing with people: disarm if possible; get tough only when there is no other choice. Jimmy Valens was a special case: He was not known for his intellect; some people thought of him as a borderline imbecile. Additionally, he had, in his nineteen short years of living, already gained the titles of "town drunk" and "hell raiser." When he wasn't drinking or wasn't too far down the path of drunkenness, he was quiet around those he considered to be "respectable folks" and knew how to be polite to people ... as long as they didn't get on his nerves. The sheriff sat down calmly, placed his hands on the table that sat between him and the prisoner, folded them, leaned forward, spoke quietly, fatherly, "You look tired, Jimmy. You had any sleep?"

Valens looked at the wall opposite him to the right of Travis's body, and said unemotionally, in fits and starts, softly, "Nope. Not much ... got drunk yesterday. Next thing, I know, I'm here."

Travis asked if Valens knew what he was accused of.

The young man said, "People wakin' me up, askin' me questions ... about the Cranby's. Was people in the cell comin' an' goin' .... Some of 'em was reporters. They started askin' questions I didn't know how to answer. Too many people. I asked the marshal what I was supposed to do."

"Did you answer their questions truthfully, Jimmy?" Valens looked away from the wall to Travis's eyes momentarily. "Didn't wanna talk to nobody. Just wanted to sleep, but marshal says I gotta talk to 'em, tell 'em what I know so's I can get outta jail. An' he was the one who started asking questions and them other people was writin'. So, I tell, but then he don't let me out."

"I'm sorry you were disappointed, Jimmy." Travis paused for a moment. "I see your hand is bandaged up. What's that about?"

Valens stated flatly as he stared at the wall, "Cut it on a bottle at the bar yesterday. Some loudmouth wanted a fight. Glass got broke. Cut my hand."

"Can I look at it? Do you mind?" Travis asked.

Like a child, Valens stared at the bandage the jailer had put on his hand sometime the previous night, stared at each layer as he unwrapped it as if waiting for something to appear he still could not imagine, like, maybe, the palm of his hand would have vanished from him. When the bandaging was wadded up on the table in front of him, he stared at his hand as if reassuring himself it was still there. Then he held it out palm-up for Travis. There was what looked like a single straight cut across the flesh just above where the fingers attach. Blood was crusted around it in various shapes where Valens' flexing of his hand had broken it open probably numerous times. It had already started to bleed anew while he held it there.

"Nasty. Hurts like hell," Valens said. When Travis lifted his head from scrutinizing the hand, Valens asked permission to re-wrap it; Valens's attention followed the rolling of the cloth about his hand until it was done as if all meaning was contained in the embrace of the rag cloth upon his skin; there was no Travis, no clerk, nothing for Jimmy Valens as his mind disappeared in the soft cloth. Travis's next question had to be loud and repeated to get the boy's attention: "Jimmy, I heard you had a gun on you. Is that true?"

The boy lifted his head briefly to look at Travis, slid his gaze off to the right again to the wall. "Yep. Twenty-two. For protection. Pulled it on the loudmouth but didn't use it."

"Have you fired it recently?"

"Maybe shot at a rabbit or squirrel a few days ago. Can't remember."

"Why do you think you're here right now, Jimmy?"

"'Cause I got drunk, got into a fight," Valens answered.

Travis noted that when Valens said this, their eyes locked momentarily, then Jimmy turned his head to the right again, yawned, and his eyes focused on the emptiness of the brick wall.

"So, you don't think it has anything to do with what you told the Marshal and the reporters about the Murders of the Cranby family, Jimmy?" Travis punctuated Jimmy's name as if he needed to keep him on track like a four-year-old, but also to accentuate the expectation the boy would speak up so the recorder could capture what he said.

"I told 'em what I seen best I can recollect it. Marshall says I can get out if'n I tell 'em. So, 'at's what I did. But he didn't let me out.

"Were you sober when you told your story, Jimmy?"

"Probly not. But I done the best I could."

"OK, Jimmy, were you there at the Cranby place at the time of the murder?"

"Yeah, like I tol' 'em reporter fellas I was. Didn't do it! Just watched."

"What did you watch, Jimmy?"

"Willie Goebel done it."

"Did what, Jimmy."

"Killed 'em people," Valens stated flatly.

"What were you doing while he was killing those people, Jimmy?"

For a moment, the boy's eyes went blank. After a long pause, Travis repeated, "Jimmy? What were you doing when Willie was killing those people?"

"Like I said, watchin'."

Travis paused, stared at Jimmy momentarily, then asked, "OK, Jimmy, do you think you could run through this whole murder thing with me from the start?"

Valens bowed his head toward the oak table dirtied by the hands of hundreds of men who had sat where he was, wiping their hands upon the table for reassurance, pounding it to proclaim their innocence, using it to brace their arms as pillows for their heads. It was an indomitable table that sat between him and the sheriff creating a space for his brain to deal with the words coming at him and for framing those he would send back. After a long pause, he responded, "I done already told this, Sheriff. I just gotta get some sleep. How many times I gotta do this?"

"Tell you what, Jimmy. You just tell it this one more time, and I'll make sure you can go back to bed, and I'll ask the jailer not to let anybody bother you for the rest of the day. What do you think? Can you do that?"

"If'n I do, then can I get outta here like the marshal said?"

Travis looked steadily into Valens' face that displayed scratches down the left side, and said, "Honestly, Jimmy, I don't think you're getting out until we get this whole Cranby murder thing straightened out. It could be a good long while yet, but I appreciate your helping me sort at least some of it out. Sooner I get to the bottom of it, the sooner things will end."

Valens paused, looked up briefly at Travis, stared at the table space between them, and sighed. "Marshal said ... should a known ... it ain't right .... I'll try to recollect it. But I'm damn tired and might forget somethin' here or there."

"Just do your best, Jimmy."

The boy spoke, pulling up details through layers of boredom. "Willie come over to my place, my dad's place, an' says he wants to go for a walk and would I come with him. I says, 'Where you wanna go?' An' he says, "Out to the coal bank, 'n maybe the woods. " I figured maybe we'd play some cards, like we do sometimes up in the woods. When we got to the coal bank, he said, 'You got money so's we can maybe get us a bottle?' 'I says 'You know I ain't.' So he says, 'You know where we can get some money?' I says 'No.' So, he says, 'You think old man Cranby got some money?' An' I says probly; he mostly always has money; I borrowed from him afore. I says, 'I don't know 's he'd loan to you since he don't know you.' So Willie asks me to borrow it, and he'll pay me back. I says, 'Sure.' So, we headed up through the woods to the Cranby place. We got 'bout to the top of the hill, an' there was ol' man Cranby comin' down through the woods like he was a headin' off to town, an' Willie, he looks at Cranby, pulls out a gun and shoots him, I think in the belly, an' ol' man Cranby says, 'Why'd you kill me for?' An' Willie says, 'So's you don't get me hanged.' The ol' man's still on his feet and tries to run up the hill to the pasture. At first he's fast for a old man with bullets in 'im, but Willie catches 'im and they fight. The ol' man, he's picking up dead branches and stuff and trying to hit Willie with 'em. Willie's looking for a clean shot but can't get one. The ol' man, he makes it up to the fence and climbs over, but I could tell he's feeling the bullets 'cause he slowed way down. Blood everywhere, blood on the fencepost. Anyway, Willie catches up to 'im, but Cranby finds a piece a metal from a machine or something and tries to hit Willie with it but misses and then he throws it at Willie 'n hits 'im in the back. Willie puts two more shots into 'im 'n then picks up the metal whatever it was and beats Cranby down to the ground and then hits 'im in the head real hard, 'n I could see he was done for—I seen the metal stickin' out his head. He was dead then, I think."

The sheriff asked for a clarification, "Did Willie use your gun, Jimmy, or did he have his own?"

"His own."

"And where were you and what were you doing while all of this fighting went on," the sheriff asked.

"Down in the woods, I helped head Cranby off so's he couldn't escape, but that's all. When they got up to the fence, I wasn't far behind Willie. They was in the pasture fightin', so I climbed up on the fence and sat there whilst they was fightin'. When the ol' man was dead, Willie put his hand in the ol' man's pocket, but, far as I know, didn't find no money. Then he went down to the creek to wash the blood off his hands, and when he come back, he says, 'Let's go to the house 'n see if ere's any money there. So, we goes to the house. When we got to the house, Willie went in the back door whilst I sat on the fence outside in the yard. Then, ol' lady Cranby, she comes walking 'round the house like she come out the back door to see a neighbor who dropped by or some-thin' like that, an' Willie's behind her carrying a axe he musta got from the woodpile out there. Here she comes walking toward me, and Willie raises the axe and plants the blade in her head. Blood and brains come out everywhere. When she's on the ground, he hits her again across the throat. Blood everywhere. Then he goes back in and this time after a long time—don't know how long it was—the girl comes out the front door, but she don't look scared or nothin' with him behind her with the axe. Then he hits her in the head, 'n when she's down, he chops her head off 'er. Then he goes back in lookin' for money, but I don't know he got any. Then him and me, we goes back across the pasture an' down through the woods home. I go home to bed; I don't know where he went."

"How well did you know the Cranby girl?" Travis asked.

"We talked some. She was fine," Valens responded.

"What went through your head as you watched her being murdered, Jimmy?"

Valens looked briefly at Travis then back at the table. "Didn't think anything, I guess."

"You didn't think anything," the sheriff restated Jimmy's words, trying to avoid overreacting to the callousness (or stupidity) of the boy's statement. After a brief pause, he went on with the interrogation. How did you come by all the money you were spending at the bar yesterday?" Travis asked.

"Been savin' it. Worked last winter. Got paid fifty dollars. I just didn't tell nobody I had it 'cause they'd all be bummin' off me for drinks and stuff."

Travis paused, and after a moment asked, "How'd you get those scratches on your face?"

"I think I got 'em in the woods, maybe when we was running around the trees and scrub brush ...."

"When you say 'we,' you mean you and Goebel chasing Cranby?"

"Yeah ... or maybe it happened a coupla days ago when the neighbor kids threw a kitten at me. It mighta happened then. I don't remember."

"Jimmy, can you take off your shirt and let me see your back?" Without any hesitation, Valens pulled off his wrinkled sweat-stained shirt, turned with his back to the sheriff. The sheriff saw a small mark on his upper left shoulder and asked how it got there.

Valens responded as he was pulling his shirt back on, "Me and the Lowry boys was drinkin' one day a week or so ago and got into a fight. One of 'em, Charley, he got mad 'cause he knows I can beat 'im in any kind o' fight, so he throws a chunk o' wood at me and hits me in the back."

"I see. Anything else you wanna tell me, Jimmy?"

"Can't think o' nothin.' Can I go sleep now?"

"One last thing," Travis said quietly. "You know, you had told other people about Willie Goebel doing all that murdering. So, I did a little checking up on him. Strange thing, Jimmy. I know that Willie was sitting in jail over in Waycliffe on a drunk and disorderly charge on the day the murders happened. He was there all day. How do you explain that?"

Valens stared at the wall, took his time answering and said finally, "Guess it weren't him."

Looking for clarification, Travis asked, "You guess it wasn't him who was with you? Or you guess it wasn't him in jail?"

"Guess neither."

"Why would you want to name your friend if he wasn't the one who did it, Jimmy?"

"I want 'im to play cards with me."

It took a moment for Travis to process Valens' response. "Who was really with you, Jimmy? Who killed those people?"

"I'm not talking about this anymore." And, when he said this, Travis instinctively knew this pronouncement was the way it would be until Valens' dying day.

When they got to the upper floor where the cells were, the sheriff told the jailer to let Jimmy sleep and to bring in some more guards. "Things could get real tense this evening with the mood people are in. I'm going to think about how we'll move him out of town if necessary."

As he was getting ready to leave, he looked in Valens' cell. Jimmy was on the bed turned against the wall, knees up to his chest, his arms around them like the center hoop on a whiskey barrel. Travis stood there and watched, thought he heard the boy humming a few bars of an old and mournful hymn, and then he was silent like an empty house. He and the jailer exchanged glances, looked back at the boy, listened, heard the first of the deep breath that would become snoring in an older man.

As he walked out the front door of the jail, Travis thought about how much he would enjoy a good stiff shot of whiskey. Maybe more than one. But that would have to wait like the bodies of the dead waiting for the coroner's release to their final resting place.

Appalachian Requiem

ONE

Houses crouch low
too near the road's edge
like impish boys
in weeds to lion leap upon
and heart-scare pound
old hen women
and rabbit-roar men
caught mindlessly
following their routine-worn paths
to who-knows-where or cares
down or up or over an' 'yond
backroads of America.
Such houses were never dreamed
beyond their births
beyond this work camp—and that,
to stand a hundred years or more.

TWO

Coal dust is written on the landscape
like slag-heap hills and rust-colored creeks,
like great- and great-great-
grandfathers for whom
those people who linger here
name children without knowing
that Hephaestus-spawned flames blinked

from the middle of ancestors' heads,
that hellish shadows lay
hundreds of feet beneath their feet
in in-bys[7] and out-bys, pillars and rooms
where ghosts have tread
or that they scratched their names
upon the stones from which they ate.
Their etchings now but detritus and debris of history.

THREE

Four-squares
and shotguns[8]
along the litter-riddled road of black-
dust, damp, and lung cancer
wait still
like feral cats
or striking men
who on their haunches
prey
wait
and pray
ashes to ashes
and dust to dust,
their own pillars sinking
in the hollowed earth
from which they came.

Black Diamonds[9]

CHAPTER ONE

Sometime in the night—well before miners had to appear for work—company lackeys posted notices at each of West Virginia's southern district coal mines: "NOTICE: Effective immediately (August 23, 1903), pay rate shall be thirty cents per ton due to diminishing demands for coal and increased costs of transporting coal to markets." As though it need to be said, the word "Management" was stated below the message. A few words on walls and posts and thousands of miners had their pay cut: No prior notice and no room for discussion. The first of the miners to arrive quickly spread the word to those who hadn't read the signs. Immediately, some walked off the job in anger and disgust. Some stayed on for the remainder of the day working half-heartedly. Almost all of them wanted to lash out at someone or something, find some way to release the pressure rage builds in the mind and body. If curses had been thrown stones, every window in the region would be shattered.

As the initial reaction subsided, cooler heads among the miners reminded the others that they had UMW organizers and members in their ranks. Though many had not joined, had not paid dues, and the union was not recognized by the companies that paid their wages, they were suddenly interested in what the union could do for them. Those who had joined the union insisted that something be done. Moze Bridges took the heat from the large number of black miners he represented who had given up part of their scant pay because they believed in him and expected he would fight for them. The time had come for their commitment to unionism to mean something.

As far as the local miners were concerned—whether union men or not (and whether black or white)—Moze had been a friend to those who accepted him and his skin color and "friendly" toward everyone else. All thought him a good miner and a trustworthy man. He and his wife—both educated and intelligent people—had worked to solve problems and make living in the coal camps more tolerable. Moze had intervened in issues between miners and superintendents and foremen to help shape fairness in the ways work was distributed. He had helped the miners to find the courage to stand against Foremen who punished workers they didn't like. He gave the miners the idea of demanding a daily lottery system that gave every man a chance at working the most productive parts of the mine. He also showed the miners how the checkweighmen who weighed and recorded the miners' haul of coal each day short-changed them in the ways the coal got screened for quality. As a result, the miners under Moze's leadership demanded standardized fair screening and got it.

Moze's wife, Ella—an Oberlin graduate—taught school for both black and white children of the miners. Moze was also educated, though largely through his good fortune of finding people who encouraged him and taught him simply because he wanted to learn and they wanted to see him be successful. Together, Moze and Ella worked to quell mistrust between the races living and working in close proximity.

However, at that time when the livelihood of the miners was on the line, focus was not on what Moze or his wife had done, but on what the miners felt Moze owed them because he had been promoting unionization and telling them they had power through the collective. In other words, consciously or not, they (particularly the black men) expected him to save them. The white men did the same with Josiah. For all of the miners, Union leaders were the best option they could think of, and though it would not be said because they hadn't thought of it yet, those leaders could be blamed if they couldn't come up with a way to do what the miners didn't know how to do for themselves.

Moze and his white counterpart, Josiah Wheeler, had spent a great deal of time trying to build the momentum for unionization. Now, in the midst of a crisis, they were somehow supposed to prove to the miners that the union could meet the challenge. They spent much of that first day calming the rage and trying to convince the men not to respond with violence against the four coal companies that owned the mines, owned the company homes that many miners rented, and owned the company stores that gave them credit so they could continue to feed their families when work hours were cut. What Moze and Joseph didn't express was their personal frustration with the majority of the miners who had not yet joined or supported the union, didn't want to give up a small portion of their pay for security, and didn't trust or believe the union could win against wealthy owners who had the state's politicians in their back pockets. Without solidarity and commitment from the miners, Moze and Josiah were in a precarious position: wanting to take advantage of the opportunity to unionize the men; wanting to make the lives of miners better and safer; knowing the miners weren't ready for a protracted battle for power; and knowing that the unions often lost fights with owners who had unlimited financial resources and friends in high places.

Moze and Josiah had worked together for many years, both as miners and experienced union men; They had seen first-hand how miners could be driven to take revenge against owners and operators who abused them. In the Hocking Valley Mine Strike of 1884-85 and some strikes thereafter, despite their efforts to dissuade workers from violence, the miners blew up railroad tracks and bridges, pushed carts piled high with wood that had been soaked with kerosene and set on fire into the mines as a way to destroy the companies' abilities to make money after denying workers fair pay and safe working conditions. Doing so, they also made it impossible for themselves or others to go back to work if they succeeded in forcing the owners to come to the bargaining table. In the Hocking Valley battle and others, they had seen miners topple and dismantle equipment and even use dynamite to blow up the homes of superintendents and their families... all of which guaranteed responses from government officials and police leading to retaliatory injuries, murder, and greater suppression. They didn't want to repeat any of those experiences if they could avoid them.

CHAPTER TWO

Moze Bridges and Josiah Wheeler called for a meeting of the miners for that same night. Their plan was to maximize the opportunity to gain union recruits and try to refocus the miners, get them to turn anger into controlled and effective action to force owners to take miners seriously and come to the bargaining table to talk about fair pay, safety and respect. First they had to sell the majority of miners on the union as a better option than rioting and violence. Simultaneously, they had to show that their plan for dealing with the pay cuts was better than simply giving in to feelings of powerlessness. It was a lot to accomplish in an evening. And it was made more difficult by the rowdiness and near-riotous behaviors of those attending—men filled with frustration that made them seethe with a desire for revenge. As the miners gathered, they broke into cliques of friends and began throwing the wild seeds of warfare, threats, bizarre ideas for vengeance into the spaces amongst themselves. Some shouted approval for every sentence that fit their frame of mind, causing other groups to cheer them on as volume increased and threats grew. Others—the more contemplative types—stood on the fringes of the gathering trying to understand what to make of the noise, the bravado, and the situation that brought them to the meeting.

As a result of the noise, the union organizers had difficulty trying to get the miners' attention for starting. It took the shock of two shotgun blasts making a hole in the wall of their words and rage before Josiah could get the men quieted down so he could be heard. He started by thanking Harvey Sunder for firing the gun that got everybody's attention, which caused the men to laugh like teenaged boys after a prank. Then he got serious: "Men, we were sucker punched today. And we've got to do something about it!"

Someone in the crowd shouted, "You betcha. Kill a few of the sons o' bitches!"

Seeing who it was, Josiah, shouted back, "Now, Benny, you don't have the money to go all the way to New York or Chicago or way over to England or wherever the rich bastards are, and you couldn't get past their steel gates if you got there."

Another man shouted, "We know where superintendents live! Where foremen live! Where the dynamite is. And we know how to use it!"

Having to shout to be heard, Josiah continued: "That's not likely to get you to the people who have the real power. We hear you! You're angry, and we don't blame you, we're angry too. But you need to hear us out. Violence is not the answer. It might feel like the only option, but it isn't. Anger doesn't solve the problems we're facing. If you want to fix the problems you and all working men are facing, you've got to let go of anger and get to work building solidarity! Standing as one! Speaking as one! Together, each and every one of us, we have a chance to change the way we get treated and to get the bigwigs to see reason. If you get all fired up, get a little whiskey in your guts ... do something stupid, you're going to have the state marshal, local sheriffs, state government and the feds all over us. They've got more guns than we have, and they're going to be on the side of the rich owners, not us. Some of you've been paying into the union for a while now, hoping your brother workers will join you. It's time. It's time for all of you to come on over to the cause. Because, if you don't, we've lost the fight before it has begun. Those rich owners don't want a union, our union: only theirs, the so-called 'syndicate' where they work together against us to hold onto their power. They're not going to give up that power if they can avoid it. They're wanting to work you to death like farm horses for the least amount they can get away with paying you. We—Moze Bridges here" (gesturing toward him) "and me—we're asking you to think of this situation as your chance to make those owners see that you have strength, that you've got backbone, and that you're all working together! When you come together with workers here, across the state, and the country, that's when you've got power that can match theirs."

Stepping forward like an actor hearing his cue, Bridges added, "That's right, men. Today they cut your pay! Some so-called 'coal men' up in New York and Chicago and even in other countries living in their mansions and being waited on by servants ... they are sitting at their tables of plenty, big old roasts of beef or turkey or pork, a pile of mashed potatoes with gravy and all the other fixings, dessert, hot coffee, maybe a glass of wine, their wives and children all dressed up in their Sunday-go-to-meeting clothes just to eat a meal ... don't owe anybody anything anywhere. And they cut *your* pay. Here you are working your fingers to the bone to make them richer and now you're working for even less than they were paying you yesterday. Those men in Chicago and New York, and wherever else they may be, they never see the inside of a mine, never have to do anything harder than lift their forks and knives off their tables or go to the bank to pull out some money for anything they want. They get rich off your labor, and they give you nothing any person with a family can live on. In these United States of America, is this right? They buy off the politicians and make the rules of the game so that they always win, and you always lose! They put your lives at risk every damned day you go down in those mines and have to work with bad equipment, breathe bad air, work yourself to an early death and then they steal what little money you make when you go to the company store where you have to buy everything you need—some of it on credit—because you can't make your paycheck cover the costs you've got. You end up owing them next month's pay before you even earn it and you still got to get through that month too. If they get mad at you or hear that you don't like how they treat you or find out you got old and can't work the way you used to or that you got sick and can't work, they throw you out on your asses. Your family too. And everything you own gets tossed onto what used to be your front yard. Why on God's green earth do we sit back and let this happen? I'll tell you why. Because you are easy to control when you are just one good man trying to reason with them. Whether you know it or not, you've been taught your whole life to bow down to their money and power. We've let them control us workers and treat us all whether we are white or black like black men were treated in the south when they could lash us to poles and tear our flesh with their whips, like when they could shackle us, pour salt into our wounds, kill us with no danger of ever having to answer for it. Today, they lowered your pay, said "take it or leave it," and then slipped away thinking they've got the upper hand and we're too stupid or too powerless to do anything about it. There are only a handful of ways to deal with this, and I'm going to lay them out for you: One, you pack up and leave and hope you find work elsewhere, knowing there isn't much of anything out there that pays anything, particularly for those of you with black skin. Two, you lie down and take what they want to give you and die working yourself to death for nothing and hating every goddamned day of your life, thinking that's just the way life is. Three, you go off half-cocked thinking you can beat them in a war and get yourselves killed by their hired guns or the lawmen who work against you; Or four, you come into the union and force the cheap bastards to bargain with you for a fair share of what your labor gives them! Union's the only way! When they cheat, we call them to account, shut them down if we have to, take away their power and their money. And we keep on demanding and striking until we get what we need to live like people instead of animals. Power is the only language those people understand, and we've only got power if we work together. We're not their slaves. There's no Abe Lincoln on the way to save us. We're on our own. They aren't going to give you anything they don't have to. You came here wanting to know what the union can do for you. I'm going to tell you a hard truth right here and now and I hope you will hear me out: The union can't do a goddamned thing for you ..." Looks of shock came over the faces of men standing in clusters around the open field. Moze felt the increasing tension as men muttered amongst themselves, before he continued. "It can do nothing if you aren't willing to stand up for yourselves and each other. Josiah and I can't save you. You—we (all of us)—we are the union: People willing to stand together and demand they get treated fairly. People at the union headquarters can help with putting pressure on the owners. They can provide us with some funds, and people with experience who will come down here and help us. If necessary, they can get other workers from other mines across the country to support us. But the heart of unionism is you and your willingness to fight smart through negotiation and good strategies to bring them to the bargaining table. Now, we—Josiah and me—we have a plan ready to go, but if you aren't willing to stand behind us, it's worthless. If you want to fight this pay cut, we need to hear that you are with us and with the union." Moze went on making his case. And when he was done, Josiah Wheeler gave the "Amen" to Moze's pronouncements.

Then, Josiah asked, "Are you ready to fight smart? Are you with us?" There was a period of silence and then a few affirmations, and finally, a chorus of yesses and yeahs and a few discordant notes of descent from those who were still too angry to give in to reason.

When the affirmations subsided, Bridges and Wheeler began telling the men how to sign up for the union and laid out their plan for men to create a total work stoppage—every man among them refusing to go into the mines until the owners agree to meet with them. "We're going to hit them where it hurts the most: in their wallets!"

CHAPTER THREE

Owners hadn't anticipated the almost instantaneous and total end to production across the affected mines. And they hadn't planned for all profit from the coal fields of the region stopping in one day, nor had they prepared themselves for the increased shipping costs they would have to pay to get coal from other locations to meet their obligations to customers. Now *they* were livid.

Both sides knew what they were facing. The owners would have to go in search of men willing to work in the mines and try to break the miners' resolve. Miners would do everything in their power to keep the scabs[10] out. So-called "guards" from the Baldwin-Felts agency[11], Pinkertons, or some other equivalent force of hired guns would be brought in to protect the owner's property and harass the miners. The owners would demand, and the miners would refuse. Miners would demand and owners would refuse. If the workers got angry enough, they would likely be driven to retaliation. State and federal governments would get involved. These were age-old, typical responses both sides knew were likely to come. And they were extremely expensive, seriously affected the owners' profits, and often resulted in workers capitulating because their resources were limited and their families were suffering from lack of food and shelter and with many other side effects of poverty.

Moze and Josiah wasted no time in alerting the press to the work stoppage and the reasons why, as well as giving reporters stories of the hardships the miners' families were facing. The press began hounding the owners for explanations about their treatment of the miners. Government officials, fearful of an all-out mine war, pressed owners for resolution. After a week of negative press depicting the owners as greedy and villainous and dealing with public censure and governmental concerns, the owners, not wanting to go through the expense of a miner's war, grudgingly agreed to meet with Josiah and Moze, and they agreed to allow Dylan Welsh from the UMW's national headquarters to attend as well, though he was to be an observer only, as the owners' refused to recognize the union.

The three union men arrived at the scheduled time for the meeting at the famous Barclay Hotel in Charleston. They did not expect miracles, but they had come believing there was hope the owners would make some kind of offer to restore at least some of the miners' pay and that there would be an opportunity to bargain so the miners would not have to endure an extended strike.

Because Moze had stated in the letter of response to the owners' syndicate that he represented the Negro miners, he assumed they understood that he too was a black man. Unfortunately, he quickly learned that wasn't the case. As they came through the door into the lobby of the hotel, an officious looking short, red-faced man came out from behind the registration desk, walking rapidly toward them, and said, "No. Gentlemen ..." (speaking to Welsh and Wheeler and pointing toward Moze). "He can't come in here."

"Excuse me," Bridges said, "I was invited here."

The clerk, looking *through* rather than at Bridges, responded as if speaking into an empty room, that it was hotel policy and Moze would have to leave.

"Sir," Welsh said, causing the man to turn toward him. Welsh lowered his brow and spoke softly, "This man (referring to Moze) is here as a distinguished member of a negotiating team meeting with the representatives of several major mining companies paying for this space, all of whom might be rather angry at your causing us to turn around and leave and their time wasted because of your policy."

"You are welcomed to stay, sir, as is the other gentleman with you."

"There are *three* gentlemen here, sir," Welsh said sharply. "How about you and I go to that meeting room so I can explain to those very wealthy men that you are making it impossible for us to attend this important meeting they invited us to attend?"

The man's face turned a brighter shade of red than it had already been as he weighed the options, choked on his anger, and said, "Follow me, gentlemen," the last word said through clenched teeth. As the men entered the meeting room, the eyes of syndicate members immediately turned to Moze Bridges as if the men had never actually seen a black man walk into a room as anything other than a waiter. Moze enjoyed watching the men attempt to gain control of their faces and look at anything but him. John Langhorn, who was to be the spokesperson for the syndicate representatives gasped and spoke immediately, directing his question to Wheeler and Welsh, his jowls quivering as he asked, "What is this Negro doing here? Is this some kind of mockery?"

Moze responded in a dignified and confident voice, "You invited me here, sir. I am Moze Bridges, the person you have been communicating with to set up this meeting."

"I had no way of knowing you were a Negro!"

"I informed you clearly that I would be representing the Negro miners." Using his educated and articulate voice to confound their expectations, Moze continued confidently. "That you assumed I was a white man, is your error. However, since you did, in fact, invite me to attend, I am hoping we might proceed as men working together to resolve our differences regarding the extraction of coal and relations between the miners and owners. Now, may we begin the discussion we came here for?" With that said, Moze gestured to his two companions, and they moved to the chairs designated for them on one side of the table facing seven men on the other.

Not having expected Moze to be so articulate and forceful, Langhorn was taken aback and had trouble getting his anger under control. He was sputtering when he said, "This is highly unusual ...." After a moment, he leaned back in his chair and turned his upper torso to consult with the two men behind him. While he was whispering with the two men, his four cohorts sitting with him at the table were displaying their discomfort in their red faces, twiddling thumbs and eyes dodging the three men opposite them. Finally, Langhorn turned back to the table and called the meeting to order. He stated his name, title, and a list of the states in which he controlled mines and then named the mines in southeastern West Virginia in which he held interests. When he was finished, he asked each of the four men sitting with him at the table to state who or which corporate entities he represented. Like him, the four men put forth lists of titles and multiple enterprises in an attempt to overwhelm the union men with their power and wealth. Then, he called on the two gruff-looking men who sat behind him, who turned out to be attorneys working on behalf of the syndicate. He did not call upon the secretary who sat at the far end of the table taking notes. Then, he simply pointed to Josiah who identified himself as representing the miners working within the area affected by the pay cut and as a member of the United Mine Workers.

Jumping on the last sound of Josiah's introduction, Langhorn stated that the syndicate did not recognize the role of the union and will assume that any talk of union will be stricken from the record. When he finished, he launched into opening remarks which would express the owners disapproval of the miners' response to the necessary pay cuts. However, Josiah interrupted him before he got more than a few words out, saying loudly, "Pardon me, but you didn't allow Mr. Welsh or Mr. Bridges to introduce themselves."

"Mr. Welsh is here as an observer and nothing more," Langhorn responded coldly. And the Negro has already made himself known.

"The *Negro* has a name, sir," Josiah interjected. "And Mr. Welsh is here as a human being as well. He is a gentleman deserving of common courtesy. And if you will not give him that, I will state for the record that this is Mr. Dylan Welsh, who has come from New York Headquarters of the United Mine Workers of America! And, for the record, Moze Bridges represents the many Negro workers in your coal mines." As he finished, Welsh smiled at him and nodded his head in a gesture of respect.

"Again," Langhorn responded abruptly, "I wish to be clear that from our perspective you and Mister," (pronouncing the word with disdain) "*Bridges* are two miners who have taken it upon yourselves to speak for a number of miners who are upset about our decisions. We do not and will not recognize a union." He said the last sentence as if issuing a challenge before returning to his scripted remarks which ultimately amounted to a restate-ment of the syndicate's position that rising costs demanded cost cutting. His comments were stated in a matter-of-fact manner as if he were speaking to uninterested children who couldn't under-stand multisyllabic words about financial issues. Then he turned to Josiah Wheeler and asked him if he wished to make an opening statement, to which, Josiah replied, "Mr. Bridges will be speaking on behalf of the miners today."

"This is highly irregular ... insulting," Langhorn grumbled over the rumble of annoyance from the men beside him.

"Gentlemen," Moze interrupted speaking with clarity and a passion worthy of a great actor, "I am sorry that my presence causes you to be insulted or uncomfortable. You obviously see me as your inferior, an uppity black man speaking to powerful men as if he is somehow equal. I ask you to embrace that feeling you are having for a moment. What you are feeling is what every man working in your mines is feeling: insulted and angry. The recent notices posted at locations all over your mine sites gave no warning, no time to prepare, and no time to at least talk to you about how your decree affected them or how the cut might be mitigated. Each and every miner who came to work on that first day learned he was getting a forty-percent cut in pay, that he was responsible for covering your increased costs over which he has no control. To the miners' way of thinking, this meant that their families must starve to make sure that company profits are main-tained at the current level. To them, it appears that their work to provide the coal which has made owners and operators wealthy is unappreciated. I imagine that when making decisions about how to cover rising costs, thinking in terms of the difference between thirty cents and fifty cents for a ton of coal doesn't sound like much to you gentlemen. But when you think of losing forty percent of your total income, it's a lot of money, especially now that the mines are only open about half the time they were just a few months ago! Whether a man makes ten dollars a week or a thousand dollars a week, losing that much money is going to affect how he will be able to maintain whatever life he is living. From their perspective, miners see this situation as unfair. They are not responsible for changing marketplaces and selling your coal. They cannot demand that companies do a better job of expanding their markets or that companies set aside money to hold them over when times are tough, or that companies pass added costs on to their customers. Miners see this pay decrease as unfairly making workers poorer to protect everyone else in the companies' sphere of influence."

Eloquently, he covered the value of the workers to the owners' and shareholders' needs for profit. He quickly disabused them of any thoughts they might have of black men being stupid and uninformed. He laid out the issues from the perspective of the miners, trying not to antagonize the men sitting opposite him while trying to suggest that working together, perhaps both sides' needs could be met. Finally, he offered, "Is there no room for finding a more just solution to your present problems?"

The looks on the faces of the syndicate men was one of indifference. After a short period of silence following Moze's question, Langhorn looked at the other syndicate men who responded with nods indicating some kind of prearranged signal of agreement. Then he looked at Moze, Josiah, and Welsh through his dull eyes and said, "We have accommodated your request to be heard. We have heard your grievances. We believe we have been fair with you and all miners. We are paying fair wages commensurate with the market value of coal. Market value has dropped, and therefore, wages must be lowered accordingly."

Moze asked, "Does that principle apply to stockholders and corporate leaders as well, sir?" It would go a long way with the miners to know that wages of corporate executives, headquarters employees, stock value, and corporate profit are all taking a forty-percent cut." Dylan Welsh smiled as indignation became readily apparent on the faces of the syndicate men.

Trying to control his anger, Langhorn, responded immediately and loudly. "We are not here to negotiate with you about the operation and decisions of our companies. We invited you here as a courtesy to provide you with the face-to-face meeting you and the press accuse us of fearing and to give the miners an opportunity to save their jobs by accepting the terms we have offered. We do not negotiate company decisions. This is America. Miners—even Negroes—are free to work elsewhere if they don't like what we are willing to pay."

"I am truly sorry to hear that response, Mr. Langhorn," Moze said. "You and we (nodding toward Josiah and Welsh), know how this is going to go over with the men. A long-term strike benefits neither of us. With the amount of money it will cost you to fight with the miners, you could easily pay each man the previous rate and still be ahead financially. We are open to negotiation. Wouldn't that be a better response?" The syndicate representatives sat in stone-faced silence. The three union men simply followed suit, knowing the reversal of their tactics would likely make the syndicate men uncomfortable. One of the men sitting with Langhorn finally broke the silence, spoke up and said, "You miners don't seem to understand. In the end, it will be you who loses. You always lose. Strikes are pointless! You only hurt yourselves."

To which Moze said, "Does this have to be about winning and losing? Why can't we come together so we both get what we need and avoid the ugliness of a full-fledged strike?

Finally, Langhorn, clearing his throat twice before speaking, muttered that there was nothing further to be discussed. With that, Moze making eye contact with each of the men opposite him said, "I am truly sorry we cannot reason together to find solutions for our mutual good." With that, he, Josiah, and Dylan got up, slicing the palpable tension like knives, as they walked out.

As he sat in the hard board seat of the train car reserved for Negroes that took him out of the city, Moze stared out the windows at the landscape passing by and thought about power in the clutches of greed, the mentality of winning at all costs, dominating others and stripping them of self and soul, emasculating men for no reason other than it could be done. He wondered what it is in some people that makes them so desperate, more animal than human. He felt the knot growing in his stomach, the anticipation of another strike. Human beings physically beating or killing one another ... in the name of self-defense and survival as defined by whichever side is doing the defining.

CHAPTER FOUR

The strike was on. And nothing was altered about the long-established patterns of mine strikes: men with nothing to their names and nothing to lose facing off against opponents who have enormous wealth and power and are determined to maintain control over their workers. Many miners had been put out of their company-owned homes shortly after the strike was called and were living in tents provided by the UMW or moved in with others who had homes of their own. All had grown weary of the relentless refusal of the owners to negotiate worker pay ... even as the price of coal was likely to increase as the winter months came on. By late October, the miners were still holding out. They had kept scabs out of the mines through reason and veiled threats and had managed to avoid most of the efforts of the "guards" hired by the mine owners to intimidate them. However, Mose and Josiah both knew that if the owners continued to refuse negotiation, it was just a matter of time before they resorted to regaining control over their mines by any means necessary: starving the miners into submission or committing acts of violence through the guards who called themselves "detectives" or through the state marshal's office asserting their "law"—as interpreted by the owners' syndicate.

The owners wasted no time in taking legal actions which had been effectively countered by UMW attorneys up to the occasion of what the owners called, "the riot": A group of miners marching from the Waverly mine to the Cabalo mine site bearing guns and shouting at the guards inside the mine sites as a show of force and frustration ... an unsanctioned action that infuriated Moze and Josiah. Though no shots were fired, the mine guards claimed the miners had threatened them. Unhappy that the local sheriff didn't see the event as anything more than a free-speech protest, company officials quickly reacted by demanding state officials intervene and put down the "vicious militia that threatened the lives of the guards." Based solely on the syndicate's demand, State Marshal, John Frothman, was sent to the region by Federal Judge Hatcher with the charge to arrest miners believed to have been involved in the "riot."

When it became known that the arrests were imminent, Moze and Josiah had a choice to make: either allow the men to be taken to Charleston for questioning and trial, knowing the courts were likely to bend to the will of the mine owners and operators, or support miners in refusing to surrender, which would likely escalate to an armed confrontation. As much as they hated the first option, they didn't want to start a war and tried to convince the miners to remain peaceful and let the UMW fight the cases in court.

Despite their pleas to the men, the miners had their own ideas about handling the situation. When Frothman and his deputies came to serve warrants, the miners were well prepared. Scouts had been watching for the marshal and his posse and relayed information to the renegade planners as the group neared. When the time and location was right, the posse was easily surrounded and outnumbered by armed and angry men with faces covered like old time bandits, their handkerchiefs tied in tight knots behind their heads to hold the masks in place. The marshal and his men were ordered to drop their guns and rifles onto the ground. Seeing no viable option, Frothman ordered his deputies to comply. They were ordered to leave and not come back. No miners would be turned over to them. Being outnumbered, cornered, and out-gunned—Frothman's threats of coming back and arresting all of them were met with derision. One of the masked men warned him that if he made any more threats, he and his men would be going back to Charleston in their underdrawers. Given the circumstances, he and his deputies had no choice but to leave. As he rode away, Frothman fumed, thinking to himself, "Oh. We'll be back. You can count on that, you sons o'bitches."

CHAPTER FIVE

Moze was standing on what he called "the veranda" of the Miner's Shack saloon observing the comings and goings of the people of the town he lived near—a town tilting toward the status of ramshackle, but better than many he had lived in or near most of his life.

He watched the merchants, the town's lone banker, lawyers, the mayor and townsfolk coming and going ... all dressed in their clean, neatly pressed clothing, men tipping their hats to one another and to the ladies they met as they made their way to wherever business or personal need took them. Most of the town's women wore long coats draped over their shopping frocks, layers of cloth that had to be held up to keep them from touching the mud and horse dung as they crossed the main street amidst the striking miners, most of whom were wearing the only clothes they had—often too big or too small, often inadequate for the weather, some wearing clothes too long worn without washing.

Ella—Moze's wife—made time amidst teaching school and raising their children to clean and repair his clothes as well as she was able with the meager supplies she could afford; her workmanship was so meticulously done that it was difficult to see the former holes and tears without close scrutiny; however, there was little even she could do now with his old gray coat worn nearly through by at least five years of hard use. Still, she tried. Poverty had not taken away her sense of pride in him, the work he was doing, or her own desire to use their lives for the good of the race.

Over the years, he had gained the face of a still-handsome prize fighter—a few small scars from mine accidents and occasional fights with those who thought a black man was an easy target for a beating or his wife too radical for the communities where she lectured on the plight and future of black people after reconstruction. What was most notable to those who knew him well was the change in his eyes, the visible dulled look of mourning mixed with intelligence, a coalescence of loss, caring, reason, and disappointment accumulated over his now sixteen years of working as a miner and a union activist and engagement with a system far more ruthless and powerful than he had imagined as a young man thinking he was going to change the world for the better through hard work, courage, and a dream of equality.

He watched striking miners from the various mine companies in the vicinity come up the blackened walkway and pass him as they went into the saloon. His eyes followed others going into Big John's across the street, another dispensary of momentary freedom from the hard-as-coal reality of being a miner. Occasionally, a miner passing by would speak a few words, but mostly they reserved their talk for those inside with whom they could share not only words, but beer or cheap whiskey. He watched townspeople moving in and out of one-story shops with façades that tricked the eyes into seeing such buildings as taller than they were and old women waddling through the slushy mud spots desperately trying to maintain their modesty as they lifted their dresses; he winced at children chasing poor old feral Toms and Queens that had slinked around corners from a night of love making and now hungrily hoping for a mouse daring to come out from beneath the weather-beaten buildings.

One of those who stopped was young Sam Matson, one of Moze's most trusted union men. He was a leader among the younger black miners, someone Moze thought would eventually become a powerful organizer if he chose to be one, someone Moze took under his wing, treated like a son. The union needed more black organizers if it was going to succeed, and the country needed more articulate and capable black men breaking down the barriers to equality. During the strike, Sam was one of the men who had volunteered to scout movements of the Baldwin-Felts "detectives" and reported back to Moze and Josiah. He was glad to see Moze and tell him briefly what he was seeing from his hiding locations.

"Saw lots of torches out at the Cabalo mine last night; more than usual. Went o'er to the Waverly too, saw some men comin' down o'er the hill this morning, 'bout ten of 'em. Guards let 'em through right quick. Strangers roamin' 'round the countryside in packs of three or four ... my guess is they're lookin' for miners out on their own. All carryin' rifles. You think they're building up to take back the mines and bring in scabs again?"

"Sure looks that way," Moze said. "Especially since they've got the state marshal coming in any time now planning to cart off a bunch of us to Charleston on trumped up charges."

"Sure didn't do no help ... that bunch of men waylayin' the marshal."

"You got that right, Sam. Boneheads! You been out watching all night?"

"Yes, sir. Headin' home now. Need to get some sleep."

"You do that," Moze said. But be careful getting there. You hear? The bastards are everywhere. Don't want you to end up like Ned Anderson." Then there was a pause before Moze said, "I'm glad you're with us Sam."

"Me, too," Sam replied quietly before walking away.

After a few moments of watching the young man walk out of sight, Moze stepped down from the plank flooring onto the street and sat down at the edge of the walkway. He liked leaning against the pillar beside the steps where people came up out of the street to the saloon doors or the stores on either side. He liked the step's centrality and how it provided a sense of connection to the people of both races as they met in their shared town—the blacks who walked in the street and the whites who walked the boards. He liked the protection of the roof that extended from above the saloon door out over the walkway to a brief flirtation with the space that extended over the top step.

He didn't know what it was he hoped to find here that he couldn't find at home. He told himself it was inspiration, something that would trigger the words he would need for the meeting coming later in the day with the other miners who were questioning the wisdom of continuing the strike when they had the equivalent of pitchforks to fight the enemy's guns, bombs and cannons. All of them wanted to win back what they had lost and wished they could get more than that if possible, but for the most part, they weren't willing to die for any of it. Some had come to believe that negotiation with heartless men was hopeless. Moze still believed that negotiation should be how problems are resolved, and he was holding on to the belief that concerted effort to defy the brutishness of the syndicate men could make a difference. But he also knew that neither he nor Josiah nor UMW headquarters had been able to conjure a solution for opening the mammoth steel door of negotiation that had been slammed shut by the owners in the workers' coal-stained faces. And time was running out.

Inhaling the clean air that had sneaked in upon the town during the night, he tried to clear his head of the fears that crawled up out of his belly and into his brain. Then, he saw Linc Adams come out of an alleyway two buildings away and turning onto the street as he dodged the worst of the mud and walked toward where Moze sat. Adams was the only black merchant in Marbora, owned the only dry goods store, and was one of the most successful businessmen in town mainly because of the services he offered and the deference he showed to his customers no matter their skin color: Whites said he knew his place; blacks said he was more like a white man than a black one but kind and didn't cheat them. He dressed today in brown: brown shoes, brown pants, brown checkered coat, but wore a black bowler on his head. "Mornin', Linc" was met with a cheerful, "Mornin,' Moze," neither man presupposing the other would offer more, both waiting to see if all that could be said had been said or if a sudden reason for more should occur in the momentary recognition of their encounter. Adams found the reason as he came forward and sat down beside Moze on the cold wood of the deck.

As if it had just occurred to him to ask, Adams let the question fall out of him like he was thinking he might be privy to the inside scoop to good news: "What do you think, Moze? Men going back to work soon?" The merchant asked his questions without seeking Moze's eyes, both sitting but a foot apart and looking out into the middle of the street as if the potential violence lay out there in the recent ruts made by heavy wagon wheels and horses' hooves.

"I don't think men can accept an empty box being passed off as a gift, Linc. I know it's not good for your business or ours, but it looks like it's where we are."

For a moment, silence took over. They sat, each waiting for something to say, perhaps a distraction to avoid dealing with talk, an opportunity to scan the activity of bodies moving along the sidewalks and street, a need to listen to the chatter of barely clad miners. "Fairness is a long way off, I fear," Moze said just above a whisper as the thought slipped out of his mouth and fell like spittle into the space between himself and Adams.

"It seems that "fair" is whatever white boss men say it is," Adams muttered.

"Ever so, friend. Ever so!" Moze allowed himself to speak openly to this fellow black man who had always been friendly to him. "Hard to explain fair to rich men who wouldn't know fair if it jumped up an' bit them on the ass. It's taken me eighteen years of dealing with them to realize they are not like common men. *Rich* means, you don't have to play fair, follow rules, honor your agreements; you've just got to win. Our needs aren't their needs. They've got the money and time we don't have, and they've bought out all the political support they need. They've got the power to keep us gut-wrenching angry and frustrated. That's their game. I'm walking a razor wire strung tight between the workers who want me to work miracles and the owners who have the tools to cut the wire. No matter what I do, it's wrong. If I fall to the right, I'm dead; fall to the left, I'm only maimed for the rest of my life, stay on the wire and slit my feet and keep on splitting until I split wide open. Don't know what I'd hang onto for up. Doesn't seem to be much winning in this world if you aren't rich, Linc."

"There ain't much winning in general. It's a tough business you're in." After a short pause, Linc said, "Wish I had answers." An uncomfortable pause rose up amidst the puniness of words. The men looked at one another briefly knowing what could not be said: like it or not, Adams had found his own way to some wealth and some security for his family, and yet, he could empathize. He contributed money to funds that helped the miners, extended credit when he could, but because of his own wealth, he was largely isolated from the pain the miners were suffering. He had nothing more to offer. Words worth saying had been exhausted over the previous two months and were like an old worn horse ready to be put down. "Guess I better be moseying on down the street. I wish you well, my friend."

Soon after the goodbyes, Linc Adams walked away, and Moze decided to get up and shake off the damp day's cold that ate its way through his clothing and lay on his skin like a moth that finds its way from the outer wool to the lining of an old coat. He walked up and down the street listening to the sounds of people talking, mules and horses braying or whinnying, and wagon axles rubbing against their clouts, as he thought about the men who looked to him for leadership. At the north end of the street, just beyond the livery stable, he looked up into the indifferent mountains surrounding the town. He thought of their shadows being like black-clad priests droning hypnotic prayers no one but them could hear.

He put his hands in his pockets, found the unspent nickel he had brought with him, and bought a newspaper in Linc Adams's Dry Goods. As he stepped back out into the street, he heard the words, "What you do matters," slip from his mind to his mouth as a whisper, as if someone other than he had put them there. As he sat down on the step leading up to The Miner's Shack, he thought, "It has to. It has to." Then he looked at the headline that had caught his eye in Adams's store, "Miners and Owners on Brink of War." When he finished reading the inaccuracies and blatant manipulation of language put forth by the writer of the article, he folded the paper, stuffed it into the space between his shirt and his coat, and stared at the chocolate-colored mud of the street. And now he did not want to think, did not want questions, did not want to answer the unanswerable "Why?" The why of human interactions, the need for greed, domination and control. Instead, he meditated upon the soggy ground at his feet, used the tips of his boots to push the more liquid portion of the mud in front of him off to one side, trying to clear a space to see beyond the slimy gel of dirt and liquid snow to what he hoped would be hard, nearly dry or still-frozen earth beneath. When he got to a small still frozen patch not too far below the surface, he stepped into it, felt the solid ground holding him up like a man on a boat deck who has been pulled from a great river, felt the weight of his own body again. He made a three-quarter turn in place and did not know why or care; and then, he reversed and felt safe for the first time since leaving home that morning. Then he sat once again on the walkway but kept his feet in the sacred circle he had made—earth firmly under his feet, a place for a man to stand if even for a moment.

He watched two men he knew: two men now stumbling out of Big John's and down the street toward the path that would lead them home. His eyes followed them until they disappeared beyond the buildings, beyond the brief open space before the woods. He felt the cold chill of responsibility, wondered what he might say when he stepped before the assembled men tonight. He hoped the words would soon wet his lips, wondered if he had them in him somewhere, perhaps in a place he had not remembered to check. "When words fail, when the hearts of good men fail, all that is left is rage," he thought.

At a loud bang of the door behind him, Moze turned to see Pearl Carver, an ancient miner—a white skin-sack of a man, a self-professed sage of the mine. Carver had almost fallen through the door. When Moze saw who it was and registered Pearl's obvious state of inebriation, he watched and waited. Pearl didn't walk straight to the steps that would have taken him down to the street to start his long walk home. Instead, he weaved and stumbled heading right at Moze, put his hand on Moze's shoulder, and grasped it like a handrail to brace himself against the potential fall. Once he got down the steps and released his grip, he stood, lilting like an old tree in a mild breeze and looked at Moze.

Suddenly aware that he knew his human banister, Carver slurred the words, "Oh, it's you. Yer Moze, right? You a ra-rab-ble rouser union man, ain't ya?" He didn't wait for Moze to respond. Like a holy man struck by the spirit of the ancient gods, Carver started singing, "There's POWER, Power, I say ... Power in yooooon-yun. Gather ye round, boys! Gather ye round! Power, I say." And all at once, dizzy ... words escaping now in decrescendo to whispers, "Pow'r, Pow'r, Pow'r," he fell to his knees. Some half-drunk miners coming out of one of the other bars in town laughed. Townspeople turned up their noses in disgust and walked away. Moze went to the man and raised his mud-covered body with ease, saying, "Come on, old man. Let's get you home."

Trying to look back over his shoulder as Moze held him from behind, Carver said, "Yer not bad fer bein' a nigger, is ya?"

Moze considered for a moment the idea of dropping Carver face first in the mud and letting him lay there. As the thought left him like vapor breathed into the cold air, he said, "No. Not bad for being a black man, Pearl. Not bad. Come on. Let's go."

For a moment as he directed, dragged, pushed, half-carried the drunken man toward home, he found himself among his thoughts imagining them as objects, tangible, things to be studied and understood. But because he hadn't found the words to say what they meant, he tucked them away, hoping the words would come to explain vicious men pouring salt on misery wounds of a gutted miner, images of frozen women and children stacked like cord wood, images of men melting like snow and soaking into the earth to be long forgotten by the time summer finally arrives. He met in his mind the eternal concept of just is—the ugliness of injustice and the unanswerable questions behind the doors of locked rooms and thoughts. As he walked, he found himself speaking words to his stumbling companion as if Pearl Carver could somehow understand. Maybe it was just the need to hear his thoughts as if sound made them more real like rain on a tin roof makes a poem: "Got to change *is* to *was*. But *how* is like trying to understand those slinking feral cats spry boys can't catch. Cats know what you're thinking ... got you figured out way before you can get near them. They're faster than you. Yet, every now and then somebody does catch one. Then, question is, 'What are you going to do with it?'"

CHAPTER SIX

Sheriff Miles Frye looked out upon the street from the window of his office as Moze Bridges and Pearl Carver made their way, Moze's hand on the back of Pearl's jacket, lifting the man like a live rabbit being returned to its cage. Carver, known for his bouts of drunkenness, was fortunate, Frye thought. Moze would make sure the old man got home safely. Frye was relieved that he wouldn't have to arrest the man on a drunk and disorderly charge again—as he had done a number of times—drag him into a cell and listen to his tales of woe until he finally passed out. Ordinarily, the sheriff wouldn't have spent much time thinking about what he was seeing—just two men he knew—one of them more in control of his body than the other. However, today, they were not just two men; they were walking symbols of Frye's predicament: coal miners on strike against coal mine owners and operators refusing to bargain. For Frye, they represented one side of opposing armies preparing for open warfare, each weighing the relative strengths of the other as the power struggle escalated day by day, incident by incident.

That the sheriff liked Moze Bridges was now irrelevant. Just the sight of him made the sheriff nervous. Early on in the strike, he and Moze and Josiah Wheeler had talked, tried to reassure one another that they would do everything possible to avoid armed conflict, but too much depended upon whether the owners' syndicate would negotiate, and every indication was that they had no intention of doing so. Frye knew that Moze and Josiah had made numerous attempts to request negotiation, and the response was always the same: "No!" Though he wouldn't say it (for fear of losing his job), Frye would have agreed with the miners that the owners were greedy sons o' bitches.

In the past few days the sheriff had received numerous tips that miners and their families were being harassed by the strangers who had come into town referring to themselves as "detectives"—men enlisted for their size, strength, pure meanness, and willingness to do what they were told by the agency that hired them. At first, it had been harassment, including such things as making threats to the miners that if they didn't give up the strike, they—the detectives—would visit the miners' homes to "have a talk" with their wives and daughters, or suggesting it might not be safe walking the roads alone if someone had a mind to make them disappear, or pretending their guns accidentally went off as bullets were fired at the ground near the miners' feet, the thugs suggesting that if the miners didn't call off the strike they might find themselves dancing at the end of a rope ... all of this when they could catch a miner alone—no witnesses. Black men were particularly vulnerable since they were well-trained by fear not to raise a hand to white men who were abusing them; they were occasionally beaten and used to frighten other black men who refused to break the strike or leave the area. The "detectives" often chose the most vulnerable people they could isolate and attack: old men, boys, and people smaller than themselves. Recently, two black miners disappeared suddenly from the camps, leading miners to believe the men had either run off—which seemed unlikely to those who knew them—or "had been disappeared"—a tactic not uncommon in the struggles between the two forces mediated by thugs. The problem for a lawman like Frye was always the same: "Where is the evidence?"

Frye played the role of peacekeeper as best he could and investigator as best he could with the resources he had at his disposal, using the law as his arbiter for respecting the rights of both sides and restraining anyone violating it ... if he had evidence and suspects. He was in almost daily contact with Joseph and Moze and tried to interact with those who seemed to be in charge of the "guards" as often as he could ... which amounted to when they happened to be on the street and he could drag them in for a chat.

He and Moze had been friends almost from the time Moze first came into the town. They liked and trusted one another. However, they both understood from the beginning of the strike that if it came to a war, each would do what was right for the people they served, the commitments they had made to those people, and the law, regardless of where it left their friendship and mutual respect. Neither man wanted or condoned violence except in the case of self-defense.

The superintendent of the Baldwin-Felts "detectives" had said the same in his meeting with Frye, even asked if his men could be deputized to help the sheriff handle the unruly miners if they got out of control, to which the sheriff, smiled and asked, "Do you think I'm daft? Would you want me to deputize the miners to help me control your men when they've gotten out of control?"

"You have no evidence that any of my men has broken the law."

"None that I can prove yet; otherwise, some of your men would be back there in the cells. You keep your men under control. Guarding is fine; attacking is not. And I've told the miners the same thing."

Frye knew the strike game as well as the miners and owners did: Set up a confrontation, state the rules for playing the game and watch how quickly angry men push the limits until rules become meaningless phrases spoken against a gale-force wind.

"We're both caught in the middle," Frye had said to Moze Bridges just a day or two ago. Today he said it out loud to his empty office. His mind roiled with concerns: *The law! A county to cover. A town to protect. A war to avert. Miners wanting a decent life. Time running out. Winter coming on. Families starving. Negotiations non-existent. Power-brokers incensed and eager to make problems go away. Rich folks who didn't even live in the state, not wanting to give up any of their wealth. All demanding their rights under the law—the law scripted by the power of money for the people of money.* His county and his town were ready to explode, and he had one deputy and a handful of citizens he might be able to count on to back him up if he needed help handling whatever might happen. He had called the citizens to service the previous day, but there was no guarantee that they would stay with him if they thought about the possibility of dying in the process of helping. Most of the citizens Frye would enlist were merchants—men also caught in the middle of warring factions—merchants who knew that miners—if they weren't reliant on the company stores for credit—helped keep the town alive by spending their meager pay with them in order to avoid the high costs of the store controlled by their employers. They also knew that the syndicate leaders could raise all kinds of legal hell if the merchants sided with the miners. *Last time around—1898—a goddamned bloody mess and nobody gained anything from it. Hell of a world. And I can't do a goddamn thing but wait.*

He watched Parson Abley walk out of the church and down the street, stopping at various groups of miners and non-miners alike to chat, every now and then resting his hand on a shoulder. The sheriff had been around Parson Abley enough to know that he was probably blessing everyone he talked to regardless of their state of sobriety or their thoughts about the two sides of the coming war. No one who knew him doubted his love of the people he served. Even the crudest among them withheld their swearing and blasphemous talk in his presence. The parson was one of only a handful of men in town who would neither think ill of miners because of the work they did or allow their ignorance or uneducated behaviors to affect his regard for them. And, most noticeable to the people who liked him, Abley wouldn't push his Jesus on the miners or anyone else ... though he might say upon walking away from the people he encountered, "I'd be honored to see you in church on Sunday if you would like to come."

I wish I could get the parson to pull a few strings with that God of his, straighten out this mess. Wish I could believe all that crap.

The Quinn sisters, two "old maid" daughters of the late Milford R. Quinn, who had been one of the richest men who had ever lived in town, were all dressed in their finery as they thumped their hard shoes on the wooden plank walkway. Frye watched them as they nodded to the parson and used their parasols to nudge the poorly dressed and inadequately-clean men. "Miscreants," the sisters would undoubtedly say, sometimes with more of a whack than a nudge as they steered around the clusters standing on the walk or in the doorways of saloons and too close to the opening of the stores the women thought about visiting. Even from his distant post, Frye could see the looks of utter contempt they had for what they would have called "ungrateful loafers and drunkards." He watched them greet Doc Leiter who was making his languorous walk toward his office; he half smiled, lifted and tilted his hat, and moved beyond them. He was dressed as always in a tailored suit, but today it was rumpled like he had slept in it after a two-day bender. Laboriously he went to the steps on the side of the Cranston Building and made a sluggish effort to get past the people waiting on the landing to the second floor for him to open his office to treat them, some of them among the many who would never pay him.

Mrs. Cranston stood at the entrance to the Dry Goods Store she and her husband had built and operated for the past twenty years. Frye watched the old woman raise her fist, squint her eyes, clench her teeth, and mouth words that—from her appearance—suggested condemnation loud enough that the words should have come to his ears. He determined she was scolding the air behind some boys who chased an old, ragged cat around the corner from Main to Fern. The sheriff guessed it wasn't so much because she felt a need to protect cats, but because boys—all boys—needed someone to teach them about the sins of being boys, someone to do what their parents hadn't done—what she would have done to teach them right from wrong had she been able to bear them.

He was watching representatives of all the people he dealt with: people drowning sadness and fears in alcohol, young men cruising for fights over women or dominance over other males, people trying to make a living and conducting business, children being children, black and white ... they were his town's people—the good, the bad, and everything in between. People coming and going, intent upon their tasks or upon their indolence as they saw

fit ... all waiting, all knowing if all-out war began, they would suf-
fer together. In the meantime, there was nothing for any of them
to do but wait and hold out hope that one side or the other—
owners or miners—would cave to the power of the opposing side
so people could get back to living their lives and accepting their
places in the social arrangement they had chosen or fallen into.

As he waited for the telegraph response from the state marshal, Frye worried. He worried about what he could do if all hell
broke loose before he could get help, and how he would handle
the so-called "help" state marshal Frothman would send. Deputy marshals had been sent once already when the miners first
decided to strike, and fights had broken out, and some property
damage had occurred. People from both sides had been bruised
and battered, but Frothman's deputies concentrated on making
sure miners got the message that the law was not their friend. In
that particular incident deputies descended on the mines guided
by Frothman's directive: "bust heads and squelch the uprising." It
was clear that the heads to be busted were striking miners' heads.
Apparently, the miners were perceived as being responsible for
their own problems and should have accepted what they were
offered. Of course, the marshal didn't say such things publicly, but
he conveyed them clearly through the ways deputies responded.
After arresting a few miners on various charges (none of which
could be proven), Frothman sent a message to the union leaders
threatening to arrest any others who caused trouble. After a few
days, when the miners appeared to be under control, thanks to
the effort of Moze and Joseph, the deputies were finally recalled,
but not without Frothman's threat to have his deputies return
in larger numbers if there were any further problems. Back at his
office as reporters gathered around him, the marshal crowed that
he had "put down the rebellion."

Then there was the most recent incident of Frothman himself and his deputies being forced at gunpoint to abandon their
mission to arrest miners accused of "rioting" as they marched
between the Waverly and Cabalo mines carrying weapons. Frye
knew Frothman well enough to know the marshal was not going

to accept that humiliation and would be plotting revenge. He wished he had any alternative other than calling the marshal back into the area.

All the pieces were adding up like sticks of dynamite linked to a central fuse. Dozens of strangers—some of whom were union reps, and many of whom were undoubtedly more owner-paid thug types—were arriving. The union reps divided their time between mingling with the miners and communicating with headquarters at the telegraph office. The companies' hired guards, on the other hand, went out to the mines to reinforce those previously assigned to protect the owners' properties. The sheriff was sure the owners' men were awaiting orders for an assault and looking for excuses. Reports were coming in that they were often out on patrol, sometimes straying some distance off syndicate property, which Frye knew translated to looking for miners to harass. He had no doubt that many more out-of-towners would come or had already arrived by horseback from over the hills.

When Marshal Frothman first became involved in the mine strike, he had made it clear to Frye that he was to be informed anytime there was a problem involving the mines or the union. Miles Frye had only done so reluctantly and only when the report dealt with something momentous. Whatever Frye sent was then passed on to Federal Judge Hatcher—the State's final arbiter of labor issues. Miles Frye knew that both the marshal and the judge had little patience for miners' complaints, outside agitators coming into the state to stir up problems, and even less patience for black men who got "uppity" enough to get into the fray in any capacity. It wasn't a great secret that Frothman and Hatcher benefited from the friendships they had with the coal mine owners and their emissaries, and both intended to stay relevant in the state's political establishment and had ambitions for more power and lucrative financial opportunities in the future.

Frye didn't share Frothman and Hatcher's dislike of the miners. In fact, he got along well with most of them as long as they obeyed the law and went about their business. However, he'd been through strikes in the past and knew how quickly they could turn ugly, and how quickly decisions had to be made—decisions that could result in men dying. He didn't blame the miners for their complaints or their desire to unionize. He saw their poverty and the unfairness of the system. He had been in the camps and seen the way people lived in the too-small mine houses where husbands, wives, many children, and, sometimes, parents, other relatives, and homeless friends were packed in like heirloom furniture—too precious to throw away, too large to store, too important to not work into the concept of "home." He knew it was even worse for the blacks whose homes often had two or three whole families pushed into them like bullets in a gun clip, lined up one after another and squeezed into a place with barely enough room to turn around without bumping into someone.

Frye didn't hate the owners either, though he could not get comfortable with the ways they treated the miners. It was their money that had built the town and supported the county—including his job—and it was their money coming through the hands of the miners that kept the area from going totally broke, and, after all, wasn't some money better than no money? It troubled him to think about the fact that when push came to shove, he would keep his job or lose his job depending on whether he pleased the owners and the politicians, not upon whether he followed the law or pursued justice. He had not chosen to play politics and yet found his job depended on how closely he could adhere to the law without alienating the various factions. He could feel the knife-blade tensions against his skin and bones. As best he could judge it, he had maybe a couple more days before hellfire and brimstone. Reluctantly, he had sent a message earlier in the day to Frothman:

> Mine situation escalating STOP Miners agitated STOP Owners bringing in paid guards STOP Union men stirring things up STOP Incident of gunshots reported STOP No identified culprits STOP Miners claim violence by guards STOP Cannot confirm STOP Union rally tonight STOP Need support STOP Check with Hatcher STOP Miles Frye Sheriff Raleigh County STOP

CHAPTER SEVEN

Deputy Sheriff John Allen's chestnut mare cantered down the street, kicking up mud with each lift of her hooves. At his "Whoa" and a tug at her bit, she stopped at the hitching post. The officer moved quickly, lashing the reins and making his way to the door, pushing it open carelessly so it bounced against the interior wall's wainscoting. "Got problems, boss," he said to the sheriff excitedly as he rushed through the door. "Fire out at the Cabalo Mine. Guard shot."

"Dead?" Frye asked.

"No. Winged him. Doc got called out there; fixed him up. Won't be firing any guns with his right hand anytime soon. Winged him good."

"What about the fire?" Frye asked.

"Doc said that the guards out there put it out on their own. He—the doc—didn't think the fire did a lot of damage."

"Guess we better go on out there and check things out," Frye said.

"Go tell Silas next door where we are headed in case anything comes up."

When the deputy returned, they walked to the stable—the deputy leading his horse by her reins. Waiting, Frye turned to his deputy and asked, "Your horse going to hold up, John?"

"She'll be fine. I was only about a mile out when I got the news from the doc himself. I told him I'd let you know about it. Molly's a little spooked, though. Acted strange all day ... kind of nervous like. She knows something just ain't right."

The sheriff chuckled. "Hell! Everybody in the county knows that. Why wouldn't a horse know it too?"

When Frye's horse was ready, the men mounted and made the trek, following the railroad tracks out to the Cabalo Mine, both men feeling the weight of responsibility they had carried over the past couple of months during the so-called "period of relative calm." The calm never was calm, of course. It was just quieter than what they knew was coming.

They talked little along the way, each caught up in his own thoughts, each remembering past strike experiences and imagining what might happen this time around, each wondering how they would manage the hostilities if they broke into open warfare.

When they finally arrived at the mine, Frye could smell burned wood but couldn't determine where the smell was coming from. There were no flames rising into the sky and no smoke billowing from anyplace other than the brick chimney of the powerhouse[12] and the chimneys rising from a couple of other buildings on the site which were probably in use by the various scab laborers the company had pulled in over the past two days.

Frye yelled before he got too close to the mine, "Sheriff Frye! Coming in! Just me and my deputy. Don't shoot!"

Guards, when they saw clearly who it was who had arrived at the site, stepped out from behind the huge upright posts that held the tipple in place, stepped out from behind the various work buildings, opened windows of the powerhouse and tipple[13] and leaned out or stood up on the roof tops ... all with Winchester rifles in their hands. They clearly had been ready to shoot had the visitors posed any threat. Many were looking beyond the lawmen as if they expected hidden forces to come riding in for a surprise attack. Even with the sheriff in their midst, they constantly scanned the landscape with their eyes just in case someone hiding in the woods or behind rocks on the opposing hillsides were to use this occasion to pick one or more of them off.

Frye let the thought flicker across his brain that something in their faces suggested that they were a little disappointed at his coming ... like maybe they had wished it had been a couple of miners brazen enough to come up the tracks like brainless deer stepping into an open field filled with hunters. This was a gut-reaction of course, but one based in past experiences. As a law man, he had to own the notion that, perhaps, he was misreading them. *Best not to judge,* he thought. *On the other hand, trust your gut and be wary; it's how lawmen survive.*

Frye engaged the guards. "I heard you boys had some problems today. Thought I'd better check it out."

One of the guards, a burly, bearded man wearing a sheepskin coat, lowered his rifle and told the sheriff to come to where he was standing behind a building. "Don't wantcha ta get shot by a miner thinkin' yer one o' us." He yelled to other guards, "Back to yer posts, boys! Don't be standin' 'round like goddamn dumb ducks! Lucas," he called to one of them, "take a couple o' men an' check 'round back agin. Don't need no more sneak attacks!" When he was done barking his orders and the officers had come up to him, he put his huge hand out and shook hands with each of them and said, "I'm Bill Cadwell, boss o' guards out here."

"Yes, sir. Pleasure," Frye responded. "So, Mr. Cadwell, tell me what happened out here today."

"Well, sir ... yep ... we had a little set too," Cadwell said. "One o' my men done got shot. See that ridge o'er there?" He pointed across the valley to a hill on the other side of the tracks. "Seems my man, he stepped out jest like these dumbasses did when you come up. He was thinkin' he heard a noise like a thud on the wood wall over yonder, an' just when he stepped out bein' stupid, *Bam!* Shot caught him in the shoulder. Rest of us got into position up front here lookin' out over the land tryin' to see where it come from an' ready in case we was being attacked by a bunch o' the dirty-ass bastard miners an' their pet niggers. Whilst we was all runnin' 'roun' lookin' to git the bastards, some son-o'-bitch must o' been sneaking in from somewheres behind. Don't know how he done it. Must o' been waitin' til we was 'stracted and sneaked over from some place on 'at 'ere mountain back o' us. Next we know, there's smoke comin' outta 'at 'ere buildin'." He pointed to a small yellow-brick building. "Whilst we was tryin' to get 'at fire

out, we sees smoke comin' outta 'at wood buildin' o'er yonder."
He pointed to another building. "We was busy watchin' out fer
a attack too. We hadda send a couple o' men to try to catch the
polecat what started the fires. We was in a real fix if they'd been
more 'n one or two sneaking bastards o'er 'roun the buildin's.
How the son-o'-bitch what did it got in or where he got to we
don't know. We don't got enough men here to be spread that thin
to be watchin' every inch o' this here mine.

"Town's been full of men coming in from God-knows-where.
I figured you'd have so many men, you wouldn't know what to do
with them," the sheriff said. He noticed the man's face redden and
his eyes look away from him. "And none of them out here?"

Hemming and hawing, the man seemed to be searching for a
lie. Finally, he said, "They was here, but ain't right now."

"Where are they?"

"Don't rightly know. Maybe had to go to one o' the other
mines. Anyhow, there we was: a man down, a bunch o' men puttin'
out a fire, and jest a handful o' us left to fight. A bunch of wuthless
recruits down in the ground tryin' to do mining what they don't
know how to do, all scairt as shit ... An' then, all a sudden, nuthin!
Not a goddamn thing. Not no more shots, no more fires, no more
nuthin.' So now I got two men out, one fer the doc to git 'em to
take keer o' our man, Arnie, an' a guy ta get a message ta other
mines ta be watchin' fer sneak attacks. Our guy got the doc, got
back with no problems. Damn fool don't think 'bout bringin' you
back with him. Doc come right in struttin' like a banty rooster,
fixed 'im up purty good—our guy what got shot—and left. Says
he's gotta git back to town. Guess that's how you heard 'bout us."

When the guard stopped talking long enough for the sheriff
to slip in a question, Frye asked, "You guys do anything to deserve
what you got?"

Cadwell had that indignant look upon his face that suggested
such questions were distasteful for well-bred, fine specimens of
humanity such as he. "No, sir. No such a thing. We was just doin'
what we's paid to do. Just mindin' our own business and the bastards jumped us."

Frye asked all the usual questions about whether the guards had any specific information on who might have done the shooting or the arson work. He asked, the obligatory question of them, "What makes you so sure it was the miners who did this?"

Cadwell looked at Frye as though he had a third eye in the middle of his forehead, "Who the hell else 'd do such a thing? O' course it's miners. I'm goddamn sure."

"But you didn't see any of those miners. Right?" The sheriff asked. "You can't tell me who ... right? Anything that might help me figure out who it was?" Cadwell shrugged. "So, I've got myself a problem trying to figure out who is responsible for this situation."

He asked the other men within hearing distance if any of them had had any run-ins with any miners that they could identify. All swore they had done nothing to deserve being shot at, and they had no idea why they were attacked. The guards—all who could be cornered to be interviewed, at least—took the opportunity to make a case for their beliefs and opinions that the miners were just a mean, ornery lot who wanted to take the owners for everything they had. Miners were, according to them, just a bunch of stupid sheep being deceived by unionists who didn't believe in owners' rights to run their businesses as they pleased. They made the age-old case of their employers, "If miners don't like the circumstances and pay, they are free to leave and find another job."

Frye was not a newcomer to these arguments and had heard both sides try to persuade him to buy into their point of view. It wasn't a part of his thought processes or job to get involved with the politics or to ask questions like, "Go where? To do what?" He knew better than to ask these guards how much they were being paid and how long they could count on work from the owners, and how happy they were with their working conditions. Had he been talking to miners, he knew better than to ask them whether or not they could understand the risks the owners took in putting their money into ventures that might ruin them financially. Frye knew men from either side of the arguments were not open to such discussions when vengeance was foremost in their brains.

Before leaving, the lawmen walked around the mine buildings, took note of the fire's destruction of a wall and part of the
roof. As they rode away from the mine, Frye said to his deputy,
"Everybody's innocent, my friend. Nobody is ever at fault. When
people differ, the good belongs to the speaker; evil belongs to the
person they're talking about."

"Sure seems to be the way the world works," the deputy said
sarcastically." Don't it?"

"I'd fall off my horse if just once somebody said, 'I did it and I
was wrong.'"

They did not head back to town right away. It was now
mid-afternoon, and Ebon was not far. Frye needed to ask Josiah Wheeler and Moze Bridges what they might know about the
events at the Cabalo mine.

"Strange goddamned world we're living in, John," he said
without any explanation to his deputy.

"Sure as hell is," the other replied matter-of-factly and without question.

***

The sheriff's coming into Ebon was not all that uncommon.
He'd been out for various domestic disturbances, and he'd been
there to enforce the law when the owners wanted somebody out.
That the strike was under way caused some of the miners and
their families to fear his visits, if for no other reason than that
the sheriff often had the chore of delivering notices of eviction
when the owners and their hired managers were afraid of serving
papers on their own workers to get rid of them. However, today
there were bigger issues to deal with, and Frye's arrival did little
to instill more fear among them.

Frye headed directly to Wheeler's house first. Josiah was
coming out the door, putting on his jacket as though he had been
waiting for the visit or, perhaps, he didn't want Frye to come into
the house. Wheeler was a tall, chisel-muscled man sculpted by
hard labor. Many called him handsome. His blond hair was just
beginning to be pushed aside by gray, but he still had a youthful
glow upon his skin. He wore personal pride like a military man

wears his epaulet, like a banker wears a new suit to impress his rich clients. His was the pride of his place in the world among the miners, his friends, and the communities he helped create simply by living as part of them. He looked at the lawmen as his equals, neither to be feared nor fawningly respected. Just men doing a job.

"Josiah," Frye said, "Just the man I came to see." Frye, having interacted with Wheeler in the past, knew there was no need for small talk, so he got right to the point, "I need to talk to you about a little incident down at Cabalo mine today. Know anything about that?"

Josiah paused for a moment looking into the face of the sheriff, "Why, Sheriff, I heard there was some trouble. Not much goes on in the mines that doesn't get known pretty quick. But you know I don't tolerate bad behavior from the men. If it was any of our guys, I don't know who, and I'd give him hell if I did."

"But would you give him up if you knew who it was?"

"Probably not if I could help it, Sheriff."

"That's what I figured," Frye said out of the corner of his mouth more to John Allen than to Wheeler. And then speaking directly to Josiah, "Anybody else might have any insights? How about Moze? Any chance he knows anything?"

"I doubt he knows any more than I do, but feel free to ask him. By the way, you might want to take a look in on Ned Anderson over there in that house with that old, rusted milk can sitting out front. He came home yesterday with the hell beat out of him. He says that he was walking home from town along the railroad tracks and a couple of those mine guards were laying wait, pounced on him and beat him almost senseless. All the time they were beating on him, they kept yelling, 'You and your union pals get the hell out of town' ... things like that. When they finally got done kicking him black and blue, he could hardly crawl home and dropped right there in the street in front of his house. It's a true miracle he didn't die trying to get here. No man should have that done to him. He did nothing to those men except cross their path. So ... I guess you can kind of see why some guys might have been a little sore at those thugs the owners call 'detectives.' Still, I'm not saying that what went down at the mine was right either. I don't want to think any miner that I know hurt anybody without goddamn good reason." He waited for a moment, and asked, "Anything else, Sheriff? I've got some work I need to do."

The sheriff couldn't stop John Allen from blurting out, "You mean like a meetin' you gotta get to, Josiah? You think we don't know what's going on tonight? We know more than you think we do."

Allen stopped when he felt Frye's evil-eye-stare pierce his consciousness, and he realized he'd violated one of Frye's cardinal rules: "When you are playing poker, keep your cards close to your chest and let no one know what cards you have to play or show them your cards when you've bluffed," and "When you are doing an investigation, don't ever tell anyone what you are thinking or what you know unless it gets you what you need to know."

Josiah remained unmoved and in complete control of his response: "Yes, John, a meeting. Yes. I know you know. And I know some of the ways you know. And we both know the men around here aren't sitting around picking their noses or their asses. Yes. We're going to meet, and we will talk and decide what we wish to do. Unless you are ready to throw a few hundred men in jail for talking, I don't see that it matters that you know. Now, is there anything else we need to talk about?" When the sheriff shook his head "no," Josiah Wheeler walked between his house and the next and out of sight as he made his way beyond the investigation and disappeared behind the people who had come out of their shacks to see what was going on.

At Ned Anderson's place, the lawmen knocked on the door and were allowed in by the man's wife. Anderson was barely able to talk. His face looked like he'd gone ten rounds with a prize-fighter. However, he was able to whisper through his swollen lips responses that he had no recollection of any particular person that he recognized who had done the beating. When asked by Frye, he shared that he'd had a few drinks too many prior to the incident and his mind wasn't as clear as it should have been. To the best of his recollection, he thought there were at least three men who had attacked him.

Frye asked him the same questions he asked Cadwell earlier, "But how do you know it was the hired guards who did this?"

Anderson whispered his tortured echo of Cadwell, "Didn't recognize 'em. Who else? Those bastards."

Anderson's wife stood at the bedside and cried, "What they done to him is gist wrong. He di'n't do nothin' worth this. Look what they done to him. She pulled the blankets back from her weakened husband's grasp and showed the sheriff Ned's naked body covered in bruises over his chest and legs and groin, one big black and blue swollen mass. "The back of 'im is worse," she said, "but it's too painful for 'im when I have to roll him. Ain't no reason to kick a man in his private parts. What kind of man does that?" She pulled the blanket over her husband and tucked it in around his neck, dripping tears into his face. "I hope you kill those men. I know it ain't Christian, but I don't care. They don't deserve to live for what they done."

Other than telling the woman he was sorry about what happened, there was really nothing more for the sheriff to do other than suggest she get the doctor out to check her husband.

"Ain't got no money for no doctor," she said. "I'll take care of 'im best I can, like I done all along."

Frye had gained nothing. No real information. No suspects. However, he still needed to check with Moze Bridges, not so much because he expected anything new, but because he wanted to leave no possible lead unchecked if for no other reason than he wanted to be the kind of police officer who tried to do right by the people of his county, no matter who they were.

When he knocked on the door, Frye was greeted by Moze's wife, Ella"—a beauty in bronze, dark brown eyes, shapely, and as well-proportioned a woman as any man could desire. There was no hesitation in her. She looked directly into the officers' eyes. As she stood at the door, her children, Denmark, Mazey, Carey, and Marcus stood behind her—her entourage of protectors—all of them exuding the same confidence and pride Frye sensed in their mother. Clearly they bore the best of both of their parents when it came to looks. A handsome lot of children, Frye thought. Behind them, black and white youngsters were sitting around the room, books in hand, staring at the door, waiting for some explanation for the interruption in their readings and discussions.

"Hello, ma'am. I'm looking for Moze. He around?"

"No, sir. He's out just now. May I help you?" She spoke like a secretary trained to shield her boss from interferences by unwanted salesmen. "I can give him a message if you like when he gets in. Would you like me to do that?"

"Know when he'll be back?"

"No, sir. He brought Pearl Carver from town a while ago. He didn't want him ending up like Ned Anderson. Then he went out again."

"Know where he went?"

"No, sir. He has his wandering ways. He doesn't always tell me what he's doing and where he's going."

"All right then. Let me try this: You know anything about the incident that went on out at the Cabalo Mine today or who hurt Ned Anderson yesterday?" he asked.

"Now, Sheriff, you know as well as I do that these men don't tell us women their business. I just know what I hear from the women folk around here, and you know how that kind of talk goes. Never know what's real, what's been made into a good story, or what's a downright lie. Best not to be passing on that kind of information; we've got enough problems around here when everybody knows what they're talking about. I just know that when those so-called guard fellows show up anywhere where miners are on strike, miners get hurt. I hope you find them and put them in jail."

"Yes, maam," he responded respectfully.

Ella wasn't done trying to make the sheriff see the miner's point of view. "Based on what they did to Ned over there, jail time serves them right. Beyond that, I don't know any particulars, Sheriff. I doubt my husband does either. He doesn't approve of hurting anyone if it can be helped. Not his style." She stopped for a moment, still looking him in the eye, still determined to control the situation, then started again. "You might want to go talk to whoever is in charge of those guards and talk to him about why his men want to go around beating up some poor old drunken man. And if there's really been a fire out at that mine, you should talk to those men out there and ask them what they've been doing that anyone would want to try to start a fire there. That's what I would recommend you do."

The sheriff knew that he had gotten all the information he was ever going to get from Ella Bridges and the people of Ebon. "Already did talk to the men out at the mine, ma'am. Just trying to follow up. If you all come up with some names of who did any of this mischief that was done yesterday or today, maybe I can get a little justice for you. Have your husband come see me if he's got any information, will you?"

"Yes, sir" she said as the sheriff and deputy walked away, mounted their horses and started on their way. They were at this time but actors on a stage, the audience's eyes following them as they exited after a poorly performed scene.

When the officers were far enough to be out of hearing range, Ella shooed the children further into the house. She turned and looked into the cold air that stood like sky-high brick walls between the sheriff's world and hers and whispered through clenched teeth, "Justice? Bullshit!" She turned to the children in the house and said, "Now, where were we?"

As the lawmen were heading out of the community, late afternoon was vanishing like crows heading for wherever the evenings of crows are spent. Men from everywhere, wolfed down their meager suppers, started gathering, talking, joking before they would walk together up the north slope of the hill to where Moze sat beside Josiah, thinking about the near future, thinking about what they might say to the miners, wishing for the mantle of leadership to pass, knowing that it would not, and waiting for the men who would expect something of them neither had the power to give. They had sold the men a a dangerous dream upon which legions from Hell would expend incalculable fury.

CHAPTER EIGHT

When Sam Matson left town after meeting Moze that morning, he was tired, and he was cold from having sat in his makeshift shelters in the hills where he watched the comings and goings of the mine guards so he could report to the strike organizers. He had spent too many hours without sleep over many weeks doing what he could for the cause, and for Moze in particular. He trudged the dirt road that would take him home—a path of chocolate-sauce-colored mud of November cold nights and morning sun beaten by the heavy feet of miners, horses and mules. Mud dragging at his heels, he succumbed to a rhythmic clomp of his feet, the splattering ooze of each step, the hypnotic pull of mind and thoughts about the strike and the impending confrontation. He was lost in thought, unconscious of the elements that burned into his brain by day-to-day familiarity: mountains looking down at him, forests slashed for the mining industry, scrub brush growing along the sides of the roads that were carved into the landscape so men could make their way to the mines for work, and the railroad tracks for the trains to cart out the coal.

He was thinking about the miners and their families. Children without enough to eat. The efforts of Moze Bridges and Josiah Wheeler to seek help from the UMW and miners in the surrounding states ... money, food, anything that could keep the striking miners going. He thought about the miners he had seen in town earlier, some of them showing signs of intoxication, and wondered where they had found money to drink, wondered what their families went without so they could swallow courage to carry on when hope was fading. He reminded himself not to judge.

Perhaps it was the thought of his mother keeping him ever mindful of abstinence that triggered the memories that took over and absorbed him as he walked. He found himself reliving those nights as a child crying in his bed, afraid for his body and his mother's life, heard his father's blubbering, blustering, inebriate-driven demands and fears still held on the surface of his brain: "Don't you be prayin' on me, Woman. Ain't no need for no fantastical God what makes those rich white folks angels an' us hell-fodder. Don't need no make-believe in this here house promisin' a life we ain't never gonna get an' no life when we die neither. You an' me an' them bastards, we all just gonna rot jest like damn dumb dead ol' maggot-eaten possums out there in the woods. An' ain't nothing prayin's gonna do 'bout any of it."

Sam cringed at the memories—their sound, his father's slush-mouthed voice. The pictures were there too like photographs behind his eyes, his mother's tears and steadfast acceptance of his abuse, his father's fists against his mother's face. Within his chest, he felt the altering of his heart rate, the tension climbing up through his chest and shoulders and neck, the rage within his little boy's body and the uncontrollable leap against his father to protect her. He remembered receiving his father's backhand for trying, his own collision with the floor, his mother's scream, her leap upon his father, her taking the beating meant for her son, the inevitability of their defeat. Then there was the defeat itself, his running, hiding deep under the porch among spider webs and shadows of cowardice where his father's body couldn't come, to wait for when his mother would call him and put him in his bed in the now still house and lie with him until he slept.

He tried to think past his cancerous memory of the man who was his father. He thought how good it would be to somehow cut the tumor of hate from his own body, let it heal somehow, never to be dealt with again: a dream he hadn't reached. Old Jake—his father—would not go away, stood there in his son's mind: a man of many selves, fewer than most men, more than some—drunk, sober, and drunk again. There were times he did not rage, simply stumbled home sober or drunk to fall into his wife's arms, press his face deep into the cleavage of her breasts, and cry himself to sleep while she prayed, "I can bear it, Jesus. Thy will be done. Make him whole, sweet Jesus." Sam could feel anger crawling across his skin like fire biting his every attempt to find good in the man. He looked up into the sky, made himself see the trees and the mountain, tried to control the boiling of his blood. His mother dead. His father dead. He was proud he did not drink.

Recollections of all kinds had a way of imposing themselves invited or not as he walked. They had a way of sneaking in like rats even when he nailed can lids over their freshly gnawed holes; they flattened their heads to slide through spaces seemingly smaller than they. And he was remembering again: after his parents were dead, the chance of adventure, going with other young men recruited for work in Ohio coal mines. At age sixteen, five years ago, he stepped over the blood of his father that lay still on the planks of the porch floor. Stepped down the stair steps of his youth into promises of good pay, food, a chance to make a life: America at last. Promises to all the young men requiring nothing more than hard work and time.

Three days travel, men tossed haphazardly like bags of potatoes upon too few wagons. Too many to stretch out legs, too many to claim more than buttock and folded leg space, the remainders of their bodies upright shoulder to shoulder with other men like too many chicks in a too small nest. Swollen bladders and bowels to be held, relieved only upon commands of rifle-bearing men. He was still a boy, could not decipher behaviors of such men. He had thought like a boy of becoming a man, making money, having things, food, friends. He had not known the word *scab* beyond dried blood covering an open wound until the day he arrived, and large groups of angry men with clubs and guns, women and children red-faced with rage, seethed beside the road to the mine, ran upon them as they neared, sound over sound all hate: "Scabs!" "Dead men!" "Stretch your necks!" "Black Leg sons o' bitches!" Epithets upon epithets like gun cracks and cannons until the riflemen guards pushed the protesters aside and the wagon went on. "Strike breaker" and "scab," had been but words until he owned them. Now they were flesh and blood. He thought somehow of his father. He remembered hearing his father's voice, "Hell fodder," his mother praying quietly to God in a corner where walls of deaf and dumb met.

Memory took him back, seeing the aching, disinterested horses plodding on before the wagon, working only for food and water. Though he might not have said it this way, he was conscious that those horses did not think of meaning; they were owned or controlled, just did; endlessly worked unto death; he hadn't thought that that was also the intended use of men in the mines. When the wagon stopped, the men were ordered from the wagon to the ground, herded to a too-small building alongside the tipple. Nothing in it: pine floor, one window high on the wall just below where the steep roof lay its body like a fat man on a skinny girl, no chairs, no tables, no chamber pots, nothing but the men, smell of their bodies too-long unbathed, too long in same-old clothes, too long baked in hot summer sun, stomach gurglings, hunger growls—sounds and feelings Sam had understood well before this. He understood waiting for as long as it takes, "piddling meals" his mother eked out of a weed-eaten, insect-infested garden she called "Eden," the occasional sacrificed chickens his father stole. It was not hunger that ate at him then, not the men's complaints. It was memory of angry people nearing his wagon. Women, even children, raising fists like sledgehammers, hating him for sitting on a wagon needing work that mine owners gave him. "I meant them no harm." To which his father's voice rose up from within him, "Rich people lock up what they have! Grasp for what they do not! Steal it if they have to just for the sake of having ... keeping it from us who have nothing!" Just beyond the edge of memory, he could almost hear his mother praying, and then himself speaking like an intruder's voice within the dust of his mind, "How has the coming of your Christ changed their world?"

All the young men, alone at last, guards out doing whatever such men do when out of sight. They talked about the travel, guards with guns, the people who had stopped them and called them names and threatened them. Where Sam found courage, he didn't know. "Men, we're being used. Ain't we? Those people back there. Their men got the boot. That's what that was all about. We're being used to starve 'em out. Ain't what I wanna be doin'. I want to be able to walk into town to buy food, clothes and what-nots, be just folk. If I'm to be a miner, that's fine, but I ain't gonna be no scab, I ain't gonna take food out the mouths of those miners' children, an' I ain't gonna live locked up like this. Stay if you want: I'm not doing it! First chance I get, I'm gettin' outta here." When the men were finally allowed to care for their bodily needs that evening under the guard of too few riflemen, Sam simply wait-ed for the nearest guard to turn his face from him, stepped into the dark of the night, and walked away behind buildings into the even darker shadows of trees.

Miles of walking and hunger took him to a little rat's nest of a town held together by the Umbrich Mine Company. Just outside the town was a grouping of tumble-down shacks where the min-ers lived. Within minutes, a red-faced woman called toward the house, telling her man to come out. It took only moments for the man to invite Sam into his home, feed him, and take him in for the night. The next day, with the miner's help giving a good word to the supervisor, Sam was hired.

As he walked, he remembered the first time he had gone down in a mine, that shivering of his body, the feeling of air being sucked from his lungs as steel clanked on stone, the elevator pul-ley screeching from high above, its sound diminishing with dis-tance and time, feelings of entrapment like a cell door to which someone else holds the key, thoughts of his mother lowered into her grave, the easing of her ravaged flesh encased in pine lowered by old men who set her down, dropped the earth over her scoop by scoop sealing her voice from his father's ears as she lay beside his rotting corpse a few feet away. Straight down six-hundred feet: he remembered it inch by inch, felt something like spirit rise from out of his body like the Archangel Michael abandoning him forever. He remembered half-breaths in dark, dense, dust-filled air as he and the others stepped off the lift. Wary and scared, he thought of prayer, let his mother's voice float up the shaft behind the ascending crate and into her God's sky. Then they walked the tunnels dug deep into the mine by other men who'd come and gone and left the chiseled paths sometimes a mile or more for walking into the next generation of paths and profits. Nothing but small flames worn on their hats to show the way in or out and without them, absolute black—a removal of a man's eyes. Cold here, he thought, but some of the other miners had told him it was always the same cold. Sam had thought that good, knowing he would work up a man's sweat carving out money for things he never had for a life he could only imagine. He could still smell that first day of coal dust amidst centuries of earth's rotting debris; at times, excrement, where workers relieved themselves of necessity in corners or out-of-the-way nooks and crannies; leavings of donkeys and horses used to pull coal cars along their rickety tracks; burned oil from machinery undercutting coal; after-cast odors of dynamite explosions upon the air moved down air shafts cut into the hills; musk smells of other men and himself working side by side extracting tonnage for bosses to count.

He thought of Mina, whom he had loved, her satin-skinned body beneath him, thought of the ache in his body when he lay upon his bed alone after she died—the thought eating at his life like black lung disease. He eyed the trees for distraction, imagined their poses like military men, swords drawn, or women reaching out sensuously to take him—their leaves waiting to spring forth like fatherless babies from their bellies into the hell of living.

Random thoughts, old thoughts, new thoughts, disjointed thoughts fell all over him like rain ... making him oblivious to sounds of the world and his own body in motion. The illusion of thoughts—sound and images in his brain making their way from one space to another in and out of time ... until the man's voice pulled him into prescience, "Hey, you, Nigger! Boy!" Unprepared by his senses, his body reacted, throwing his broad shoulders up and twisting his head sideways as his mind raced to choose between fear and friendliness. He had worked with many men now. He did not like being called "nigger" or "boy." Though he was young, he had worked hard enough to prove himself a man to anyone who bothered to know him. Some of the people he worked with still called him "boy" to joke with him, and for that, he forgave them, accepted their respect behind the taunt. When he turned in the direction of the voice, he did not know the four men he saw: Strangers with guns—one on horseback, smirking, the other three on foot wearing sardonic smiles. Two of them had snuff-drooled whiskers; and all were glassy-eyed—the look of men who had been drinking. The shortest man of the three who were on foot said it again, "Hey, boy. Come over here; talk to us." At that moment, Sam knew exactly what a stray cat felt when a pack of dogs was on the loose and not far off. He could feel it in his bones and his brain. He did not know or care to know these men or their reason for calling him. He knew like an animal knows fight or flight. He did not take time to ponder the fears that competed for attention in his brain. His young, powerful body did his think-ing for him, not caring to contemplate being a coward or martyr once he saw the noose slung over the rider's saddle and the grin of the man on horseback. He bent his knees, turned toward the woods and pushed against the earth with the grace and strength of a stag, pumped his strong, long legs against the downhill slope, leaping as best he could over brush piles and briers that grew before the scarred forest. When he had cleared entanglements of brush created by the mine developers, he ran through the trees between the spaces they created—spaces cleared by years of a canopy's control of light.

The horseman maneuvered the half ton of flesh beneath him, pushing the beast beyond pain of brier sticks around the thorny, man-made apron to the forest, clearing a path for the three who ran behind him. He too had broken into canopied spaces. And now, these he-wolf hunters saw Sam ahead of them. They made screaming banshee cries, made threats and cursed. Sam could hear them coming, knew he was no match for the speeding bloody-legged horse or bullets. Leaping over fallen logs, Sam made sud-den shifts in direction when he could, instinctively thwarting the men perhaps lining up rifle shots, but it was slowing him down. He ran in straight lines for speed when he dared, trusted the trees to protect him, but the horseman was gaining on him fast. He reached the creek at the bottom of the hill with the rider nearly on him, the yelps of the other men running at full speed. Luck had run out.

The creek was ferocious and roaring, flexing its muscles against the banks. Sam had no choice but to attack it as the lesser of two monsters to be fought. Momentum alone carried him halfway across. Then the water monster leaped, threw him down into the ice-cold water, punched his body with hammer-hard fists, mauled him over and over ... the men on the shore now shouting obscenities worthy of his beating, but the lion roar of rushing water obliterated the sounds of those words from Sam's ears. He was thrown and slapped hard against huge rocks as the raging creek put its teeth to his throat and yanked his breath from his lungs. Pain sped up his spine to the base of his skull, and he was gone from himself.

When he awakened, he was naked beneath a thin saddle blanket, hands tied behind his back, feet bound together like an animal waiting for the knife blade across its throat, the bleeding out, the casting of its entrails upon uncaring ground. He was beside a fire made of dead wood hastily gathered. The four men stood over him.

"He's coming 'round, boys," one of the men said.

Then the man he remembered as the shorter man of the four spoke: "Ya feelin' better now we warmed ya up, boy? Nice o' us, don't ya think ... warmin' ya up like that? Warn't no kind o' fun with ya out like that?"

Words climbed up weakly from Sam's lungs to his throat: "Why are you doing this to me? I don't know you. I haven't done anything to you! What have I done to you?" He looked up at the smarmy grins on their faces, the glances of one to the other ... bully boys tormenting a captured cat.

"You a miner. That's what you done. You a miner what's on strike. That's what you done, boy. Shoulda been happy makin'

what you was given. But no! You had to go and git all uppity lis-
tenin' to 'em 'ere union pricks. You gonna learn yer place, boy."
There was a savageness to the voice that was deep and personal.

Sam already knew that to say anything was probably useless. Such men would do what they were going to do. And still he
hoped, tried reason on unreasonable men: "I mean you no harm.
I'm just a miner. I got no power over anybody. Just let me go.
Please! "Even added "sirs" at the end as a plea to whatever potential they had to forgive his state of unworthiness in their eyes.
He heard his father's voice from within the nearby fire flames:
"Reason ain't got nothing to do with nuthin'. Only question, 'You
gonna die like a man?'"

The littlest of the men who had taken control of him seemed
to be the angriest. He spoke through rotted and broken teeth,
"Somebody gotta pay for you nigger miners all gettin' uppity. An'
you gonna pay fer 'em all. Stand 'im up, boys. Let's see what 'es
made of." Two of the men pulled him upright. At their lifting, pain
shot up and down Sam's back, down his legs, into his toes. The
beating by the creek had done its work. He leaned into the hand-
holds of the men, cried out in pain, could not yet find balance on
his feet. His knees tried to give way, but the men lifted him up
straight, carried him away from the fire to a tree. Above him was a
thick protruding branch almost straight out from the tree like the
top rail to the gallows three or four feet above his head. Three of
them held him. The fourth—the horseman—retrieved both horse
and rope.

Sam pleaded, "No, no, no. Please. No," as the horseman
slipped the noose over Sam's head, snugged it against his neck,
tossed the rope coil over the gray skin of the tree branch and let
it dangle momentarily before Sam's eyes—a taunting torturous
threat to heighten his fear. Sam felt the weight of the rope's rough
hide against his throat, as he watched the horse pulled into place
by the man who would give the rope its meaning. Then the man
picked up the loose end of the rope and tied it to the saddle horn
while the little man spoke, "Whatcha thinkin', boy? You ready to
die today, boy?"

Sam did not know where his words came from, but they came, useless though they were, and yet somehow essential. Perhaps there was something in words that must escape the body before it dies: the confessions of dying men, the easing of the soul, proclamations for innocent men to clear their names, spewing seeds of longings for a life that will not be. Words somehow mattered at times like these to some men. To others, they were but a waste of breath, an admission of acceptance of this awful place upon which they have tread. Words mattered to Sam, though no one who could save him would hear. Words had always mattered to him. Words must be said upon the universe, he thought, captured there for some far-off time. Perhaps he hoped his mother's God would smile upon her, grant her another fish or loaf. Or perhaps because he could not save himself, he said what was too dangerous for any common man to say out loud to those with power. Perhaps he said it for his father: "I am a better man than any of you, even dead! Do what you're gonna do, but it won't make you better men. Fact is you're barely men at all."

The littlest man, the rotted-mouth man punched Sam's jaw, knocked him back against the men who held him, the sudden movement startling the horse, causing it to rear up and dance nervously under the hold of the man with reins. "You son-a-bitch," the little man said, "String the bastard up, Roy. String 'im up!"

The man called "Roy" walked the horse forward pulling the rope taut. The noose tightened around Sam's neck. Sam's feet—heels first—lifted from the earth heavenward. For a moment the men held him, toes pointed, Sam standing upright on them, then heard a command to take him up, kicked his bound legs into space desperately trying to kick one of these bastards as his last act on this earth. His throat closed. Darkness began to come over him.

He came to consciousness as the men threw cold water in his face and slapped his jaws hard one side and then the other. He heard the voice he was now coming to know would be his main tormentor, "Ain't done with you yet, boy!"

A red-bearded, scraggly, sweat-soaked man helped to raise Sam from the ground and held him in place while a nondescript other held him from the left. He had felt his knees buckle, his body wanting to slip back to the ground, but the men would not allow it. He could feel the slightly slackened rope against his neck as the rotted-mouthed, little man stood before him breathing his fetid breath into Sam's face Roy stood beside his horse, smiling like a mean-spirited, ill-bred boy who just set a cat's tail on fire for no more reason than to hear its pathetic cat screams, enjoy watching its agony as it raced through the night somehow trying to escape its tormentors who were now a permanent part of its flesh.

The man spoke again. "So, ya still think you a better man now, boy?" As he said the word *boy*, he punched Sam's stomach and laughed at his groan of pain and his attempt to fall while the others held him up against the pull of the rope at Sam's neck. "Be glad I don't cut yer nuts off, boy."

A part of Sam was beginning to move beyond pain. He was at the point when a tortured man pulled inward and endured—stopped caring about hurt. He was like a soldier ready to take the bullet for the cause of freedom, like the woman willing to die so her newborn child can be saved. He had accepted the inevitable. He tried to drag sound up through his now constricted, blood-clotted throat to claim something for himself before death: "Do what you are going to do. I am still a better man than you."

The little man's face lit red with rage. "Take 'im up agin, Roy! Teach this bastard who's a better man!"

Again, Sam was lifted off his feet, life fleeing from his eyes, sound dissipating to a hum, decrescendo into silence, blazing cold white light of death beyond him. And then, again, cold water was being thrown upon him. The men were slapping his face. Then the voice again, "You still think you a better man, boy?"

The thought of begging clawed at Sam's will to survive. Just tell them "No." Give them what they want and die finally. But again, a voice that was not his own whispered into the ears of the beasts, "I'm a man. As good as most. And better than you." The rope pulled tight.

When he came to consciousness this time, he had been let down all the way to the cold, wet ground like a sack of rotted-mush-brown and fetid apples. Now Roy spoke to him. "See, we didn't kill ya, boy. We's just havin' fun with ya. You be gist fine in a bit once ya heal up. We gonna let ya have a chance to live yer wuthless life. But this here is yer one an' only chance. Now ya go back an' tell 'em union men we ain't gonna stand for no union an' no strikin'. Once you done that, you git yer black ass outta this area and don't ya never come back, ya hear, boy?"

Sam could not speak or move as they cut ropes from his hands and feet. He could not feel his body. Then, the little man kicked Sam in the chest and then in the stomach. Sam wretched, pulled his knees to his chest and cried out in pain. He did not hear them leave. They had simply walked away, horse in tow. They had left the flaccid noose upon a rock like a cross upon a church altar. When the agony in his body decreased, Sam slowly, achingly, rolled himself closer to the dying fire, wept, and passed out.

When he came to, he was shivering. The sky had darkened. He lifted himself slowly and painfully upon his arms, his elbows but inches above the muddy earth, his body having collected to itself layers of cold mud as he tried to drag his legs behind him, thinking he needed to get his clothes on though he had no idea where they were, and all he could see was a blur of light. His eyes refused to focus. He knew he had to stand and then to run, but the best he could muster was the attempt to say it though he could not hear the words: "Get up! Get away! Survive!" He passed out again.

Early evening tapped on Sam's body, tested his flesh for death. He heard his mother from some far-off place, "Wake up, Sam. Wake up, son." He was shivering. He tried to open his swollen eyes. Swirling, black, white, and color lay in his eyeballs like water, oil, and paint stirred in a pot. He closed his eyes again, tried to clear his vision, tried to remember where he was. His skin and flesh ached. Pain squeezed its fingers all over his body. Muscles burned. Neck screamed pain. Head throbbed. "Uhs," "ahs" and "ohs"—the words of his pain unable to rise beyond a rasping gurgle within his throat or crawl across his tongue to his lips. Tears began to wash away the kaleidoscopic designs that blocked his vision, slid them away as he gained a sense of the place where he was lying. Slowly, excruciatingly, he forced his legs from their fetal position. As his legs stretched, his arms unfolded from across his chest, new pain shot at him from every angle. The thought of giving in, lying there to die screamed at him from the universe, challenged the whispering of his mother—that call to life from within.

He could now see the last wisps of smoke from the fire's ashes, though it was as if each of his eyes was seeing an incompatible version and the two versions of reality would only slowly became one. He rose upon an elbow, tried to shake his head, clear his brain. Rolled upon his back, bore the pain to stretch his body out, to look up into the oncoming evening sky. The cold would not let him lay there long. It prodded him with razor sharp swords: *Rise and survive! Or lie here and die; it makes no difference either way.* Just choose! He howled at his pain and sat up despite it, his eyes rapidly scanning the space around him, the mountain behind him, and the trees before him.

Sam knew the path home was just beyond the ridge he could identify. He rose unsteadily to his feet, found his clothes nearby, pulled his wet shirt over his head, tried to step into his pants and fell. He pulled them over his ankles from his sitting position, rose again to finish ... "Better to be naked than wet," he thought as he worked the cold, clinging wetness of inhibitions over his body. He staggered to his coat and shoes, pulled them on, thought again of laying down, letting go, and then stumbled as best he could toward home.

By the time he got back to the road, it was already hardening its ruts and ridges of mud. He staggered like a drunk over the washboard earth, saying over and over as if words can defy death: "I can take just a little bit more. I can; I can ... for as long as it takes!" Time had been lost to him. How long it took to get home, he had no idea. His eyes had blurred; he was barely moving anymore; just tiny pigeon-toed steps were carrying him as he neared the houses of Ebon. Ahead of him, he could see a shape—a person on a porch holding a lamp.

Young Marcus Bridges came out of his house holding a lantern. He paused before stepping off the porch. He was sixteen, a young version of his father, Moze, a boy Sam was as close to as a brother. However, in the state Sam was in, he could not have recognized him, or anyone else, from a distance; all he could grasp was that there was a dim lantern before him shining like the beacon of a god. He tried to call out, kept trying to make his legs work; he just needed to make them go fifteen or twenty feet to fall into the lantern light. But sound would not come from his throat. His legs had done all they could do, and he collapsed.

The boy had heard sound but could not interpret it as the thud of the body or a gasp expelled from Sam's lungs. Marcus raised his lantern high in hopes of seeing deeper into the dark, tried to think what it was he heard and whether it was worth the risk of investigation. He, like the children of all striking miners, had learned that he had to be cautious, the company thugs were willing to use anyone they could, hurt anyone they chose to, and murdered people if the miners were recalcitrant. He and the whole community knew the dangers of becoming careless. Marcus first started to move toward the sound, then stepped back, assessing what he should do just like his father had taught him. Was this the sound of the men returning from the meeting in the hills? But it was too early and too quiet. There was no man-chatter or laughter. Thoughts of the men who hated miners sneaking into the camp crossed his mind. He waited listening for more sound, some verification that there was something to be concerned about. After a moment or so, he decided that maybe he had just imagined something that wasn't there. But now he had to decide whether or not to do as his mother had asked: go to the wood pile for fire logs, and there was still a boy's fear of the dark lingering in his brain, but it annoyed him that he experienced it.

Then came a harsh guttural gasp. This time, Marcus knew he had not imagined it. He reached back inside the door lifted the shotgun his father had placed there "just in case." His mother, Ella, had seen the back of his head, his right arm and his lean upper body coming back through the door reaching for the gun.

She spoke just above quivering whisper, "Marcus, what are you doing? What's happening?"

The boy looked back at his mother still in her rocking chair by the wood stove, put his pointer finger over his lips, shushed her and whispered: "You lock this door and wait. I've got to check something out."

Ella swelled with a mother's fear, a miner's wife's fear, knew what was being said without saying. She had been through strikes before, knew what can happen when bosses are determined to win at any cost. She tried to say in loud whisper as she gasped for breath, "Don't you go out there now!" But Marcus had already escaped her. "God, please. No," slipped quietly from her lips. Then, ignoring her son's command, she ran to the door, and pulled it back, fast and hard, ran oblivious into fate at the lantern light, saw her son trying to lift Sam Matson from the ground. He had raised him to a sitting position, was kneeling behind the slumped body, his arms wrapped around Sam's chest. With strength he had inherited from his father, he lifted Sam up and held him in a standing position. "Get alongside him, here, Mama. Put his arm over your neck and shoulders. I'll do the carrying. You just guide."

Ella felt some of the weight of the man and grabbed hold of the wrist that dangled before her. Marcus picked up the gun and lantern in one hand and slid to the other side of Sam, his strong young arm holding Sam's back, lifted Sam's arm and pulled it up over his own shoulder, grabbed the wrist and held as much weight as he could bear.

***

In coal towns there are no secrets. Eyes watch ubiquitously from windows and doors porches and play yards. They penetrate the night and linger at the windows of day. Neighbor women and teenage boys started coming out—many with guns. Marcus commanded boys to take up his gun and lamp and carry them. He had one of the boys take over for his mother and help get Sam into the house.

Several people had followed the boys in and were trying to get a look at Sam's condition. Marcus had no patience for them, told them to go home as he and the other boy carried him beyond Ella and two other women to the little pallet bed in the corner of the room. And there, they laid the body down.

"We've got to get him out of these wet clothes, get him warm. You women back away," he barked. "I'll tell you when you can come near. Sam wouldn't like you women seeing him naked."

The boy worked fast in the lantern light to strip Sam of his clothes. The other boy held the lantern as Marcus worked. He demanded some dry cloth and warm water from his mother to clean Sam with; Ella handed what passed for towels to the lantern bearer along with a pan of water that had been sitting on the cast-iron stove that heated the house and cooked the family's food; then she left the boys to their task. As the clothes came off, Marcus wiped Sam down with the warm water and dried him immediately, all the time looking his body over for wounds and broken bones. He saw the boot prints that lay on Sam's chest and stomach, saw his neck was rope-scorched all the way around, gently bent his fingers, elbows and knees looking for breaks. He surmised that Sam would become a mass of bruises shortly and would likely be in a lot of pain, but Marcus couldn't find anything that was obviously broken. With that, Marcus covered Sam with his only blanket and his own coat. Then he announced to the room, "He doesn't look like he has any broken bones, but he's hurt bad, and he's cold. Real cold. I need some blankets ... more than this one little one I use. The implication of his command being that it was needed even if it had to be borrowed from somebody who had an extra.

Marcus told the other boy to go home. There was nothing more to be done. One of the women said Doc Leiter needed to get called out for this. Marcus turned his head from the bed, told her, "No! Too dangerous unless you women want to end up like Sam here. I'll take care of him at least until the men get back tonight."

He pulled the flimsy blanket up under Sam's chin. Some of the waiting women went to beg for blankets from the many who had so few. Sam's teeth chattered uncontrollably as the boy stood by thinking about what else he might do, told the others to go home now and let Sam sleep. Most of the boys left; most of the women didn't. The boy who had held the lamp put his hand on Marcus's shoulder and said, "You done good, Marcus," then walked away and out the door with the others.

At one point, it seemed like Sam was beginning to come to. He was trying to talk through his chattering teeth, but Marcus couldn't understand him. When he asked him to repeat, Sam muttered unintelligibly.

Marcus lowered himself down upon his knees beside the bed and spoke in Sam's ear and whispered what he was sure were lies: "You just need to rest, Sam. You'll be okay." The weight of his self-imposed responsibility to this man as much friend and brother as any man he knew pressed pinprick-like into his chest. Marcus thought about the times he and Sam had talked about all kinds of things, about hopes and dreams, fears, living in a world that gave so little and expected so much. Only Sam knew some of his secrets. Marcus looked down upon the now bruising face. He thought of Sam's good looks that attracted people to him, the glint of his eye, the little turned up corner on the left side of his mouth that always seemed to express joy in others' talk, the way he had of leaning forward to hear everything and focusing his deeply caring large brown eyes right on Marcus's eyes, like he was looking into his soul.

Marcus watched Sam's uncontrolled moving lips and wondered if he was trying to talk or just reacting to whatever he'd been through. "What has he been through?" He watched Sam's eyes roll, open and close, over and over as if deciding between waking or sleeping—between life and death.

After a few moments, ignoring the faces and voices of the women gathered here in this now altered and somehow holy place, Marcus simply lay his own body into the bed space beside Sam, lay his arm and leg over Sam, and pressed his whole, strong young body up against him, held him tight. The boy leaked tears, felt them slide off his face onto the blanket that covered Sam's chest until the women came with the blankets. Marcus rose and laid them gently over Sam and then lay down again holding them tight against Sam's skin.

The women stepped away from the bed, talked quietly amongst themselves, left Sam and the boy in the dark corner of the room like the prayers they would give to their gods.

CHAPTER NINE

As the meeting neared its end and the assembled men re-affirmed their resolve to carry on and combat the forces against them, a number of miners' sons appeared. While Josiah was wrapping up, the boys informed Moze about Sam. Moze stepped back in front of the miners and announced that another from within their midst had been beaten. He used the occasion to remind the men what they faced and reminded them to be ever vigilant before dismissing them. As soon as he could, he went quickly down the hills and around the rocks and trees with Josiah Wheeler keeping pace and many others from the Ebon community as well. Though he and Joseph would not have said it in front of any of the miners, they knew each other well enough to know what the other was probably thinking about: concern for Sam and concern for the miners and the outcome of the strike. Though the miners had committed to continuing the strike, it had been clear during the meeting that the miners were nearing the end of their patience with union efforts to get owners to nego-tiate. The union wasn't strong enough and was running out of resources for supplying food for the miners' families. Soon the men would decide their options were limited to choosing from amongst four evils: yield to the profiteers, sacrifice themselves and their families to eternal poverty, run to who knows where (to do what?), or fight, even knowing they would likely fail.

The Ebon miners returned to their homes in a parade of dim lantern light. When the group got to Moze's place, he stood on the porch, raised his lamp up over his head and looked out over the gathered men, and said, "Go home now and get warm. Josiah and I will take a look at Sam, and we'll let you know if there is anything to do about this tonight. Go take care of your families." Some of the men walked away. Others, mostly black miners, their anger palpable, made it clear they weren't going to leave until they got the report on Sam's condition. Moze promised he and Josiah would return to them as soon as they could see Sam and get a better sense of his condition.

As the two men entered the house, Ella moved to Moze, wrapped her arms around his waist, pressed her face up against his cold coat, and said "Looks like they tried to hang Sam. He's bad off. Marcus took good care of him ..." but before she could finish, Moze had put his hands on her shoulders and gently pushed her away. He lifted the lantern he had set on the table and went to the bed in the back corner of the room. Josiah followed. Marcus, now sitting on the edge of the bed, looked up at his father, "He's so cold, Dad. I wanted to make him warm."

Moze put his huge, hard-skinned hand out for his son, lifted him up off the bed with ease. Marcus took the lantern, stood over his father who had gone to his knees to look at Sam. Marcus spoke authoritatively, not as a boy to his man father but as a man speaking to another man and was making a list of what he had done. "Checked him out. Ran my hands over his body. Didn't find any broken bones. Wiped him down. Trying to get him warm. He's been beaten badly. Looks like they tried to hang him. Look at his neck." Then he paused, his clinical assessment giving way to passion, "Why? Why would anyone do that?" He felt the urge to cry but fought against it.

"There is a lot of hate in the world, my son. You did the right things. That's all there is to do: do right things."

Moze pulled back the covers. Marcus held the lantern above the body, holding it like the eye of Christ upon Lazarus as he was called forth from the tomb. Sam was now looking up glaze-eyed and trying to talk. He shook less now, Marcus noticed. As Moze checked him for broken bones, Marcus handed the lantern to Josiah, neither of them conscious of the shift in status, just did what needed doing. Marcus had claimed his space among them pointing out all the various things he had seen on Sam's body. He showed the men the boot prints on Sam's chest and stomach coming out in deeper shades of red than even an hour earlier. He helped his father roll Sam to his side to show his back and the massive bruises that were making their way to the surface. He gently lifted Sam's chin to show the rope burns high up in the skin beneath his jaws and under his ears.

Josiah looked on while the boy and his father worked like skilled medical men carefully assessing facts, diagnosing potential for the patient to survive. He thought about his own sons, thought about having seen Sam earlier in the day: this good looking, strong young man—a good man. He, like Marcus, could not hold back, the word, "Why?" He had seen enough. "I'm going to get the doc. Get him up here."

"No!" Moze commanded. "We don't need you getting yourself beaten or killed. Too dangerous. We've got enough problems here with men being picked off one by one. Ned a couple days ago, others before that. Now Sam. They're not likely to stop there. I need you here. I think Sam's going to hurt pretty bad for a few days, but he'll be all right. We'll take care of him. Right now, we've got to keep the hot-heads amongst the men from doing anything stupid. They're going to want revenge."

"We better go out and talk to 'em," Josiah said, "But I'm thinking they're about talked out. It's getting tougher and tougher to hold them back."

"I know. But we've got to. You know what's going to happen if we get into an honest-to-God fight."

Josiah didn't respond. He knew.

Marcus remained silent and worried.

Before leaving the bedside, Moze put his large heavy arm around his son's shoulders, pulled him against himself, reached up to the back of the boy's head and coaxed his yet whiskerless face against his own and then released him. He and Josiah walked out the door to fulfill their promise.

***

Marcus, lying beside Sam, awakened with each of Sam's groans as the battered man tried to shift his weight away from one pain to the lesser of another. Marcus had wedged his body as tightly against Sam as he could to keep him warm and to keep him from thrashing. They were both covered in blankets now. Sam had stopped shivering and chattering sometime after Marcus first fell asleep next to him. Then Sam made a painful groaning that Marcus heard as, "Pleeeeeeeeese ... No! ... Don't."

Marcus asked in whisper, "Sam, what is it? What can I do to help?"

Sam now becoming more conscious, tried to take in, sort through the confusion of where he was, who was beside him, what was being asked of him, what had happened to him.

Whispering, the boy said, "It's me, Sam: Marcus. You're safe. You are safe, Sam. Do you hear me?"

Sam tried to speak through the pain in his throat, eventually raspy whispered, "Water."

The boy got up, moved through the light from the moonlit window to the water bucket on the table in what they called "kitchen"–just another corner of the main room. He lifted a dipper full, balanced it against spill and took it to Sam. He raised Sam's head gently, heard him groan before he sipped from the edge of the metal cup end of the utensil. When he had had enough, he looked up into Marcus's face like a baby suckling from its mother's breast in the glimmer of moonlight. After a moment, he whispered, "They hurt me bad."

The boy controlled the desire to cry, "I know, Sam. I saw what they did to you. I cleaned you up, fixed you up, best I could. You need to rest now. You're safe. Don't talk. I won't let anything hurt you again, Sam." Marcus lay there in the tinge of moonlight that had crawled its way from the window into the room highlighting Sam's anguished face looking up at him.

Then, he did not know or question why he did it, but Marcus stood and took off all his clothes. He pulled the covers aside long enough to climb into the bed beside Sam skin-to-skin like ashes-to-ashes, wrapped his arms around him, and pulled his body gently to himself. Marcus felt the tears from Sam's eyes falling onto his chest as Sam slowly lifted his arm over the boy and held him. Their tears mingled on the boy's face and chest, sliding down the smooth surfaces of their bodies into minute canyons and caverns of oblivion like time across their fathers' fathers.

CHAPTER TEN

In a move to end the dispute in their favor, owners called on their longtime champion, Federal Judge, John Hatcher, to issue a blanket injunction forbidding the union from interfering in mining operations. When it was done, it came as a severe blow to the miners and their hopes of a successful stand against the owners. When Moze and Josiah were informed by union headquarters, Josiah said to Moze, "This routine's gettin' old."

"It does get discouraging," Moze said, with an unusual sound of pessimism in his voice.

"Proverbial rock and a hard place." Josiah said more to his coffee cup than to Moze who knew all the clichés as well as he did. Both men felt the strain of their years working to get some fairness for the miners.

Moze sipped his coffee, his mind struggling with concepts, the invincibility of an idea worth fighting for, even dying for, knowing that even dying doesn't make it so. "We've got to deal with the fact that the men are tired of hearing 'negotiate' when negotiating is not going to happen. They're not stupid. They're going to choose defiance just like you and I have in the past. It's all they've got. It's all any of us has when it's all said and done." As he said the words, he realized that *defiance* would translate to *violence* when the miners stopped believing that reason can win against those who won't be reasonable, who believe that the already-rich owners' desire for wealth and power is more important than allowing others to exist ...

"So, what do you suggest?" Josiah's question called Moze back into his presence. "Where do we go from here?"

"I say just keep telling our men the truth about what they're facing and why standing up is better than giving in," Moze answered. Let it be their decision to give in if that's what they want. From where I stand, I don't see anything else to do but try to keep the pot hot but not boiling over."

What Moze didn't add to the end of that sentence but both men understood, was "too often and too much." Both men lamented that death and destruction had been far too often what forced both sides into negotiation. They didn't want that on their consciences if they could avoid it. However, with Hatcher's order, time was running out, and they knew the miners would most likely fight solely for the reason of being men, for the reason of saying, "No! If I die in trying, so be it!" Many had already crossed the line in the sand between themselves and the owners and operators of the mines—a line between "We are men!" and "We are your beasts of burden."

Both men knew the owners had more than enough money to outlast the striking miners, but they also knew that the strike was having an impact on company profits and making it impossible for the owners to skirt around the heavy costs of paying for guards to protect their properties. However, owners were determined to win and keep the unions out, even if it cost a fortune. The thinking seemed to be that money could be made again, but power—once it is lost—might never be regained. On the other side of two opposing forces, UMW headquarters leaders were using their much more limited resources to solicit support for the cause from political influencers who put pressure on owners to negotiate and West Virginia government to be fairer in administration of the law.

Moze and Josiah had been taught well that feeding news to the press throughout the campaign was a way to gain public support and put that support to use for taunting the owners to come to the bargaining table and as a means of making the miners feel their cause was just. Recently, they had contacted *The Charleston*

Gazette by telegraph inviting someone to come get the real story of what the miners were facing and why they were committed to continuing the strike.

Arthur Banderman, a top reporter for the newspaper, arrived by train two days after the union meeting and Sam's beating. Moze took the reporter to his home, let him meet and interview Sam and then took him to Ned Anderson's. Then he and Josiah sat with Banderman for a long interview, laying out their position and their perceptions of what the owner's syndicate was doing, all the while trying to appeal to the reporter's sense of humanity and justice.

Josiah laid the groundwork, reminding the reporter of the history of the strike, and then explaining the many actions of the guards waylaying miners' families, making threats, roughing up various miners, and maybe "disappearing" a couple of miners who vanished; he finished with the statement that, "Owners will do anything they can to stop unions and will go to any length to control a strike. They are employing men to threaten, maim, and even kill miners. They are paying them more to keep us from a living wage than it would have cost to pay us what we're worth. They say our pay eats into their profits and a union takes away their right to control their own business and gives workers a sense of undeserved importance. We say, miners give the muscle and sweat of their bodies to provide the means for owners to gain wealth and, therefore, have a right to a fair portion of the profit. But what do we get? We live in mine camps at the will of the owners, die in the mines, get no compensation for our widows or children if we die or are injured. When we grow old and can't work anymore, they throw us out of our homes because we're no longer of use to them."

Moze contributed that he perceived the owners' approach to mining as a system of continued slavery that came out of Reconstruction. He also pointed out how the "Truck System"[14] was being used as another form of control of workers, paying them in scrip rather than cash, forcing them to buy at the company store at high prices and having to borrow against coming paychecks to feed families on wages that won't cover costs, and then, "owing-'til-you-die." To emphasize his point, he said, "It's Jim Crow for miners ... black and white."

They went on to talk about the absurdities of the syndicate: a union of owners working to dismantle unions for workers.

"So, you see it as a power struggle more than a money issue," Banderman summarized.

Moze, animated in his response to what he saw as Banderman's misunderstanding of the issues, responded a bit more aggressively than he knew he should, "The money's definitely an issue with miners. We're not talking about us getting filthy rich, but we need to make enough money to take care of our families. We can't afford to live on what they pay us. As to power, if you call demanding to be treated like human beings a power struggle ... if you call wanting not to die in unsafe working conditions and demanding companies pay attention to bad equipment and bad air we have to deal with a "power struggle," I guess it is! I just call it asking for basic human decency."

Josiah heard uncharacteristic sarcasm in Moze's words and changed the subject, giving Moze an opportunity to rethink the tone of his remarks, just as Moze had done for him in the past. The men had both bristled in previous interactions with others over the issue of power vs. fairness, and the interpretation that fairness could only be achieved through domination and not through reason—a perception both men saw as a sad commentary on humanity.

The interview continued for well over an hour before the reporter made it clear he was ready to move on, get back to Charleston, and begin the process of fact checking the claims that the organizers had laid out for him. Before leaving, he asked a final question: "These battles between owners and workers have gone on for a long time, so what is it going to take to fix these problems that nobody seems to be able to fix?"

Moze responded with, "Change of the human heart! Learning to view workers as fellow human beings with families and needs just like the owners."

Josiah jumped into the answer with, "Give us a living wage! But they don't want to do that. They see us as parts in a machine, not human, and easily replaceable."

Moze tagged onto Josiah's statement with, "That's why the answer to your question has to be unionization. A union allows men to be men, to have some say in their working conditions and get fair pay so they can take care of their families and educate their children." And then the interview was over.

The resulting article provided a fairly close rendition of what was discussed and what the reporter had seen with his own eyes. Banderman's verbal description of seeing Sam and Ned—both men covered in bruises over much of their bodies and obviously in great pain—combined with telling their stories of their beatings was powerful. His words about the reasoning of the two sides for their stance on the strike and their beliefs about power made it clear that the reporter saw little hope a peaceful solution would be found. His comments about the injunction and the unfairness of it were tempered as a result of interviews he did the following day with company representatives, resulting in a subdued article that concluded with his interpretation that ...

> ... Union officials continue to make claims that West Virginia coal owners and operators are unfair and own politicians, the law, and the state. "Owners and operators have stacked the deck like card sharps clipping suckers," according to Wheeler.
>
> The miners have a particular dislike of Federal Judge Hatcher. According to union men, Hatcher's blanket injunction would keep his friends warm through the coming winter while the "horny-handed sons of toil" starve.
>
> Mine owners argue that coal is too unprofitable if they have to pay the wages being demanded.
>
> Miners say that what they are being paid cannot sustain them and their families.
>
> We fear war is about to let loose!

And it was.

***

The families of Ebon slept warily. Sam, healing slowly, still shared Marcus Bridge's bed. Marcus was the first of his family to hear the shot—the wake-up call. Then came the shouting: Marshal Frothman demanding of the camp that Moze and Josiah surrender themselves. Marcus got out of the bed, went to the window and looked upon the army of men just beyond the houses. His father came out of the back of the house, dragging his pants up above his waist. Sam was rising painfully from the bed as Moses yelled out the door he had opened just enough to be heard, "Don't shoot! I'm coming out unarmed!"

As he pulled the door open, he felt a bullet's heat slung past his head, slammed the door shut screaming, "Stop shooting! Stop shooting! I'm surrendering!" But the shooting didn't stop.

Mozes could hear Miles Frye yelling, "Stop, goddamn it! They want to surrender. What the hell is wrong with you?"

"Miles? Miles! Get them to stop!" Moze was yelling, hoping that the sheriff had some means for getting through to Frothman to stop the attack. What Moze couldn't know was that Frye had been trying to stop the marshal. Frothman was ignoring him, even when Frye threatened to make charges against him.

The shooting didn't stop even when Ella and other women nearby were screaming, "Stop! Women and children in here! We're not shooting!"

Frothman hollered back through the whine of the bullets, the "thwuck" sound they made as they entered the wood siding and crackling and tinkling sounds of window glass exploding into the rooms of other homes where panicked children cried. "Women and children will have to take care of themselves!"

"We are not firing!" Moze screamed over the top of barrage of bullets. But it wasn't true. Many miners were now firing into the dark where the voices of the marshal and others came from in an effort to fend off the attack and to protect their families.

"Too late now, nigger," someone hollered back.

The crack of rifles was now coming from everywhere. The marshal's posse of deputized mine guards had surrounded the collection of houses and were continuing to shatter homes with their guns. Moze grabbed Ella and pushed her back toward the bedroom, telling her and the other children to get under the bed. Then he ran back to Marcus and Sam who had fallen to the floor and told them to stay there. He picked up his double-barrel shot-gun before trying once more to plead with the men outside, "Stop! You're going to kill women and children here. We will give up!" But no one was listening.

Bullets pierced the door. Then voices of the attackers grew louder. They were making their assault on the houses. Moze, see-ing no other option than to protect his family, went to the broken window and fired his gun, both barrels roaring into the darkness before receiving the volley of return fire throwing him several steps backward before he fell to the floor. Marcus pushed himself up and threw himself at the place where his father lay. Sam was trying to rise. As Marcus held his bleeding father, Sam tried to reach for the shotgun, but as his hand reached the gun stock, the door flew open, and wild men came rushing in still firing.

***

When the posse had done enough shooting to satisfy Froth-man's anger, and no return fire was coming at them, The mar-shal gave the signal to stop the onslaught. As the smoke from the gunfire began to dissipate, he shouted orders for the miners and their families to come out with their hands up. Deputies then checked for anyone who might be hiding in the houses. The men who were not dead or severely wounded were then taken as prisoners whether they had participated in the battle or not. The women and children were left to fend for themselves and answer the UMW representatives and the reporters who would descend upon them the following morning:

WEST VIRGINIA RIOT QUELLED: SEVERAL DEAD

INDIANAPOLIS, Nov. 20.—About day-break on Thursday officers and their posse surprised rioters in their camp calling them to surrender. The reply was a gunshot, and a furious battle ensued. Four of the rioters lay dead when the fighting ended. Numerous others were wounded, two of them likely to die.

Ten people arrested were taken by Deputy Frothman and sixty-three others by Sheriff Frye. All prisoners were taken to Beckley for a preliminary hearing and held for appearance in court.

A representative of the United Mine Workers Union, Dylan Welsh, went to the scene on Friday and reported he had gone to a home occupied by a woman, Ella Bridges and several small children, where he observed dead bodies of her husband Moze, her son Marcus, and a man named Sam Matson ... all previously known by Welsh as "good men."

This shooting took place without warning, and the men—all Negroes—were found dead on the floor from multiple gunshot wounds..

Welsh stated, "We also visited another house where Josiah Wheeler lay mortally wounded and then died, having been shot as he was dressing to come out to surrender."

"During the shooting men and women of the camp pleaded for mercy, but pleas were met with derision and curses. Our investigation proves conclusively that no effort was made to shoot until miners were left with no choice but to defend themselves against premeditated violence of the posse instigated by its leaders. All would have surrendered had they been given the opportunity," Welsh said.

Local sheriff, Miles Frye, who was at the scene, suggests that Welsh's version has some merit, though he did not elaborate.

It is believed the strike will now end and remaining miners will accept the pay cut that had set it in motion.

Ella Bridges folded the week-old newspaper and stared out the train's window. Soon she and her remaining children would be back in Ohio amidst the remnants of her husband's family, bringing with her a tattered bag of personal belongings, already fading newspaper clippings worn thin from reading, and the three embalmed bodies to be taken to a priestless burial in the Golgotha Hill Cemetery.

When the monument finally arrived a few months later, she watched and waited as it was being set. Once the workmen walked away, she went to it and ran her fingers over each indented letter—the names, the births, and the common death date—as if the touch were skin and would somehow bring them out from the stone to be with her again as if words and longing had magic within them ... and her wishing it could be true.

The cold of early March pressed upon her, burned her fingertips and toes. She had children to attend to and lessons to prepare. She got up off her knees and stared at the hard, cold stone a moment longer. Into the silence of the graveyard, she said their names one by one and then pronounced them collectively as "far, far better men than most," before walking away across the greening grass and home.

Elaine

Elaine Davis went to her car and wept through her lunch hour as she had done each day for well over a week. When time was up, she pulled another tissue from the box in the passenger seat and dabbed the tears from her eyes. She turned the rear-view mirror so she could reapply the faint hint of blush to her cheeks and tap the powder brush against her face to absorb the remaining moisture that lay there. Drops of Visine helped with the redness of her eyes but could do nothing to restore the long-departed spark. Makeup wasn't going to fix that. As she got out of the car, she fluffed her auburn hair, then let the tufts fall into places of their own making. She pulled at her navy-blue skirt, matching jacket, and white blouse to minimize the wrinkles the car seat had made. As she reached the entrance door of the Foster Company regional office, she avoided her reflection in the tinted glass. As if walking out of the wings and onto the stage, she did what she had to do for the audience's pleasure—another performance—faked a smile and walked through the door as if she owned the world and loved everybody in it.

Within half an hour of her return, she was in the all-staff training room greeting people as they arrived—mid-level management and the public relations and sales teams—with a joyfulness that disarmed the snipers amongst them. When the meeting had started and she finished making a joke about some perceptions related to the usefulness of meetings, she said, "We're going to play a game. I'm going to tell one person a secret. I'm only going to say it once, and I'm not going to answer any questions about it once I've said it. When I'm done, that person is going to tell the next person the secret following the same rules. We'll do this until everyone in the room has been told the secret." She waded through smart aleck comments, tittering amusement and the grimaces and groans of the snipers, made a joke that if this felt like a grade-school game, it was. "There is method in this madness," she proclaimed. "If it bombs, I'll take the hit!"

As Elaine approached Kathryn Nelson, Kathryn, playing to her colleagues, jokingly begged not to be first. Elaine asked the roomful of people to be quiet before she whispered in Kathryn's ear, "The Washburn Building on Fifth Street has been bought by Weser, Inc. It's a fire trap. Current employees will be moved to another Weser site. Weser is going to demolish the building and replace it with an apartment house called 'Liar's Corner.'"

When the last person in the group had been told, Elaine asked the woman, Anne, to tell the secret that had been passed. Anne began by laughing nervously and apologizing if she "screwed up the secret" but, as best she could understand it, "Some geezer was going into a corner and lying about firing some employees who wanted to build an apartment house."

When the laughing stopped, Elaine read the statement that she had originally whispered. Again, everyone in the room, including Elaine, burst into a fit of laughter. She began taunting them with, "All right you guys! Who screwed it up?" Almost everyone said it was the person who had whispered it to them. Then she got serious.

As a game, it's funny, but in real life it can be a big problem. That's really why we're here today ..."

Jim Handly, always the clown, imitating an overly exuberant grade-school student, started waving his hands and interrupted, "Oooh, Oooh, teacher? Teacher?" When Elaine acknowledged him, he said, "I heard a rumor training sessions are going to be canceled forever."

"No, Jim," Carol Evans piggybacked on his silliness, "I heard that we're all getting a fifty-percent increase in pay and a huge Christmas bonus!"

"Really?" Elaine wrested control, "I hate to burst your bub-
bles, guys, but no one from on high has given me any information that those rumors are true. Sorry. I don't recommend holding
your breath waiting for those things to happen."

Then Chuck Lassiter spoke. "All joking aside, there's been a
rumor floating around here over the past few days that Foster is
pulling out of Columbus in the coming year. My wife also heard it
from someone she knows—somebody who doesn't work here. I'd
like to know if there's any truth in it."

Scrunching her face, trying to look like she had just taken in a
mouthful of sour milk, Elaine growled like cartoon bear, "Grrrrr.
It's true ...." Giving the audience a few seconds to react, she blurted out, "Not!' Feeling the tension in the room release, she laughed
out loud. "It's true that that rumor is floating around," then she
became serious: but it is not—N-O-T—not true that Foster is
planning to leave Columbus anytime soon. However, we do have
a problem. The rumor has caused some of you concern and, if it
is out on the streets (and it is, unfortunately), it can harm our
relationships with customers, our friends in city government, and
our relationships with the community as a whole. How the rumor
started and gained traction, I don't know. I spoke with headquarters in Phoenix yesterday to reconfirm what I've just told you.
What is true is that there is a proposal at corporate headquarters
to restructure community relations activities to make messag-
ing more consistent with the company's national approach, and
there will likely be some jockeying of positions within community relations. But Corporate has already stated that we here in
Columbus are exemplars and they want to use our system as a
basic model for organizational restructuring and effectiveness. At
the moment, it's just a proposal and nothing is finalized. It's an
idea, not a done deal!

When Elaine finished explaining what was being done to
squelch the rumor, she explained how rumors hurt customers,
employees, and the community and what employees could do to
assist in killing the beast that had come upon them. Her presen-
tation included handling rumor control and counter-messaging

made more palatable to the group as she likened each of them to Dragon Slayers, Knights of Faerûn, and joked that they needed to put on their armor and mount their armored steeds. The participants applauded to which she made a bow like that of the coloratura soprano at the end of Bellini's "Casta Diva" followed by her best rendition of Porky Pig's "That's all folks."

As the employees began getting out of their chairs, Jim Handly shouted humorously, "Next time, can we play Duck, Duck, Goose?" Elaine laughed and made a joke that if he wasn't careful, he would have to *duck* for cover when she came after him. As she was picking up the markers she had used to emphasize a few of her key points, several people thanked her for making training fun. As they passed by, she slid the markers into their plastic case abruptly like guns that had slipped out of their holsters. She was making herself appear too busy to make small talk, gathering up materials, folding the easel with the pad still attached, and returning her props to the storage room. When she came out of the closet-sized room, and busily straightened chairs and picked up the debris of other people's making, the hangers-on took the hint that she didn't have much time for chit-chat and went out the door to their offices.

As the laughter of employees walking down the corridor began to fade, Elaine allowed herself to feel the exhaustion of the actor after a bravura performance and felt the fake smile getting sucked away by the emptiness of the room. She had pulled it off: the rumors game that she settled upon only fifteen minutes before she took her lunch break. She had entertained them and taught them: Don't jump to conclusions; know the sources of rumors and innuendos; check facts. What she hadn't taught them was how painful the process can be when a rumor turns out to be true.

Back at her office, Elaine asked Wendy, her secretary, to run interference and give her half an hour before letting the usual parade of the insecure and the lonely in. The door was unusually heavy, had to be dragged behind her as she stepped through and pulled it shut and twisted the wand that made the blinds close over the door's glass panel. Then she cranked the wide louvered slats into place flat against the window-covered walls on two sides of her office. The overhead fluorescents went out with a flick of her middle finger, an unconscious "flipping off" of an obnoxious imposition on her space. At her desk, she couldn't decide whether she just wanted to sit and stare, try to take on a work task, or lay her head on the desk and cry. For a while she sat, rocking in her comfortable leather chair, the motion somehow soothing, but her eyes kept going to the photograph of her husband she kept just beyond her desk calendar. Without ceasing the back-and-forth movement, she picked up the frame and held it at her waistline. She touched it, leaving fingerprints on the glass that covered his face, the strong jawline, his whisker stubs, his lips. She started to cry again, a few tears dripping onto the picture frame as she pulled it closer to her face. She stopped rocking and quickly wiped the surface with a tissue before holding the frame against her breasts for a moment as if the frame really were him. Then she put the picture frame gently into her desk drawer face down, closed the drawer, and started rocking again, the back and forth and up and down motion somehow primal and soothing as a counter to her thoughts, the almost constant feeling of wanting to crawl into a dark hole and disappear from the world.

It had all come at her too fast: the end of her marriage. She was trying to be reasonable ... "So goddamned reasonable," she told herself as she drifted back into recent experiences playing themselves over and over in her head like a bad song set on endless "repeat."

***

"Are you alone?" Elaine's best friend, Mary Ellen, asked over the cellphone. No, "Hi" or "How are you?" It was asked with urgency and secrecy as if something sinister was going on between them.

Caught by the surprise of Mary Ellen's question, Elaine responded cautiously, "Joe's not here if that's what you're asking. What's up?"

"I have something to tell you, but I wanted to make sure Joe isn't around. Is he going to be out for a while?" Mary Ellen's voice was noticeably strange, deadly, like there was no humor anywhere in her.

Elaine assured her that Joe was at a meeting that wouldn't get him back into town before ten o'clock. "This sounds serious."

"Can I come over?"

Elaine said hesitatingly, "O-kaaay" in a way that was equally statement, exclamation, and question. "But can I have some idea what's going on?"

"Best to wait 'til I get there."

In the ten minutes it took for Mary Ellen to arrive, Elaine had imagined any number of potential scenarios, mostly related to Mary Ellen's life, but she couldn't imagine what any of that would have to do with Joe not being home.

***

"Come on, Elaine! You believe her? Mary Ellen Maynard is a fucking busybody troublemaker who has nothing better to do with her life than make up shit about people!" Joe was crying and yelling at the same time.

"But you can't look me in the eye for more than a few seconds without turning away, Joe. If it's not true, why are you so upset," Elaine's volume matching his.

He turned away from her and shouted into the empty space of their living room, "It's a lie! And you believe it."

"I didn't want to believe it, called it a lie when Mary Ellen told me what she'd heard from Linda Mason. So I called Linda and heard it from her. It was her son that told her." Realizing that she was yelling, she subdued her voice, tried to find the voice of reason and said quietly, "I went to see him. I made him tell me everything he knew. He says he has seen you at that bar several times—a gay bar, you and other men. He says he saw you with somebody who's a regular there, somebody he knows, saw how you acted, and it wasn't just two guys with a few drinks under their belts acting stupid! He knows gay when he sees it! And, maybe by whatever code of behavior gay men have about outing other people, he shouldn't have done it, but he did!" I would love to believe he's a liar, that none of this is true. But I need you to tell me the truth."

He just stood there, his body quivering.

She could feel the pain her question caused, the surprise, the hurt. Seeing that he was not going to respond, she continued. "I love you. I do! I want you to be happy, but I can't ... won't ... share you. If you're a gay man or a bisexual, it's time you get honest with yourself and me." Her voice started to rise again as she said emphatically, "You can't live with a lie, and I'm not going to live in a lie. Which is it? Gay or straight? And if you're straight, tell me why that young man says you're not. Are you gay, Joe?"

He turned and faced her. Tears increased, flowed as rivulets down his cheeks and over his face, his body convulsing. Torrential rains spun within the windstorms of sobs and repeated attempts to say in almost whispers, "I'm sorry." He fell into the cushion of a chair and dropped his face into the broad palms of his hands. The answer to her question was obvious. And then he spoke in a voice that wove between his sobs, "I tried so hard not to be."

***

At the end of thirty minutes, Wendy called to say that people were waiting to see her. Elaine reached for and clicked the "on" button of her small desk lamp and felt a brief moment of peace in the soft light of the thirty-watt bulb. She took a moment before she turned on her computer, pulled a file from her credenza, spread the papers on her desk, and finally got up, turned on the overheads, opened the blinds and then the door, swinging it open to whomever was there. The work she should have been doing would have to wait.

For the remainder of the day, she met with her staff, answered questions about projects they were working on, reviewed news releases and answered telephone calls. Apparently the rumor about the company leaving Columbus had gone viral. She and her staff had to deal with phone calls from various news agencies, counter social media stories, and provide supervisors and head-quarters with updates about what they were doing to undercut the spreading disinformation.

When staff left for the day, Elaine was exhausted, but she stayed. She had work to do, and she didn't want to go home to an empty house, all the reminders of Joe, and all the questions she needed to answer about what she hadn't been able to see in him, what she needed or wanted to do now that he had left her, and how she would deal with the overwhelming loneliness she was feeling. "Anyway, I've got work to do," she said as if trying to convince someone other than herself.

The proposal from headquarters she had mentioned in the meeting—the proposal she had read previously and didn't like—needed a response before Wednesday of the following week. What she hadn't said at the training session earlier in the day was that at the heart of the document was a belief that regional sights didn't need PR people and that all PR work could be handled at headquarters. The plan would eliminate at least half of the staff spread out among various locations, including her own. It was true that the processes she and her staff instituted were to become the model at headquarters as well as the impetus for taking the jobs away from her staff. On the computer, where she was trying to make notes to herself in preparation for a response to headquarters, she wrote, "No good deed goes unpunished." What she needed was an argument that would hold up to scrutiny, one that wouldn't sound like she was protecting her job or her staff rather than working to make the company more efficient and effective, an argument that would make a case for continuing to engage and build relationships with locals who trust that the company cares about them and not just the company's bottom line.

Shortly after seven o'clock, Don Benson, knocked on her door, startling her. Elaine looked up, recognized who had been knocking and tried not to show her annoyance with being interrupted. He was looking through the glass door with an exaggerated, "I'm-being-playful-and-cute" look and expected to be welcomed. Thinking, "Oh, God, I really don't want to deal with him," Elaine knew dismissing a vice-president of the company was not a wise move. Pulling a half-smile to her face, she raised her hand and motioned for him to come in. In the past, she might have spent a moment admiring the man, carefully groomed, impeccably dressed in a tailor-made gray wool suit, still handsome at forty. She might have taken time to noticed how his smile exaggerated the slight crow's feet made at the outer corners of his eyes, the movie-star-whiteness and perfect alignment of his teeth, the strength of his jaw and chin. She might have enjoyed the flicker of desire she felt on those occasions as long as there were other people around. He was one of those men that women love and hate:

too good looking for his own good, and dangerous ... the kind of man that made her feel like women were potential sexual experiences rather than people.

As Benson entered, he said, "I saw your light was on. I'm glad to know I'm not the only person here. Place is kind of depressing when there's nobody around. Mind if I sit for a few minutes?"

Elaine watched him settle his long body into the armchair beside her desk before she had time to politely respond to his question. Still thinking about her work, she said, "I've been reviewing the proposal from headquarters. I'll have my responses for you in the next couple of days so we can discuss them before the meeting next week."

Suddenly animated, he said, "I already hate it ... the whole idea of it." Elaine was surprised by the animation in his voice, the sudden rise in volume.

When she asked him why, Benson looked at her and said, "I have no intentions of letting you go if they try to coax you into moving—being their trainer ... I mean, ... that is ... unless you want to go. I'll find a different position for you if it will keep you here." The way he said these words with his head bent downward to keep his eyes from meeting hers made her feel like they were sitting in a sleazy bar over a couple of cocktails talking about their spouses' inadequacies as a prelude to an affair. She could feel her nerve endings sending reactionary red pigment onto the surface of her skin, the tightening of her chest, and a wariness splashed against her brain cells.

She looked away from him, put her eyes on the proposal, picked it up nervously and spoke more to it than to him. "I don't like the proposal or what they want a trainer to do. It's too prescriptive. I am trying to look at it from the standpoint of what's best for the company, not what a change might mean for me. The proposal is sloppy and seems more like somebody's whim than a real proposal. There's no data to back up anything, no clear explanation of what is wrong with what the regional offices are doing. I sent an email asking for clarifications, but I'm not sure I'll get what I need before we go to Phoenix next week."

Benson looked at her, told her he knew she would do an excellent job of presenting her point of view. When he finished, he sat and waited, watching Elaine set the proposal on her desk and then fidget with the pen that she picked up and held in both hands.

After an uncomfortable silence, she asked, "Was there something else you needed to talk about, Don?"

He began to shift in his seat, pull his arms from the chair's arm rests, let his hands rest on his knees momentarily; then, as if he didn't quite know what to do with his body, he pulled himself up straight, let his forearms lay back on the rests. The skin on his face moistened and reddened.

"Yeah. There is. I've been looking forward to a time when you and I could talk. I've picked up on some vibes from you ..."

"Vibes? What kind of vibes?"

"I think you know what I mean," he said.

"I don't know what you mean. What are you talking about?"

"I've seen how you look at me. I heard you're going through some tough times, and I thought you might like to have someone to talk to ... or maybe help take your mind off things for a while. I was thinking we might go over to Louie's have a couple drinks."

Elaine looked at Benson's sheepish smile, his inability to look her in the eye, and told him, "I can't. I'm married. And I never meant to suggest ... I really have a lot of work to do."

"From what I hear, your husband is out of the picture. If what I heard is true, you're better off without him."

In a flash of anger, she asked, "What do you mean by I'm better off without him? How do you know that? You don't know anything about him or how I feel."

Unruffled, he responded calmly, "I know lots of things ... maybe more than you think. Let's just say a little birdy told me he threw you over because he prefers men. Why would you want to waste your time on that?"

"That little birdy of yours has no business talking about my private life and neither do you," she flashed her barely controlled anger again."

"Now, don't go getting all worked up. I just thought maybe you would want to talk about it. I'm a good listener."

"The last thing in this world I need right now is you!"

He sat there looking at her as if she had said nothing. After a moment, he said calmly, "Need I remind you, Elaine, that I am a vice-president in this company, and I can be anywhere I wish to be. You can't throw me out. And I can fire anybody I want to, so I encourage you to take a different tact. Would you like to try again?"

Gritting her teeth, she responded slowly. "Yes, I would like to try again. You need to leave now, sir! Fire me if you want. I'll file a harassment complaint while you go to hell where you belong."

Benson lifted himself up out of the chair, walked slowly to the door and opened it; he turned back to her, put on his mischievous little boy smile, and asked her, "Is there anything I could do or say that would change your mind?"

She looked up from the desk and said, "No. There isn't. And I don't ever want to have this conversation again." Then she picked up her pen and began turning pages of the proposal.

He looked at her, recognizing she was rattled, smiled at her, and said, "I'm sorry it didn't work out; perhaps another time."

She did not look up. Instead, she fantasized about throwing her metal stapler at the glass of the soon-to-be-closed door just to hear the plate glass sheet fracture and fall in a heap of tiny glass chunks behind Benson. She thought of doing better yet: throwing the stapler's weight against Benson's head, watching him, his being, his maleness break into shards of glass.

"See you in the morning," he said casually, cheerfully, ignoring all that had occurred between them.

As he walked away, the door began closing and eventually struck the door frame. The wall's metal pillars, posts, and their panes of glass rattled arrhythmically on Elaine's mental state. She thought about leaving, picking up her keys and her purse and walking out but realized there was nowhere she wanted to go. She allowed her hand to move toward her desk drawer as she considered pulling Joe's picture from it to look at him once more but thought better of it. Instead, she walked to the door and locked it, closed all the blinds and returned to her desk where she fully intended to develop a list of data she needed from IT and get the "goddamned response to headquarters" as finished as she could make it before midnight.

Abdication

D ave Nichols and his little brother, Luke, stepped off the school bus in front of their house. As they often did, they instantaneously set about the task of determining who could get to their front door first. Caught up in the chase and the rough and tumble of siblings, they didn't have time to think about or care about their father's battered and always unwashed car: a 2004 green Subaru that sat on the weather-worn, cracked and broken pavement of the driveway. They paid no attention to the drained color escaping the house's siding or the bulging weeds taking over the lawn. The routine of it all enough to remove young boys' consciousness.

Dave, with his long gangly legs, had caught Luke in three bounds. Luke's eight-year-old running gait was no match. When Dave had Luke pulled to a stop, he wrapped his long arm around his brother's neck and tickled him mercilessly all the way to the unlocked entrance door. Then he dragged him in and released him to the living room where Luke fell laughing wildly and calling his older brother a "Butt Head," for which he received another application of Dave's fingers against his ribs, belly and underarms.

When he had finished with his brother, Dave remembered what he had been taught somewhere along the line by his parents—those two people pretending to be adults. He was supposed to call out to let somebody know that he and his brother were home. Logic suggested that yelling at this point was "lame." He and his brother had made enough noise coming into the house to notify anybody within a hundred feet of the door. He yelled anyway, "Parental Unit, we're home!"

Having glanced out the front window to see whose car was in the driveway—the one he hadn't noticed on the way in, he expected to hear that distinctive man voice of his father coming back at him like an echo from the canyons of loneliness that is always a teenager's home. Only the humming of the dying refrigerator's compressor and the creaks of the floor beneath his feet spoke to him. He checked the house, its bedrooms and basement, wondered if his father had gone somewhere on foot ... somewhere Dave couldn't imagine. His father didn't walk anywhere except when it was required for his work, or necessary for getting around the house or required to get to and from his car or the mailbox. For whatever reason a fourteen-year-old boy would think to check the least likely place his father—Mr. Mechanically Inept, Mr. I-Don't-Do-Manual-Labor-If-I-Can-Avoid-It" would be hanging out, he decided to go to the door at the end of the hall that went to the garage and opened it.

With that simple turning of his wrist on the door handle and a quick pull of his still underdeveloped upper arms, the demon— that image of his father lying in a pool of blood—burrowed its way inside him. His scream brought Luke running toward him, but Dave, still standing at the door, had the presence of mind to push it closed, lock his brother in a body hug and take him by force back into the living room. Through his horror and tears, he said, "It's just a dead rat, Robby. I'm sorry I yelled. It scared me."

"I'm not afraid of a dead rat, Davey!"

"No! Do you hear me? I said no!" He heard his own voice like that of a man, firm, forceful, parental. "You stay here and watch TV now. It's a horrible mess. I've got to clean it up. Don't come out. You'll have nightmares. Promise me you won't come out!"

"But I want to see it, Dave! I saw a dead cat once."

"No, you stay here and watch TV. This is too gross for you. I mean it. You stay here!"

The younger boy finally accepted his brother's command. At that, Dave went into the kitchen where the phone hung, the

receiver in its cradle with the sixteen-foot-long, curly cord twisted up beneath it. He had to tell someone. He had to get someone
to take over, deal with this, take it off his shoulders. Someone
had to do something. Police? Ambulance? Hospital? Somebody.
He thought about calling his mother at work, making her come
home and deal with it. But then she would have to see it. "Dad
is dead," he heard the words in his mind, imagined the screams
coming into his thoughts snatching the words before they could
be spoken out loud. He couldn't think of the phone number or
where to find it. Fog-building confusion was wrapping its numerous writhing arms around him to restrain him, making it difficult
to focus on finding the phone book that managed to hide in the
kitchen drawers or on the counter or refrigerator, or any of a doz-
en other places. When he couldn't find it, he cried as quietly as
he could. "Maybe it isn't true. Maybe none of it is true. Maybe I
was wrong. Maybe he's not dead. Maybe he's just hurt. What if
he isn't dead?" He looked again for the phone book. "He's dead.
I know he's dead. But what if I'm wrong?" He found himself at
the door to the garage, unaware of how he had arrived, or how
he had opened it and stepped through. He pushed the door shut
behind him, went quickly to the body. It hadn't moved, still lay
in the same dark red liquid that was already drying at the edges
to a blackish brown where it had stalled after the initial pull of
gravity onto the concrete. A shotgun lay amidst the ooze where it
too had fallen. When he got past the feeling of nausea and a desire
to run, the boy walked around the body, made himself look at the
blood-covered face, the ragged skin of the neck where the slug
had entered under the chin. His father's mouth hung open and full
of blood, the eyes had lost their sheen and stared upward at the
roof rafters. He looked away to the chest hoping to see some kind
of motion—a slight rise or fall. Through his tears he imagined
he saw something move, reached down, blubbered words to the
flesh nearing his fingertips, "Don't be dead." He felt the rigidity
of the body, the thingness it had become, and he stifled his desire
to shriek, scream at the disintegration of all meaning in one loud
voice that would shake the world, and then, choked on the desire

for Luke's sake. Instead, he sobbed as quietly as he could, not yet understanding that he was weeping not only about his father, but about his childhood that had come up out of his lungs, rising above his father's stare, floating off into the rafters like smoke.

Dave returned to the kitchen, found the phone book in the broom closet behind the dustpan propped against the wall. It took what seemed a long time for him to stop sobbing enough to be able to see the buttons on the phone. He wiped his eyes with the T-shirt he had pulled up over his belly and chest between every two or three buttons he pressed. When he had finished dialing, he stretched the long phone cord back out into the garage where he waited for his mother to answer. He heard Luke off in the living room laughing out loud and trying to imitate the voice of Elmer Fudd. When his mother finally answered and he blurted out that his father was dead, his mother screamed into his ear as he knew she would though he had forgotten to prepare for his body's reaction to her. He dropped the phone. When he picked it up, she was still screaming; he yelled for her to stop screaming and call whoever needed to come. She yelled again, "He's not dead. He can't be dead!"

He responded in the cracking voice of a teenage boy speaking too rapidly through sob-induced phlegm and swollen sinuses "Yes, he's dead, goddamn it! Call somebody and come home! I can't do this by myself. You're supposed be the adult, not me!"

He listened to his mother telling him he was wrong, he didn't know what he was doing, he was lying, pulling one of his crazy stunts. "I'm on my way, and Goddamn you if this isn't real." The phone went dead. Dave stared at the phone, watching it moving in his trembling hand as he tried to stop the echo of his mother's voice still reverberating in his ears. "Goddamn me either way," he would have said had he been able to think it.

As if believing that, somehow, maybe he had failed, been wrong, he went to the body again, wondered if he had missed some life somewhere in it that he could save to assuage his mother's wrath. He walked around the body again, pushed once more on the stiff flesh that confirmed what he already knew: His father—

the man he had shared with his brother and mother—had fled from them. He turned and braced himself at his father's "work-bench" where his father never worked. A folded piece of paper was propped against a paint can. Scrawled in large letters made by a magic marker on the outer face were the words, "How you killed me." He picked it up and read the indictment: his father's accusations against a wife he didn't love and who didn't love him, a family that kept him from being who he might have been, who kept him living like a poor man, a family that included unworthy children who demanded too much of him and were so tainted and over-controlled by their mother that he wanted nothing to do with them any longer.

The message was clear: Dave Nichols had caused disappointment, been a disappointment, and had contributed to his father's death somehow. The thoughts burned themselves into his flesh as he read the letter's end, "I'm glad it's over!" Loneliness deeper than anything he'd known, deeper than the canyons of his home life and of his mind's ability to fathom crawling inside the boy's brain and looking out through his eyes.

He carried the ugly final words of his father into the house along with the blood that had stuck to his shoes. After he banged the hall door shut behind him, he could hear the television and his brother's talking back to it. He wanted to go into the living room, lift his brother into his arms, and hold him tight, thought there might be comfort in that. Instead, he went to the kitchen and soaked the letter in hot water until the heat was too much for his reddening hands. Laying the wet paper into the sink momentarily, he opened the cold-side handle so his hands could bear handling those words some more, picked up the soggy mass, scrunched it with his fist, watched ink run off his hand like blood as he squeezed. And when he couldn't squeeze it any tighter, he started picking at the mushy wad-flesh, using his fingers like vulture jaws to rip and tear. When he could no longer hold onto the flesh of the thing, he brushed the shreds with the side of his hand into the mouth of the garbage disposal and listened to the sounds of its eating. The morning's dishes left in the drying rack rattled and clacked to obscure the sounds of rage that gurgled in his throat.

***

Over the next few months, his mother's mourning spun itself out of the unanswerable whirlwinds of "Why's?" and the night-after-night alcohol-induced cries of regret. She proclaimed to anyone who would listen that she accepted (though she obviously didn't) the unknowable about a person who suddenly decides, without explanation, to end his life—a life she lied was a good one. Within minutes of stating her so-called acceptance, she would often complain, "He could at least have left a goddamn note." When she said it in front of Dave, he would often get up and leave the room, his face flushing red, the images of wet pulp paper squishing in his hand, and the words no one else would ever read or hear being eaten by the InSinkErator.

His mother told herself and everyone else, including her sons, whatever lies she needed in her attempts to erase any responsibility for her husband's decision. The more lies she told, the more she invested in cheap whiskey that helped mold her memories to what she wanted to believe and that helped move her toward her early grave and Dave picking up the slack in parenting both his brother and his mother needed, but only Luke would accept as he and Dave watched their mother fade and die.

Luke had Dave to comfort him, make sure he had food and clothing, protect him from their mother, and tell him necessary lies about their father: "Our dad loved and cared for you and would want you to grow up happy and healthy."

"And you, too, Davey. But if he loved us, why did he kill himself?" Luke had asked not too long after the funeral, the coming and going of relatives, and time had given both boys the space they needed to process their thoughts and feelings.

"I don't know for sure, Luke. I think maybe he was sick and thought we would be better off without him."

"That's lame, Davey."

"You're right. It's just the best guess I could come up with."

"Maybe it was just an accident. You ever think about that, Davey?"

"You know? You might be right. Maybe it was."

"I think it was," Luke said as he lay his head against his brother's chest and felt Dave's arms wrapping themselves around him.

"Okay, let's believe that."

"I'm scared."

"I know, but I'm going to take care of you."

"But you're a kid,Davey."

"Not anymore, Bro."

Labyrinth and Minotaur

At thirty, Dave Nichols had done his duty as primary care-giver to his brother, Luke, who was about to graduate with a degree in engineering from MIT. In addition to the pride that came with helping Luke survive the loss of their parents and giving him a future, Dave had been proud of his own accomplishments: BA and MA degrees paid for with hard work, what little he got from his parents' "estates" (he found the word *estates* ridiculous in his parents' cases) and student loans; a job working for one of New York's oldest advertising firms; a great income; a plush apartment in Bay Ridge; and what looked like opportunities for advancement in the near future. Though he didn't necessarily love advertising, he felt like he had made good on his childhood determination to "make it" despite his early experiences and the struggles that came with trying to negotiate the world without parental support for the past fifteen years.

He enjoyed having money, buying high-quality products and services, and being able to afford to splurge on himself and his brother occasionally. And now that his brother was graduating and would soon be working and taking care of himself financially, Dave was anticipating new ways of enjoying the extra money he would have ... right up to the day he was told that his services at the VML agency were no longer needed.

When Dave asked for the reason, his supervisor stumbled across phrases such as, "We hold our employees to the highest standards of conduct particularly in their interactions with clients" and "sometimes we have to make decisions that we don't like, but which become necessary ...." When the imperious, pinch-faced little man finished stumbling through the many words that amounted to "You're fired," Dave said, "Cochran complained, didn't he?"

"You called him a moron."

"No. Actually, I called him a *fucking* moron." As Dave said it, the supervisor's face started turning red. "I've told you a number of times about him and the way he treats me, making demands of me that aren't in the contract, coming up with constant changes he wants made that contradict what he had agreed to in previous meetings ... all while belittling me, swearing at me, treating me like a child. I asked you to straighten him out. You kept saying you would, but you did nothing. And now you're going to fire me for doing what you wouldn't do yourself?"

"We will not have a client treated that way ... calling him a moron," the man said.

"'Fucking moron,' that's what I called him." Dave's temper getting the better of him, he continued, "As far as I'm concerned, you are the one who should be fired; you aren't as smart or as capable as that fucking moron Cochran. I smell a lawsuit in the air. Can you smell it, you idiot?" Smells like satisfaction to me. With that, he walked out of the door strutting with a young man's cock-sure belief that he could go down the street, walk into another agency and be given a great job at a much higher salary. Reality would take a while to set in.

Over the next couple of weeks, he worked full time searching for a job amongst New York agencies, but when potential employers called VLM for references, they didn't like what they heard. It was readily apparent that his former supervisor put the word out on the street that Dave Nichols had committed the unpardonable sin of infuriating a top client, and the client had threatened to move his lucrative account to another agency. Word spread like a confession in a what's-said-here-stays-here AA meeting out into the local community faster than the confessor could get through the hand-holding end of the meeting, out of the building, and into the parking lot.

After numerous polite rejections and non-responses to his applications, calls and queries, it became obvious that there wouldn't be any interviews, and no offers, from top paying advertising firms. The blackballs had been thrown in all directions, and Dave would keep falling on his backside as they rolled under his feet. Meanwhile, the bills came in and tore at the flesh of his savings. The apartment took a huge bite out of what he had; utilities chomped away steadily, demanding their usual portions as did laundry service and food costs; then there was the insurance company and the storage facility that held his car ... all these gluttonous beasts adding their mysterious service fees that fed unnamed entities deep within their systems that even the employees who worked there couldn't explain.

From the day of his firing, Nichols estimated he would go broke within two months if he didn't find employment, and that was based on the belief he would probably have to live on Ramen noodles and bologna for some of that time. He gave up everything that wasn't necessary, packed his nightlife at the clubs into a mental box to be stored amongst his hopes "to be opened soon" and gave all his energy to looking for something he could do that would pay well.

Like a PT boat in a war zone, Nichols dashed around the lumbering behemoths of New York, applying to publishing companies, agents, corporations of all kinds looking for writers and who offered salaries that would allow him to keep his apartment and pay his expenses. He was meeting with people he knew who might know the people he wanted to know and brazenly making pitches to people he could find unguarded by their overzealous office staff, and he was "working" his phone and computer for many hours each day trying to make connections.

Early in the second month of what he called "the job search shuffle" (search, apply, make follow up calls, hear nothing or be told the "position has been filled"), he allowed himself to think of moving, going someplace where he could afford to live even if the pay was less, even doing something else for a while. Jobs he never dreamed he would consider suddenly started sounding more appealing to him. That's when he began toying with the idea of government work.

It made sense to Dave that selling political ideas was not all that different from what he'd been doing with promoting products and services. The challenge was to find a position that would pay him well and stretch his talents. The research skills he had acquired in college, his excellent writing abilities, and his experiences working with high-profile individuals (other than Cochran) led him to believe he might qualify for the position of communications assistant he found posted on the U.S. Senate Employment website. "What the hell," he told himself. "It's just another application. Worst they can do is say 'No.'"

A week later when his phone screen showed he had a call from Washington, D.C., he took a moment to contain his surprise and quell the nervousness that scattered like the beads of a shotgun shell throughout his body. He waited through four rings while he calmed himself. "I can sell ice to Eskimos," he told himself as his self-confident, carefully practiced, "Hello. Dave Nichols," fell out of his mouth and onto the phone's receiver, and the process of schmoozing the caller began.

***

It had taken some time and effort for Dave to justify his deci-sion to hit the send button at the end of the online forms the caller had sent him. He had to first convince himself that he didn't care that the senator was a Republican. He would have preferred to work with a senator from the "other side of the aisle"—as poli-ticians refer to the supposed "colleagues" they also called "sons o' bitches" behind closed doors. None, other than Senator John Bedsloe, needed a communications assistant at the time and Dave needed a job.

Dave's personal belief about politics was a cynical one: the party of the moment drinks from the shot glasses of power and self-importance until its adherents become so drunk that they start tearing the house down around themselves just for fun. In some cases they get so wasted that a drunken lout among them leads a chant to find somebody to lynch. With that, they run off into the night with pitchforks and torches and burning anger, ready to destroy everyone who isn't them. When they wake up the next day, they try to cover up their obvious crimes, get indict-ed by the press, lose public support, and create an opportunity for the "other side" to step up and repeat the process.

But he was running out of options and beginning to believe he could adapt. Other positions he had applied for weren't coming through. He had moved out of his apartment the previous week, stashed his belongings in a storage building, and was now staying at the YMCA in Washington, and had just enough money to eat for a few more days. Given his circumstances, it wasn't difficult for him to decide that politicians were simply faces of a political party line. They were not all that different from non-politicians whose faces get printed on cereal boxes or toy packaging or on wanted posters. He told himself that politicians and political parties were no different from the producers of "Superior Brand" dishwashing liquid trying to displace another company's "Ulti-mate Brand" dishwashing liquid. Both, just soap. Both made from the same basic ingredients. Both poured from similar bottles. Both created about the same amount of suds that would last for about the same amount of time. But each wore its uniquely designed label, and each claimed to be much better than the other.

Outside of Texas, Senator Bedsloe was not much liked even by the people of his own party. His wealthy campaign donors thought him boorish, a wannabe sophisticate bereft of the essen-tial skills and delicacy required, a battered bull thinking of itself as an elegant steed. But that slight majority of Texans who both-ered to vote him into office liked his tough guy image, what they called his "tell-it-like-it-is" style (whatever that was supposed to mean) and his pride in declaring himself white, conservative, anti-immigrant, damned-sure proud to stand up for the "forgot-ten middle class" and a "real" American. He had a long-standing reputation for spoon feeding his constituency what they wanted to hear, and they ate up whatever he dished out and then, licked the bowl he had served it in. He got his donors what they wanted, voted the way they wanted, and promoted their agendas for as long as the money and the "atta-boys" rolled in the way the senator wanted.

"It doesn't matter one way or the other," Dave mumbled to himself as he stated that he was a loyal member of the senator's party and hoped no one would take the time to check his voting record. As he pressed the submit button, a phantom pain shot deep into his belly.

***

A couple of days later when he told his brother over the phone that he was in the final round of interviews for the position with Bedsloe, Luke begged him not to take the job, called the senator all the filthiest words he could pull into his consciousness, laid out a litany of reasons to hate the man and his politics as he pleaded with Dave to wait until a better opportunity came along. Apparently, Luke believed any opportunity was better. Dave faked a laugh at his brother's intensity and his commitment to political beliefs that would be appalling to the senator and his ilk.

"When did my hotshot, little brother, smart ass, college graduate become so passionate about politics?" The question was asked and followed with another fake laugh. "Anyway, I'm not taking a political stance, I'm taking a job and I'm going to take it if it is offered. At least it will be interesting.

Politics: It's not all that different from what I did in advertising. I was a slut for them, wrote what they needed written because it paid. I'll be doing the same thing for him. Being a whore pays well!"

After a string of reordered expletives and a few comments about Dave selling his soul, Luke gave up, stopped talking, sighed, and said, "I love you in spite of yourself, bro," and ended the conversation with an excuse for cutting the call off. As the phone clicked to silence, Dave realized that he "felt green" … green like when as a boy he had tried smoking three unfiltered cigarettes one immediately after the other and felt the nausea and regret as his stomach and chest rebelled and his skin turned gray—a feeling only understood by those who have felt it and never want to feel it again. He hadn't liked what he had heard himself say, and he hadn't liked the way the conversation ended ... "in spite of yourself."

He sat down on the hard red park bench outside the deli where he'd brought his pastrami on rye wrapped in white paper, and the hot, paper cupped coffee he needed for surviving the day. As he ate, he watched the street filled with traffic and the sidewalk teeming with bodies moving like racing ants among patio stones performing tasks that humans don't understand. He found himself thinking about the concept of a soul and wondered if he'd ever had one.

***

"It isn't political," he had said, trying to convince his brother in their previous conversation. "It's just writing what he wants said and getting paid for it. It's not like they're my thoughts. They're his. I just dress them up."

"And your writing helps Bedsloe bring more people over to his way of thinking even when they're fucking themselves in the process. You'll be as guilty as he is, and you know it." Luke had spoken with a layer of heat in his voice.

"It's just a job, and after I get on my feet again, I can look for something else without losing what little I have left of my things!"

"I'd rather have nothing ...." Luke's words from their last conversation had bitten his brother. Dave found himself being somewhat defensive about them. Though he pretended to slough them off, they roiled in Dave's mind during his interview with Bedsloe's Chief of Staff. However, he had managed to focus enough to impress the interviewer who set up a face-to-face between Dave and the Senator at the Senator's fourth-floor office in the Russell Senate Building the next afternoon at 2 p.m. "The Senator likes to have the final word in hiring staff that he might have to work with directly."

When he left the office, Dave was still hearing his brother's arguments, arguments that stayed with him throughout the remainder of that day and into the next.

***

He arrived for the interview wearing his New York tailor-made charcoal gray suit; his red, white, and blue checked tie; his large turquoise ring; a matching masculine-looking bracelet; and brilliantly shined shoes. He made a striking figure with his handsome face, strong chin, blue eyes, and dark brown, carefully trimmed hair, his broad shoulders, slim waist, and powerful muscular and toned body. He walked confidently into an office where he was met by a woman who introduced herself to him as Mrs. Kepper, the senator's secretary.

Mrs. Kepper was an early-middle-aged blonde, dressed in a tight-fitting business suit, short skirt, white blouse, and a jacket. Hers was a straight-lipped face carefully made up to reduce the appearance of wrinkles at the corners of her eyes and to lighten the dark sacs under the lower lids. She spoke as if she were a tape recording of the type that can be found at a museum: eliminates the docents and can do their jobs until the machines that hold their voices die. Dave Nichols noticed her doing a quick head-to-toe scan of him. He sensed that she had made her decision as to his value and wasn't impressed. He'd been around enough to know that secretary's run organizations; they just let their bosses think that they (the bosses) are the powers behind their operations. He could feel his confidence fading when his attempts to make small talk with this woman wasn't going to be reciprocated, so he walked along behind her as she proceeded officiously and silently across the room to the senator's massive red oak door and its inches-thick ornately carved moldings. She knocked and within a few seconds, a booming voice came from the other side of the door saying, "I'm ready. Send him in, Ruth." Mrs. Kepper, Ruth, pushed down on the latch, walked the door open on its hinges, then stood like a butler motioning for the applicant to step inside the room.

As he took several steps toward Senator Bledsoe to shake his hand, Nichols heard the door close behind him. The senator had risen from his chair and was walking toward him with that politician smile on his face that said, "You are the most important person I know at this minute in time, and you and I both know that's not true but let's pretend, shall we?" The senator stuck his paw out like a trained dog waiting for the treat that was sure to come after such a well-practiced gesture. The men exchanged their strong handshakes like gentlemen before a wrestling meet, trying to out-squeeze and intimidate the other.

"Come in, young man. Have a seat here in this big old leather chair and lets parley," the senator said. Nichols sunk into the chair, felt it envelop him, the Texas-twanged "parruhlaay" still ringing in his ear; he wondered if he was perceived as being an opponent or the senator didn't know the meaning of the word. The senator walked away briefly, returning to his desk to pull out a bottle of whiskey from a drawer. He studied Dave like prey, removed the cap from the bottle, took two engraved whiskey glasses from the side table and held them in one large hand as he poured whiskey into both. Then he brought the glasses toward Dave, handed him one, said "Cheers," clinked his glass against Dave's. Both men took a swallow, and then the senator sat down, dropping his weight into the chair opposite Nichols, causing the sofa to groan at the attack by his backside. The men sat looking into one another's eyes as if checking to see who would blink first.

Nichols was impressed by the size of the man. Bedsloe was large, not fat, just large, maybe six feet two or three, broad shouldered and big boned. His face was perhaps a little rounder than a man of his stature would like, not strong-chinned, but it was hard like a stereotypical Texas cowhand, a Marlboro Man, an oil rigger, or banker's face when he denies a loan; he had the look of exhaustion around his brown and sunken eyes, the skin darkened almost to the color of burnt umber under his heavy protruding brow. He had one of those thickening, slightly bulbous noses typical of heavy drinkers. His expensive suit looked somehow badly fitted for a body in a sitting position. His big bones pushed at the fabric and pulled the jacket up behind his large neck and the sleeves high above his wrists; his pant-legs showed the bare skin of his legs above the socks.

After thanking the senator for the excellent whiskey, Nichols expressed his appreciation for the interview. Then he waited while the senator looked over the top of his whiskey glass. Bedsloe had swallowed the remainder of the liquid in one large gulp, but he held the glass in place barely beyond his lips as he looked at Dave as if studying something in his face that he hadn't quite figured out but intended to. Then, he lowered the glass to his lap and said, "Nice suit. New York?" As Nichols began to respond, the senator talked over top of him, "You'll need to tell me who your tailor is. Might want to get myself a couple of new suits."

In the pause at the end of the interruption, Nichols said he would be glad to provide the information. And then he waited again. After the forever that a long silence can be among strangers, the senator spoke: "Is it true that you called Sam Cochran a fucking moron and got fired for it?" The senator rattled off the question almost as nonchalantly as asking, "Where are you from?" Nichols could feel his pulse speed up.

Dave's brain tried to process the surprise of the question, allowed the thought to enter his mind that the job was slipping away. In an attempt to match the senator's style, Dave swallowed the remainder of his whiskey, set the glass down on a coaster on a side table, took his time, looked into Bedsloe's eyes and said confidently while controlling any shame that might escape to his face, "Yes, sir. I did." And then he waited for the senator to ponder his response.

"Is it true you said the same thing to your boss?"

"Yes, sir. It is true."

"So, are you likely to say that to me?"

"Senator, I have no intentions of saying it, especially if it's not true. If either of those guys had just had a bad day, I could have accepted that and kept my mouth shut. Problems had been going on for a long time, at least a couple of years, and my boss wasn't doing anything to help. What Cochran wanted was to be his own advertising agency and use me as his personal whipping boy, and my boss let him do it."

"Your boss told you to bend over and take it for the good of the company?"

"I probably wouldn't have said it quite that way, but yes."

"Sam Cochran is a fucking moron, and I've told him so myself. You've got balls. As to your former boss, I can't say, but from what you just said, my guess is you aren't wrong." Bedsloe got up, picked up both glasses, and refilled them as he continued talking. "I like my employees to have balls. Even the women. I've seen the work you gave to my staff, liked the way you rewrote a couple of press releases and made me sound pretty goddamned good. You've got a flair for words, son." He had brought the glasses back, handed Nichols his hand-warmed glass, and smiled as he sat down. "You think you can make me look good, spin me when it's needed?"

"Yes, I could."

"Good." The senator paused. Then he repeated himself before moving on, "Good. That's good! Now tell me about your politics. Tell me where you stand."

"Stand on what, sir?"

"Oh, how about you telling me about your coming over to the Republican Party? You voted Democratic in New York for the past four years. What is it you decided you like about us Republicans.

"Well, sir, I ah, ah," struggling for words, "I ... well ... to be honest, I figured marking that on the application form was the only way I would get a chance for an interview, and I hoped I could impress you enough once I got here that my voting record wouldn't matter. It was wrong for me to do that ... but I couldn't see what difference it made. Truth is, I am a good writer, and I can create what you want words to say whether or not I personally agree with them. Isn't that what you would be hiring me to do?

"I've got to know that my staff people are with me a hundred and ten percent. The job is about loyalty to me and to my vision. Total commitment, son. I can't be worrying you'll stab me in the back. You're either all in, or I can't use you."

Something about the way the senator said, "use you," hit Nichols like a flash fire—the hot breath of the Minotaur as it prepared to eat its prey. He remembered his brother's assessment of the senator, what he himself had known but tried to dismiss as unimportant. In those few seconds, the thought occurred to him that he had become a walking sales pitch, a man ready to sell himself to another man who had succumbed to his own delusions of power and control. Bedsloe's phrase about bending over and taking one for the company came to mind.

As he looked at the senator, he could almost hear his brother's voice crying out like the voice of a gull above the ocean crying out to nearby gulls. He had no words prepped and ready for saying. Yet, they fell out of his mouth as if placed there by someone else, surprising him as he said them as easily as he might have said he had enjoyed the whiskey: "Senator, I have wasted your time, and for that I apologize. But I can't give you what you want. I'm not willing to give you my soul. Come to think of it, I'm not sure I want to work as a whore for anyone anymore. Think maybe I need to go in a different direction."

The senator's face first turned brilliant red and then drained to a ghastly gray, the slits between his eyelids narrowed, and his forehead acquired wrinkles that had not been there even a moment previously. He set his drink down and said, "Yes. You have wasted my time. Now get the hell out of my office." He walked to his desk, pressed a button on his phone. Mrs. Kepper opened the door and once again stood like a butler waiting for a command. "Mrs. Kepper, we are finished here. Show him out."

As Dave walked across the threshold, he heard the senator utter, "Fucking moron," before the door hit the doorjamb. Mrs. Kepper maintained an unreadable face as they walked. He found himself smirking, feeling on the edge of laughing out loud as he walked toward the door that would release him to the hall . He looked sideways at Mrs. Kepper as she closed the door behind him without saying a word. A strange sense of joy stayed with him as he rode the elevator down to street level and stepped out into the light of day. And there in front of him, a phantom image

of himself sitting on a low bough of a manicured tree, the grin-
ning boy he had once been, dropping to the grass as only a gawky
teenager can, to walk alongside him toward home, wherever that
might turn out to be.

My Father's Eyes

I look at my father's eyes of dissipating clouds,
his time-sagged face
jowls falling off his bones like unbuttoned pants
two sizes too big.

He does not know me, calls me "buddy."
Whispers hoarsely to whomever buddy is,
"I want to let go."

I tell him he can
whenever he's ready,
but he stares through me.
Gone somewhere
he cannot remember long or share . . .
paws his right hand with the left,
scratches the withered hide.
leaves white lines of dead cells.

I sit and wait, imagining myself
the body in his bed
my own bones there
wondering in final moments of lucidity
if there was something more
I might have done or said,
knowing full well the answer
is always yes.
Another anonymous chaplain
makes his rounds to sell his death-bed god with prayers.

I do not tell him I eschew eternal life
not liking company I'd have to keep
and reject his hell as well. Tell him, Can't
stand too much heat.
Fine with getting out of the kitchen.
I think oblivion is not too bad an option.

Not much now to do but wait some more
for him to awaken
or not, as he sees fit. I
thumb through a yellowed album
searching for photos
maybe I never had, searching for
the young man
my father was or was not—
an image I thought I had
years ago: the eyes
cutting the stained, fragile paper of dream
his defiant stance
eternity cast
like a straw from his coat
the speed of his life
—and now mine too—
careening across the universe
he and I with no particular place to call a home
nowhere in particular to go,
no idea what to do were we to arrive.

Backstage

M arc Esper stripped down to his underwear. After an hour and a half of performing under hot stage lights he welcomed the removal of the now dampened wool business suit and soggy shirt he had just worn for the second act, welcomed the coolness of the dressing room's tile floor where he lay briefly to let the sweat evaporate from his body as the overhead fan spread waves of cool air over him. He watched the blades spin, listened to the mesmerizing whirr of the motor and the whoosh of air it created, used it like a mantra for letting go of performance stress. After a few minutes, he lifted himself up from the floor and watched himself grow larger as he walked toward his dressing table with its huge mirror. He was pleased with what he saw: body still firm, muscular, well kept, moving confidently like a self-possessed athlete. Flickering images of other men of his age—other actors he knew—played in his brain ... men who had succumbed to flabby bellies from too much indulgence in Bacchanalian revelry and their weak commitments to preserving the most essential tool of the trade ... at least if they expected lead roles. He touched the now tousled hair on his head, felt the thinning, and reminded himself it would have to do for now; he would be able play the roles written for young men for a few more years ... and maybe longer if he kept himself fit, even if he had to give in to the idea of a toupee at some point. As he turned sideways to admire his smooth and hardened abs, he smiled at the notion that it would take a lot of work and makeup to become old enough to play Willy Loman or Lear.

After he sat down, he reached for the dimmer switch and reduced the intensity of the mirror lights: A simple action that still gave him pleasure whenever he thought about the days when he had to make do with a lamp sitting beside a too-small mirror that someone had set on a rickety, scarred desk, and he could only hope that he looked reasonably put together as the curtains opened to the audience. He removed two clean squares of cloth from a drawer, wrapped one of them around two fingers and pushed it into the wide mouth of the Noxzema jar. He rubbed the white cream over his face to remove the first layer of makeup. He picked up the second and was wiping the residue from his face when the door to his room burst open violently, the shock making him rise up out of his chair as if ready to fight or flee. "Whoa," came out of his mouth as if he were trying to bring a team of runaway horses to a dead stop by a single word. In those seconds of initial shock, he hadn't thought about the fact that all he had on were tight blue, almost see-through briefs.

The man leading the charge turned out to be his old friend Bill Marley pulling a woman along like a recalcitrant puppy learning to adjust to a leash. She was laughing like she was half drunk pushing at his hand wrapped around her wrist in an attempt to make him release her. "Now, Billie, you can't make a lady in heels walk that fast! I'm going to fall on my ...." When Bill let go of her, there was an awkwardness to her attempts to regain her balance. Then she pulled down the dress that had risen on her torso as she was dragged through the door, pulled it back into place over her hips and walked the last few steps with an air of dignity and a hint of seduction.

"Jesus Christ, Bill," Marc said loudly, "you scared the hell out of me!" Seeing the woman, he continued with, "I'm not dressed," as if it weren't obvious enough, and instinctively put his hands over the front of his underwear as instantaneous red flush spread across his face.

The woman, now in front of him, looking him up and down his body spoke: "My. My. You were right, Billie. He is a handsome man!"

Like mischievous children, Bill Marley and this woman with him were taking pleasure in antics. In those seconds of confusion, Marc's only options were to yell at them to get out, throw them out, or accept the intrusion for what it was—Bill being Bill—and regain control to perform—bluff—through the embarrassment, or pretend that an interruption such as this was a normal part of an actor's life and make light of it.

Bill was in one of his many tailor-made thousand-dollar suits, a three-piece charcoal gray, with red silk tie, starched white shirt with French cuffs, and black Italian leather dress shoes: shoes that looked like he had paid a shoeshine boy to follow him to the dressing room door, do a shoeshine then and there, and receive a five-dollar tip for making the leather radiate rather than just shine, no sign of wear and tear whatsoever. Had appearance been the sole criteria for stardom, Bill could have been among the best of the best: heartthrob handsome, physically fit, self-confident, and always very well-dressed. In the business arena, Bill was as much a star as Marc was in the world of theatre. Bill had mastered the skills of his trade, knew how to play his money-making roles like an actor knows what he is to say, how he is to say it, what expression must be on his face as he speaks, where he's supposed to stand, and when—and how—he is supposed to make his body and facial features work for dramatic effect.

Before Marc could take two steps, Bill caught him and wrapped his long, powerful arms around Marc's body and hugged him, ignoring the awkwardness of Marc's arms and hands still trying to cover the center of his body.

"You should have called," Marc half-whispered. "I could at least have put on some clothes for the lady."

"I wanted to surprise you," Bill said. "And she's no prude."

"I hope to hell you didn't just get makeup all over that nice suit," Marc said. "I was just taking it off when you came in. ... How did you two get in here? House crew is supposed to throw bums like you out into the back alley." Turning to the woman, he said, "I'm sorry. I don't mean you're a bum, I don't even know you. But I know he is," he says gesturing toward Bill. "If you don't mind, I'm going to finish getting this makeup off and grab a quick shower. Then, maybe we can all go out for a drink or something." Accepting the awkwardness of the situation, he returned to his chair at the make-up table and began once again to remove his stage face. Bill stood behind him, looking at himself in the mirror, checking his suit coat for smudges, each of the men looking at one another's image, their history revived in the meeting of their eyes.

Though the two men had been together sporadically over the previous ten years when they happened to be in the same city at the same time, they still made frequent telephone calls. They got together for holidays when they returned to their aged parents, both men trying to fit too much into the little time they had with one another amidst their commitment to their families and ever-present work responsibilities. The click and clack of the phone hitting the cradle or the closing of doors after goodbye hugs often punctuated their sense of loss.

Marc's acting opportunities had kept him busy throughout the last half of the fifties, and he was making good money, landing good roles, and receiving accolades for his work and intended to keep it that way as he was making his way through 1964. He was often on the road with a show, preferring live theater to television or movie acting. Bill was constantly lost in the rat maze of deal making, catering to the monied elite, traveling the world, meeting with his bosses and handlers, and raking in as much money as he could while standing arms akimbo with one foot on either side of the razor wire that divides the "good guys" from the "bad guys," ultimately leaning toward the ethical side of wheeling and dealing, at least leaning enough to keep himself out of significant danger.

They had first met in 1932 when Bill's parents bought the house next door to the Espers, Marc's family. The realtor told Bill, "There is a boy next door about your age! Maybe you can be friends." Seven-year-old Bill took that to heart, determined it was going to happen, and planned how he was going to start the friendship. On the day he and his family pulled up to the house, Bill waited until his parents went in the house, marched past the movers who were carrying the furniture and household goods from the street, and went up onto Esper's porch and knocked on the door. When Marc's mother opened it, he didn't say "hello" or who he was; he said, "Will you please send that boy outside so I can play with him. I want him to be my friend."

His claim upon Marc held. Now thirty-two years later, he expected his best friend to be happy at his arrival, and he expected the privileges of their youth to be honored: he had a long history of dispensing with trifling things like announcing his arrival, knocking on doors, or thinking about what Marc might be doing behind a closed door. It had been this way through all the years of their youth and continued whenever they were in the same place at the same time and a door was unlocked. Bill was Bill.

Taking hold of Marc's shoulders, Bill used both hands to massage as he spoke, "Great show, my friend! Phenomenal! Had the audience by the balls!"

Marc tried to interject his "thank you," and repeated, "I didn't know you were in town; I wish I'd known," but Bill talked through the repetition as unnecessary blather among old friends.

"I think the women wanted to rush the stage to save you when that guy pulled out that gun. You could feel it! The anger. Probably a lynch mob waiting for that poor guy when he gets out of the theatre. You know, if you're not careful, you just might make it as an actor one day!" Bill was following the basic rule of masculinity that compliments must be undermined to make sure they can never be perceived as somehow too sensitive and caring.

Marc responded the way he always did when Bill undercut the praise: "Ya think, Bill?" and followed up with the perfunctory "thank you" for his friend's reactions to his work. "Now! Are you going to introduce me to this young lady you brought with you to catch me naked?"

"Oh ... yeah! This is Kesey Lane," he said. The woman, stepped forward into a space at Marc's left side. She looked into his eyes, braced her backside on the edge of the table and put her hand with its crimson-colored nails out in front of her as if he were to kiss it like someone might be expected to kiss the hand of a queen. Marc, wishing he had slid his chair further under the table, looked up at her overly painted face, chuckled, lifted his right hand to clasp the offering, and lied about how happy he was to meet her. He watched the slight shift of her eyes that went from seduction to annoyance as he let her hand fall. Then he let his right hand rejoin the left to cover the bulge in his underwear. "I trust you'll forgive me for not standing up again," he said.

She was in many ways Bill's kind of girl, early to mid-twenties, petite, around five feet tall, big busted, tiny waist. But Bill usually went for the blondes with lots of hair to fling around. This one had bobbed black hair and dangling, over-stated two-inch long, diamond-shaped silver earrings with what was supposed to look like actual large diamonds in the center of each. Marc recognized them instantly as rhinestones and painted tin, the kind Woolworth's sold at eight dollars a pair on cards hanging off a rack somewhere near the jewelry counter ... the kind of earrings a props manager might buy to look good on stage where no one would be close enough to see the quality.

As he looked at the woman's reflection in the mirror, Marc thought that, apparently, she had not been taught subtlety in any aspect of her appearance. She had large brown eyes with enough eye shadow, liner, and mascara to be worthy of a bit-part actress playing far upstage where harsh lights would wash her face out without gross exaggeration of her features. She wore a tight-fitting black dress that showed a lot of cleavage. She had a pleasant enough face, a tiny nose and large eyes and moist, red-colored lips that made the upward curve in the left corner that worked like a foghorn from a lighthouse to tell all sailors in listening range that sexuality was on the high seas.

"You must be forgiven everything, darling—a man of your talents. You are simply too marvelous an actor," Kesey Lane said, as if she'd watched too many old movies in her short lifetime and absorbed the worst dialog from the worst of them. Marc was accustomed to dealing with people who said stupid things out of nervousness or who just needed to express what he called "the joyed its"—people saying as best they could—or as they thought they *should*—that they appreciated ("enjoyed") watching the play and/or his acting abilities. Maybe it was the drawn out, over-emphasized use of *darling* and *marvelous*, which came out more like "dahhhling," "maaaahvelous," and the attempt at feigned elegance in her phrasing that raised his hackles. Or maybe it was something about her eyes as she talked, her gaze dropping a bit too obviously to his mid-section where he had placed his hands. He liked her even less when she said, "Now that we are friends, darling, stand up and kiss your newest fan! You needn't be shy. I have brothers, darling, and I've seen them in and out of their underwear."

"Well, that's straight forward," he said, "but I'm not your brother. And I'd prefer to remain sitting."

Bill laughed out loud, "Oh, stand up and kiss her, Marc. It won't hurt you any. Probably do you some good."

"No, really, I can't," Marc said.

She looked at him pouting, "You don't like me, darling? You refuse my kiss? You would make a poor girl cry?" It wouldn't have surprised him at that point if she had tried to add what she thought was an exotic foreign accent to her interpretations of the dried-up lines of yesteryear, maybe a hint of Russian or French. He almost blurted out his thoughts and then pulled back at the last second for Bill's sake. This woman was probably somebody Bill was trying to impress, though Marc couldn't imagine that she needed much impressing.

This was to be a performance, the actor decided. *Just go along,* he thought, *and do whatever it takes to have some time with Bill.* He had barely got to his feet when she wrapped her arms around him, locked his arms to his side like a human straitjacket. She pulled him tight against her as she nuzzled her face into the hair of his chest and pressed her body against his. When she finally released his arms, she immediately reached up and pulled his face down to hers and kissed him as if he were the sexiest man she'd ever met and the last piece of flesh she was ever going to get. He could feel her efforts in his groin. This was someone who had studied the art of the kiss, the art of the tongue, the art of soft moaning as she held their lips locked together.

Many men would have found her aggressive approach utterly irresistible: a hot fling. Marc just wanted her gone. When he found himself unable to breathe any longer, he had to physically break from her. He turned to Bill and saw his Cheshire Cat grin as he was taking off his jacket and vest and hanging them on the coatrack near the door. Bill walked over to a chair in the corner of the room and sat down, loosening his carefully knotted tie and undoing the top button of his shirt. He sat there smiling as the woman pulled at Marc's face and tried to kiss him again, and this time, he could feel her hand at the front of his briefs, then suddenly pushing his briefs down to full exposure. At this, he took her by the shoulders and pushed her back a step, pulled his briefs back up, and said, "What are you doing? I don't know you."

He turned, speaking with agitation verging on anger in his voice to the smiling face in the corner of the room, "What's going on here, Bill?" When there was no instantaneous response, he turned again toward the woman who was still scanning his body, her eyes stopping momentarily at the underwear and letting that little mouth-curl thing happen where she lifted a corner of her lip that speaks without words, "I want it."

"Thought you might like a little pick-me-up after the show," Bill said. "Kesey here likes to do pick-me-ups, don't you, Kesey?"

The girl nodded, and, in one motion, bent her knees, leaned slightly backward, pushed her hips off to her left and her torso to the right and upward to accentuate her breasts. She put her hands behind her head to strike her best impression of a 1950s screen siren pose while pressing her lips together in a smiling heart-shape.

Bill had bought him a gift that was unwrapping itself. Perhaps at another time in his life, he could have—would have—accepted it for what it was. He understood why some men would revel in it, would unquestioningly let this woman take them to wherever she was going to take them. He had bought himself such gifts in the past, hoping they would somehow make him feel something he didn't seem able to feel. However, when the girl came at him again, he looked at Bill, then at the girl, and said in his booming stage voice, "Stop. I've tried to be polite, but ... enought ... I'm not ... I'm not prepared for this." Looking to Bill, "I can't. I'm not ready. Put an end to this."

Bill asked, "How prepared do you have to be? Enjoy it."

"I can't, Bill" Then he turned to the girl, "I'm not going to do this. Do you understand?"

"You don't want me, darling? You don't find me attractive?" she asked.

"I just can't. It's not you. It's me. Let's let it go at that." As he said it, he looked to Bill as if asking for him to intervene.

There was a long pause. The girl looked to Bill for guidance; Bill looked at Marc confused about his response; Marc looked back and forth between Kesey and Bill wondering who was going to make the first move to get all of them out of this situation. Then, Bill cleared his throat, looked at Marc, looked at the girl again, looked around the room as though he'd wasted part of his life watching a badly written play directed by an idiot and performed by amateurs. Then, he looked at the girl, told her, "Go ahead, honey, go on. You can keep the pay I gave you." He pulled out a folded pad of bills from the inside breast pocket of his jacket, separated a twenty-dollar bill and gave it to her. "Here. This should get you home. Take a cab." She took it, looked back at Marc, squinched her eyes, abruptly turned her head away from him like he was some kind of urine-soaked, filth-covered street bum, too offensive to bear, and walked out.

After the door closed, Marc asked, "What in hell was that all about?"

"I told you! A treat for a pal! Thought you'd get a kick out of it."

"Just what the hell did you expect would happen here?" Marc asked, "Did you think I was just going to drop my shorts and lay her on the spot with you sitting there watching?"

"Sure! Why not? Probably would have been a great performance."

"Seriously, you thought you'd just sit there and watch, and I'd be okay with it?

"I guess. Yeah."

"Jesus, Bill! What are you thinking? Do you go around watching other people having sex?"

"Not without their knowing it. If you were too shy, you could have said, 'Leave!' I would have left. Whatever." I just thought it would be interesting. That's all. It wouldn't have been the first time I've seen you naked ... or her, for that matter."

"I don't know what to say, Bill. I thought I knew just about everything about you. I didn't know you were into that sort of thing."

"So, are you mad at me?" he asked.

"No. Of course not. I just don't know what to say."

"Then, don't say anything," he said.

"I don't feel good about myself after being with a girl like that, using them," Marc responded. "Look, you can enjoy whatever makes you happy as long as it doesn't hurt anyone or abuse anyone. No judgments from me."

Bill got up and moved to Marc, embraced him, and said he was sorry for offending him. "I'm sorry I used the girl as a prop."

Marc hesitated, looked up into the bigger man's face, then laid his face against the starched shirt and said, "I miss you. And maybe a part of me was jealous of her being here and taking up the space between us. I miss being young with you. The intimacy. I just don't find that in the women I've been with ... never have really. Maybe I've just never grown up."

"Being a grown up is overrated," Bill whispered against the side of Marc's head. After a moment, Bill gently pushed Marc back so they could look into one another's eyes as if to find something there he'd forgotten. Then, he pulled Marc back into himself. They wrapped their arms around one another as they had done many times long ago in the darkness of night as they faced the unexplainable changes in their minds and bodies. Bill released his tight hold on Marc's back, slid his hands slowly down along Marc's torso until he could slip his fingers under the elastic waistband around Marc's middle, put both of his hands on Marc's buttocks, and pulled him tight. Then he let out a subdued laugh. "I lawve you, daahhhhling! All of you!" he said, as he let his hand glide in gentle circles upon the skin he had exposed as he pushed Marc's briefs further down with his knuckles.

Marc reminded him that it might not look good if someone else came crashing through the door and caught the two men holding one another this way. He said maybe they should at least lock the door. But Bill didn't let go or back away, and Marc lost the thought in the midst of whispering, "I've loved you for as long as I can remember."

"And I, you," Bill whispered back.

Grayson Family Gathering

CHARACTERS:

Tom Grayson: Male, 70+, a playwright
Mary Grayson: Female, 70+, Tom's wife
Craig Grayson: Male, 45-50, oldest son
Mike Grayson: Male, 35-45, second son
Ginny Sardis: Female, 30-35, daughter
Ben Grayson: Male, 22-24, Craig and Carrie's son
Carrie Grayson: Female, 45-50, Craig's wife

TIME:

Present. Friday evening through Sunday.

SCENE:

All action takes place in the home of Tom and Mary Grayson in either the living room or dinette area (a portion of the kitchen), both of which can be on stage throughout the play.

———

Writing is an act—a performance—played for coins tossed into a harlequin's sack as he works the crowd, distracting them from the always that is today with its terrors lurking in the shadows. —The Author

———

ACT ONE
Act One: Scene One

Friday afternoon. As the curtain opens, Tom Grayson is sitting on the SL side of the sofa reading a newspaper. He is dressed in a tee-shirt and slacks and has socks on his feet, but no shoes. His wife, Mary, comes from SR, through the kitchen, and through the kitchen door into the living room. She is dressed in a good-looking dress and is wearing jewelry—she is ready to entertain. They have been married for a long time and still enjoy engaging in playful talk and ribbing.

MARY: Tom, they're going to be arriving any time now. Did you finish cleaning up the bathroom?

TOM: *Without looking up from the paper.* Yes, my sweet.

MARY: Did you put the car in the garage so they have more room to park?

TOM: *Answers mechanically.* I did, darling.

MARY: How about the . . .

TOM: Yes, dear.

MARY: You don't even know what I was going to ask!

TOM: You were going to ask me if I swept the porch.

MARY: You don't know that. You didn't wait to hear the question.

Tom pulls the newspaper down from his face and looks at Mary.

TOM: You're right, Mary. What did you want to ask?

MARY: I wanted to ask if you had swept off the porch. But you could have at least let me ask it before you jumped right into the answer.

TOM: Sorry. I'll do better next time.

MARY: You will not! After all these years, you think I don't know you?

TOM: No. I suppose you know me pretty well, Mary! Was there anything else you needed me to do?

MARY: You could put on some nicer clothes.

TOM: Why?

MARY: Do you want them to see you like that?

TOM: Why not? They're our children for Christ's sake. It's not like the British royal family is stopping by our house.

MARY: Carrie will be here. And Ben. What about them?

TOM: Carrie is our daughter-in-law. Did you catch that "daughter" part of that. She doesn't count as royalty even if she thinks she does. And Ben is our grandson and is fine with us being who we are. Are any of them bringing their dogs?

MARY: Of course not! Why would you ask such a question?

TOM: I would have dressed up for the dogs. I don't know them very well.

MARY: You try my patience, Tom! At least go put on a shirt.

TOM: What's the big deal?

MARY: Just do it! Just do it because I asked you to! Could you just do that?

TOM: Yes, I can do that.

Tom folds up the paper, lays it on the sofa. Gets up and disappears down the hallway to the bedroom. Mary goes over to the sofa, picks up the paper, puts it on the coffee table. She looks around the room to see if everything is in order. Tom yells from off stage.

TOM: Tell me again why Ginny's half-wit husband isn't coming!

MARY: *Yelling back at him.* Probably because you treat him like a half-wit, dear.

Tom comes back in buttoning up a shirt.

TOM: I suppose that could be it.

MARY: It is it! Last time he was here, you told him he was dumb as a coal bucket.

TOM: Well, he is! He didn't even know what a coal bucket is.

MARY: He's an attorney for crying out loud. He can't be as stupid as you seem to think he is. What if they ever have children? He won't want to let them come see us.

TOM: You can go visit with them! I'll stay home. Anyway, I don't think he's smart enough to figure out how to have sex. Our daughter's probably still a virgin.

MARY: Even stupid men figure that out. For some men, it's the only thing they ever learn to do well.

TOM: Now, how would you know about that, Mary.

MARY: Let's just say, I've seen enough so-called families in my lifetime where the female is carrying the load and the free-loader husband doesn't do much of anything worthwhile, but they keep pumping out the babies.

TOM: Obviously, the guy is doing something the woman likes. Maybe he's just so good at it that the she's willing to keep him around just for that. I thought that's why you kept me around

MARY: You flatter yourself, my dear!

TOM: You could at least lie to me once in a while.

MARY: You know I married you for your money. Everything else is just a bonus.

TOM: I guess you lost on both counts then, huh?

MARY: You've become a habit. I'll try to hang on to the end!

TOM: *Feigning being hurt by her words and exaggerates his pain.* I am cut to the quick! He stops the performance. At any rate, I'm looking forward to seeing Ben. It's been a while. Only seen him a couple of times since he got out of the hospital. It's been a while.

MARY: Don't forget that Carrie is coming too. She's part of the package.

Tom goes over to a sofa or chair that has a throw pillow on it, picks up the pillow. Pushes it against his face and screams. "Noooooooooooo!!!!" Mary is amused.

TOM: Well, I feel much better now! But Craig's not all that much better than she is.

Tom is still holding the pillow and screams into it again. However, Mary is not so amused this time.

MARY: That's our son you're screaming about.

TOM: If I'd known back then what I know about him now, I'd have insisted on an abortion.

MARY: Stop it, Tom. That's just mean.

TOM: Yes, my sweet.

MARY: Where are your shoes?

TOM: In the bedroom.

MARY: Well, go get them on!

TOM: Why? Are we going to dance?

MARY: You just stop trying to rile me up. Go get your shoes on!

TOM: Okay, okay!

Tom exits to the bedroom. The doorbell rings. Mary opens the door. Craig, Carrie, and their son Ben come in. Ben is carrying a gym bag or small over-night bag. Mary greets each of them by name, hugs Craig first with genuine joy, then Carrie dutifully and quickly, and finally Ben. She holds him an extra bit of time. Craig and Carrie are dressed as though they have come to a for-mal business luncheon; he is wearing a white shirt and dress jacket, and she is dressed in a designer dress. Ben is in a tee-shirt and jeans/slacks; he drops his bag off to one side of the door.

MARY: It's so wonderful to have you home again! I didn't know you were coming together.

CRAIG: Ben flew in separately but waited for us at the airport so we could drive over together.

MARY: Please come in and sit down. I can't wait to hear what you've all been up to. Craig, you look so healthy. Must be Carrie's taking good care of you.

CARRIE: *Speaking without humor. A note of annoyance is apparent in her voice.* I have always taken care of him, Mary.

MARY: Of course, you have, dear. Just making conversation. And you look marvelous too, Carrie. I love that dress you are wearing. That's a lovely color for you.

CARRIE: Thank you. But you needn't look for things to compli-ment me.

MARY: But I meant it. That is a lovely dress.

CARRIE: I'm sure you meant well, of course. But why is it that people must comment upon a woman's clothing as if that's the most important thing about her? You didn't say that you loved

Craig's clothes or hated Ben's clothes, as you should. We women shouldn't feed into old ways of thinking about our status.

MARY: I didn't mean to offend you.

CARRIE: You didn't offend me. I am simply pointing out a fact if for no other reason than to help Ben to appreciate women as human beings and not as objects of lust. It is so important that women convey that message at every opportunity, don't you think?

Ben is rolling his eyes. Craig is clearly uncomfortable.

MARY: You are right, Carrie. Just a thoughtless old woman brought up in an old-fashioned way trying to make conversation. I'll try to be more careful in the future. *To Ben:* Ben, Honey! How have you been? Your grandfather has been looking forward to seeing you!

Tom has walked out from the hallway.

MARY: Here he is now. Tom, they're here!

TOM: I see that, Mary!

Ben gets up and goes over to his grandfather and affectionately hugs him as they talk. Craig has risen, waits through Ben's interactions with Tom. Carrie remains seated.

BEN: Pops! So good to see you. I've missed you.

TOM: *Full of joy.* Ben! My boy! Great to see you. It's been too long.

As grandfather and grandson embrace, Craig comes to them. Ben steps aside to make way for his father. Craig puts his hand out for a handshake to make it clear that he won't be hugging.

CRAIG: Hello, Father.

TOM: *Taking Craig's hand. Speaks in a matter-of-fact way.* Craig. Hello. You're looking good. Love that shirt. Just the right color for you. Brings out the color of your eyes.

Craig looks at his father then to his mother as if to ask, "What's up with him?" Then he catches on.

CRAIG: You were listening, weren't you? Very clever, Father.

TOM: And, Carrie, you are here as well. So good to see you.

Tom walks to Carrie and puts his hand out as if for a handshake. Carrie looks a bit confused but takes the hand limply. Tom shakes it up and down once before releasing it.

TOM: How about that game last night, Carrie? You watch it? Cowboys by ten. Unbelievable last-minute touchdown, eh?

CARRIE: I have no idea what you are talking about, Tom.

Carrie looks to Craig with some confusion about what is happening. Ben is chuckling.

TOM: Sorry. Thought you would.

CARRIE: Ben, what is so funny?

BEN: Nothing, Mother. Something just struck me.

CARRIE: You're enjoying your grandfather's mockery of my comments about respecting women! I would be ever so much happier if you would kindly return to being the boy I raised instead of whatever this is you've become.

BEN: Sorry, Mother, if I'm a disappointment to you.

TOM: Oh, leave the boy alone, Carrie. He's fine the way he is.

CARRIE: He is my son, Tom, and I'll thank you not to interfere.

CRAIG: How about we change the topic.

TOM: You're right, Craig. Let's talk about the grown man that Ben has become and how he gets to make his own decisions about his life. How about just letting him be who he is?

CARRIE: We've only just arrived. Are you actually going to attack right away?

CRAIG: Father, really! Please drop this.

TOM: Sure. Drop it. I'm sorry, Carrie. *Facetiously:* It is always a pleasure to have you around! Hey, Ben, you want a drink?

BEN: What do you have?

TOM: Whatever you want.

BEN: I like Cognac! Got any?

TOM: Sure! Craig? Carrie? Can I get you anything?

CRAIG: No thank you.

CARRIE: Certainly not!

TOM: *Mocks Carrie:* Certainly! *To Ben:* Come along Ben. It's in the pantry. *They exit.*

CRAIG: *To Mary:* I see he hasn't changed any.

CARRIE: I cannot, for the life of me, understand why he feels the need to challenge me at every turn.

CRAIG: It's just his nature, dear. It's in his blood.

MARY: Now, Craig. He's your father. You know he jokes about everything. Doesn't mean any harm! He loves Ben so, and, after all, Ben is old enough to decide for himself.

CARRIE: Just because Ben's of age, doesn't mean that he should become a drunkard.

MARY: But, Carrie, we're talking about a drink, not about getting him drunk. Surely you don't begrudge him that.

CARRIE: I would prefer he took after my side of the family.

MARY: I see. *She turns to Craig and changes the subject.* How is business, dear. Are you doing well?

CRAIG: Yes, very well, Mother. Company's making money. Or, I should say, I'm making money for them. There's talk about another raise coming up soon. They're expanding. Lots of room for moving upward and maybe into a top executive position.

MARY: It sounds like they are fortunate to have you!

CRAIG: I'd like to think it's mutually advantageous. How is father doing? Are you and he in good health?

MARY: For being in our seventies, I would say we're in excellent health. We have our aches and pains, of course. Your father is still a spitfire.

CARRIE: That's fairly obvious. Aches and pains just come with the territory, I am told. All the more reason for those of us who are still young to do everything we can to minimize the effects of old age.

CRAIG: Yes, of course. *To Carrie:* Thankfully, I have you to take care of me, dear.

CARRIE: *To Mary:* Is Tom still writing his smutty plays?

MARY: Why, Carrie. They're not smutty. They are often works that the critics admire.

CARRIE: Let's just say that they're not my cup of tea. I like things that are uplifting and cheerful. He always seems to be dragging people into his plays who are on drugs or living terrible lives or are undressed or almost undressed.

MARY: I am sorry that you haven't looked deeper into his work. I think you would find that there's a lot more to it than you are giving him credit for. To answer your question, yes! He's always working on something. Sending submissions here, there, and everywhere. One of his plays is being produced in New York this fall. He's excited about that.

CRAIG: Will he go to the city for the opening?

MARY: Actually, he's going up for a couple of weeks to meet with the director and producers, sit in on rehearsals and such. He'll probably stay through opening night. That's what he usually does. I think he's looking forward to getting away.

CARRIE: Will you be going with him, Mary?

MARY: No. I think he needs a break. And I know I do. Men! They can get on our nerves, can't they, Carrie?

CARRIE: I can't really say that Craig gets on my nerves. Ben, on the other hand, is a different case.

CRAIG: Be careful with what you say about men, Mother. You brought two more of them onto this planet. Not that Mike quite fits the mold.

Carrie smiles. She looks at Craig with approval.

MARY: Craig, don't demean your brother. *To both Craig and Carrie:* I don't care that he's gay. I love him. Let's not talk badly of him.

CARRIE: I am not in the habit of casting aspersions on anyone as long as they keep their perversions to themselves.

MARY: Perversions? Carrie, please. That was a very unkind choice of words.

CARRIE: You are right, Mary. A poor choice of words. I will attempt to be more cautious when Michael arrives.

CRAIG: Sorry, Mother. I'll try also. When is Ginny getting here?

MARY: Anytime now.

CARRIE: Why is she coming alone? Why isn't Vince coming with her? I always enjoy his company so.

MARY: As you know, my dear, he and Tom don't really get along. I think Vince is happier not coming and Tom is happier when Vince stays at home. Those two are like gas and flame. Best for all of us if they stay apart.

CRAIG: You have to admit that Father has taken every opportunity to make Vince feel unwelcomed.

CARRIE: He has a way of making people uncomfortable.

MARY: Unfortunately, many people have a way of alienating other people. It's not just Tom. Vince hasn't made it easy for your father to like him. The way he treats your sister sets Tom off.

CRAIG: Maybe, if she were more of a wife, he wouldn't act the way he does.

MARY: What do you mean by that, Craig? Ginny is a wonderful person.

CARRIE: What he means, Mary, is that Ginny flits about. She doesn't stay home. She's always with one friend or another. She runs her own business. It's as though she prefers the company of others to her own husband. You can't blame a man for wanting his wife with him.

MARY: Perhaps she does prefer the company of others. There could be a reason for that. I don't know. Probably best we don't speculate about her marriage or how she behaves. And she seems perfectly happy to me.

CARRIE: But what about her poor husband?

MARY: Poor husband? He's got a nice home, lots of money, fancy car, nice things. I'd like to talk about something else.

Tom and Ben come back through the kitchen. They are carrying partially filled cognac glasses; Tom has the bottle. Sets it on the kitchen counter. They are laughing and joking. Before getting to the door to the living room, they have a moment.

TOM: Now don't tell your mother what I told you. She'll have a conniption fit.

BEN: To say the least!

Tom and Ben enter the living room. They are happy. They walk in and see the dour faces on Craig, Carrie, and Mary.

TOM: Looks like a fun discussion going on in here. *To Ben:* Ben, did you bring a camera? Looks like one of those fun family moments you want to keep forever.

BEN: Sorry, Pops. Forgot to bring it.

CARRIE: Ben, I do wish you would not call your grandfather "Pops." You're a grown man. Call him "grandfather."

BEN: He's been "Pops" all my life. I'll stop if he tells me to. But I like it.

CARRIE: Well, you have certainly taken on a disrespectful attitude toward your mother!

TOM: I'm fine with it. He likes it. I like it. What's the issue here?

CARRIE: *Speaking to Tom:* Why must you always side with him against me?

TOM: Because you treat him like a twelve-year old child instead of a twenty-two-year-old grown man. Why can't you just leave him alone?

MARY: Please let's stop this! We're going to have a wonderful weekend together.

CARRIE: That is debatable.

MARY: We don't need to squabble. It will be so nice to have the family together again. Can we, please, agree to try to be kind to one another for just one weekend. *To Ben, changing the subject:* Ben, I'm putting you in with your Uncle Mike. You can take your bag up and put it in his old room: the one you usually stay in when you come to visit.

BEN: Sure.

Ben gets up, picks up his bag and takes it upstairs.

CARRIE: Really, Mary. Is that a wise move?

MARY: Whatever do you mean, Carrie?

TOM: What she means, Mary, is that because Mike is gay, he's likely to impose himself on his nephew and turn him gay too! *To Carrie:* Do you really think Michael would do anything to hurt Ben?

CARRIE: That was a rather crude way of putting it, Tom.

TOM: Then, please, explain what you meant.

CARRIE: I suppose Ben will do whatever he wants anyway.

TOM: As he should, Carrie. He will be fine. I'll make them both wear chastity belts to bed.

MARY: *To Craig:* Craig, you didn't bring your bags in. Why don't you go out and get them? You and Carrie can have your old room. I've made it all up for you.

CRAIG: Thank you, Mother. But . . . well, you see . . .

CARRIE: What Craig is trying to say is that we've decided to stay at the Hampton on Westchester. We dropped our luggage off on the way here. We will be more comfortable there.

MARY: *Disappointed.* I see. I wish you had told me.

Ben has returned.

CRAIG: I am sorry. We just decided during the flight. But now, Ben can have his own room.

BEN: I'm fine sleeping in Uncle Mike's room.

The doorbell rings. Tom starts heading for the door, but before he can get to it, Mike and Ginny come into the house. Each of them is carrying an overnight bag.

MIKE: Look what I found lurking about outside!

TOM: Mike! Ginny!

Mary and Ben join Tom in greeting the new arrivals. Travel bags are set down during the greetings. Hugs all around.

TOM: Come in!

Craig stands up. Mike goes to Carrie and shakes her hand. Then he puts his arms around Craig to hug him, but Craig is stiff; it is clear he is uncomfortable.

MIKE: Good to see you, Brother!

Ginny comes over and hugs Craig; acknowledges Carrie without touching her.

MARY: Ben! Would you take their bags upstairs?

BEN: Uncle Mike, I'm sharing your room tonight. That okay with you?

MIKE: Of course, Ben! We'll have some guy talk later, heh?

CRAIG: That ought to be interesting.

BEN: Father, give it a rest, will you?

MARY: Stop it, Craig!

Ben picks up the bags and takes them upstairs to the bedrooms as Mike speaks.

MIKE: *To Craig:* I just got here, and you're going to start already. Believe it or not, brother. I'm still a guy! I'm gay, but I'm a guy. Can we just not get into this age-old bullshit and stay civil?

CRAIG: No problem, Mikey! Civil! That's me. *To Ginny:* So, Ginny, how's Vince doing these days?

GINNY: He's fine. Sorry he couldn't come. He had some business to attend to and sends his regrets.

CARRIE: Really? I was under the impression that he doesn't like coming here.

GINNY: He's busy. Lots of clients. Court hearings. Meetings. Lawyer's life.

CARRIE: Court hearings on the weekend?

GINNY: No. Of course not. He's got prep work to do, briefs to write.

Ben returns from the hallway.

TOM: What Carrie is getting at, Ginny, is that she wants to make sure everybody remembers that Vince doesn't come here because he doesn't like me. And that's okay. I don't like him either.

GINNY: Well, we're off to a great start, aren't we? All right. Vince didn't want to come. I did. Here I am. Can we just get past this and try to enjoy our time? If that's possible.

BEN: Aunt Ginny, I for one am glad you're here.

GINNY: Thank you, sweetie! It's worth it just to see you. And I can't wait to hear all about what you've been up to.

BEN: Not all that exciting. ... I'm not crazy anymore.

CRAIG: Ben. Please don't get your mother started.

CARRIE: Get me started? Why does he do these things? Tells everybody he was crazy. He wasn't crazy.

BEN: I might get crazy again if you keep up this needling crap you're doing.

MARY: *Shouting.* Everyone, stop! I thought you were all grown-ups! Can we please all stop picking at each other? I had hoped we could all get together and have some quality family time for once. I've been looking forward to this day for months. We've been together for twenty minutes and we're already at it. Please! If you won't be pleasant for one another, do it for my sake. I can't take an entire weekend of this bickering! If that's the way it's going to be, I'm going to ask you to turn around and leave.

Everyone is looking uncomfortable except Tom.

TOM: I'm sure everyone is just travel fatigued. To Mary: I'm sure no one means to upset you, darling.

CRAIG: You are the one who set this whole thing in motion, Father!

TOM: Really? I thought Carrie . . .

MARY: *Shouting.* God, help me!

TOM: You're right. Let's restart. I apologize for offending anyone here. I, for one, am going to do my best to be pleasant. Let me just say that I am happy to have you here, each and every one of you, and I am looking forward to a pleasant weekend with you all.

MARY: That's the spirit, Tom. Thank you! How about coffee or tea? Anyone?

TOM: Or something a little more interesting?

BLACKOUT.

Act One: Scene Two

Friday evening after dinner. Tom and Ben are sitting at the table talking. They are sipping glasses of Cognac.

TOM: I'm glad this place has quieted down so we can talk a bit.

BEN: Me too. Thank God, my parents are staying at a hotel. I don't think I could take it with them on top of me all weekend.

TOM: You've got your hands full with those two. That's for sure.

BEN: Was my dad always such a dork?

TOM: Actually, your dad's quite smart. I just don't know what he's about anymore. He never really talked to me much even when he was a kid. Didn't talk about his thoughts or feelings. I think he did with your grandmother some, but not with me. After he left home, he just seemed to drift away. Never seemed all that interested in being close. But to his credit, he didn't keep you away from us. I think your mother would have been okay with you being mostly connected to her side of the family, but your dad was able to convince her that we weren't axe murderers or anything like that. At any rate, I know he cares about you.

BEN: He sure has a strange way of showing it.

TOM: We don't get to choose our parents, Ben.

BEN: Sometimes I wish I had had that option. When I got out of the hospital, that's when I knew I couldn't deal with them anymore. I couldn't live with them. That's why I hit you up for the loan. I had to have my own place, some peace and quiet, or I'd end up right back in the looney bin.

TOM: I've got your back, buddy.

BEN: I intend to repay you, by the way.

TOM: *Joking.* Damned straight! I'll send my goons out for you if you don't.

BEN: You talking Big Bubba and his sidekick Lefty with the twisted lip?

TOM: Ah! You know them! Best not to have them visit you.

BEN: Do you remember when I was little and we used to make up those goofy stories about all kinds of things? I loved coming here.

TOM: We loved having you. And, by the way, they weren't goofy stories. Some of them ended up in my plays or gave me a theme for a play or triggered some playfulness in me. Even old men like to play sometimes. I'm a writer. That's what I do. I play with words. I make up goofy stories that some people like. Seriously, just in case it needs to be said. I don't care about the money. I care about you.

BEN: That money paid the rent, bought groceries, paid the bills while I went out looking for jobs. I'm doing well now, actually.

TOM: Glad to hear it, Ben. You feeling okay?

BEN: You mean with the crazy stuff? I'm fine most of the time. I get depressed sometimes, but not like back before I went in. My shrink is great. He has helped a lot.

TOM: That's great. And by the way, you aren't, and never were, crazy, and you know it. The world got to you; that's all. It can happen to anyone under the right circumstances. You know I'm here for you, right? Always! No matter what.

BEN: I know. Without you and Gram, I'm not sure I would have survived it.

TOM: Yes, you would have. You're tougher than you think.

BEN: You think so? When that was going on, I felt like a total wuss!

TOM: Stop beating yourself, Ben. You're a good man! You have people that love you. Not everyone has that, you know?

BEN: Thanks, Pops.

TOM: You said you've got a job. What are you doing?

BEN: Selling dope! *Tom is taken aback.* Just kidding, Pops!

TOM: Don't joke about that shit! Especially if your mother's within a hundred miles of you. You think she's a pain in the ass now. I hate to even think about the hell you'd face if she even heard you joking.

BEN: Seriously. I'm working for a small ad agency in Columbus. Mostly I'm a glorified runner. Drop things off. Pick things up. But once in a while they let me try out some of my ideas. Mostly, they think I'm full of crap. But every now and then, they seem to like what I have to offer. It's only been a few months, but they treat me well and pay well; so, I can't really complain too much.

TOM: You're probably too smart ... overthink that stuff. You've got to think like a moron to write some of that advertising crap, obviously.

BEN: Get a beautiful woman in the shower washing her hair and making orgasmic moans and sighs and talk about the "organic" experience. Brilliant writing, Heh? It's hair soap for Christ's sake packaged in a sex fantasy.

TOM: I guess it sells. Writers! We all sell our souls in one way or another. Same thing in theater. Sometimes it seems like the crap is what people want. "Fluff," I call it. You write a serious play, and they say it's "depressing." I'm so sick of hearing that. What that means to me is that serious work makes them have to think about how shitty life can be sometimes, and if they have to think about it, they'd have to think about doing something about it. Most people don't want to think. They want to laugh themselves to death or be angry that someone else doesn't do the hard work of living for them. Nothing wrong with laughter, don't get me wrong. I'd just like to think we could get audiences out for something weightier than a romp.

Mary, Mike and Ginny are returning to the living room. They have been upstairs unpacking, chatting, etc.

TOM: Sounds like the mob is reassembling.

Ben stands up.

TOM: Wait a minute Ben. I want to tell you something. He rises. Pulls Ben into an embrace. I love you! More than you'll know until you have grandchildren of your own. I will be here for you for as long as I live. Please, please don't ever try to take your life again. No matter what. Please don't do it.

BEN: *Laying his head on his grandfather's shoulder.* I love you too, Pops. And I'm sorry I hurt you and Gram.

Subdued laughter is still coming from the living room. They separate. Each wipe tears out of their eyes.

TOM: You want a refill on the Cognac, or are you all right?

BEN: I'm fine for now.

He hugs his grandfather again, kisses his cheek. They go through the door into the living room. The others are sitting at this point, still chuckling.

TOM: Okay, you birds. What's all the clucking about?

As Mike and Ginny tell the story below, they do a lot of laughing.

MIKE: Ginny and I were reminding Mom about that time we climbed up on the roof and tied a rope to the chimney, and Ginny tried to rappel down the wall and ended up kicking out the window in your study when you were in there trying to write.

GINNY: The look on your face!

TOM: I'd never been attacked by Ninjas before that.

GINNY: And then I had my leg all wrapped up in the rope and you had to reach out and untangle it before pulling me in.

TOM: Actually, I was just trying to move it up to your neck and push you back out the window!

MIKE: Then Mom came running up into the room. I could hear her screaming down below while I was up on the roof laughing like a damned fool.

MARY: Well, forgive me for having concern about my children's survival! You were both a handful. What one of you didn't think of the other did. Ginny, I swear you were more Tomboy than most boys are boys! And you, Michael, always egging her on.

BEN: If I'd done anything like that, my mother would've had me in reform school for sure.

TOM: *To Ben:* You've got that right, Kiddo! *To Mike and Ginny:* By the way, you two still owe me forty dollars for the window repairs.

MIKE: Good luck collecting, Dad.

TOM: I'm taking it out of your inheritance!

MIKE: I guess zero minus my half of the window costs puts me at owing the estate twenty bucks. Some attorney can chase me for it.

BEN: If I have any part in the estate, you're paying up, Buddy! I'm not footing the bills on my own.

TOM: Relax, I'm going to win the Lottery any day now. I'll leave each of you a few bucks.

MARY: *Changing the subject.* Tom, Michael was telling us some good news when we were upstairs. *To Mike:* Tell him, Michael!

MIKE: I'm seeing someone, Dad.

TOM: You've seen lots of "someones." What's the news? Maybe you could elaborate a bit more.

MIKE: I'm living with a guy. I've been with him for about a year now.

TOM: Still not news.

MIKE: I love him. And we are planning to get married!

BEN: That's great, Uncle Mike. I'm happy for you.

TOM: Mike. That's wonderful news! So, why didn't you bring him along? Did you think I'd bite him?

MIKE: No. I didn't think that. I guess I just wanted to fill everybody in and let them get used to the idea.

TOM: When we've talked to you on the phone, you've never mentioned him. Why has this been a secret?

MIKE: We just made the decision to marry recently. As you know, I haven't had the best of luck finding Mr. Right. I didn't want to say anything until I was certain he was the one. I was maybe afraid I'd jinx the relationship by blabbing about it. I thought about asking him to come with me, but I didn't want to get into a big stink about it. I thought it might go better to just let people get used to the idea.

TOM: Big stink from whom? Who needs time to get used to it? You knew none of us here would have a problem with it. Now let me think! Who's left? Who's not here at the moment?

BEN: Uncle Mike, it doesn't matter when you tell my father. He's going to pull his judgmental crap, and you know my mother. She's not likely to change all of a sudden. They're just going to have to deal with it.

MIKE: You're right, I know. Maybe I just didn't want to hear their crap. Didn't want Alan to hear it either. That's his name, Alan Wilson.

TOM: Your brother will get over it or he won't. Doesn't change anything! We're all happy for you. Have you and Alan set a date?

MIKE: Not yet. We'd like to get married this fall. But I wanted to know what your schedule is. I want you to be there.

TOM: Of course! I've got a lot going, but I'm sure we can find a time that will work for you. I'll make it happen. We'll look at my calendar sometime over the weekend. Now tell me. Is the father of the groom supposed to pay for this or is the other father of the groom supposed to pay for it? If I'm paying for it, I'm deducting twenty dollars you owe me for the window. I'm not paying anything until I meet the guy.

MIKE: I think we have the wedding costs covered! And, no, neither father is going to walk us down the aisle. And you haven't met him because I've been too caught up in my own stuff. Hell. I haven't seen you for close to a year now. I'm going to do better, I promise. By the way, he doesn't have two heads or fangs or anything. He's good looking. Incredibly good looking, and he's a great guy—smart, funny. I think you'll like him.

GINNY: So, when do we get to meet him?

MIKE: Soon! I promise.

GINNY: *Joking.* I hope Dad is going to be nicer to your husband than he has been to mine.

TOM: I tried with Vince. You know that.

MARY: Fire and gasoline. That's the sum of it.

GINNY: I do know you tried, Dad! But Mom's right. You two were on a collision course almost from the beginning.

MARY: Any time you get two strong-willed men with opposing views of how the world should work, you're headed for trouble. There's no cure for it. It's just the way they are. Best thing is to just keep them apart. *To Mike:* Ginny and I will keep them separated at your wedding.

TOM: Now, come on. I'm not going to cause a problem at my son's wedding.

MARY: I know you're not. I'm going to see to it ... keep you on a short leash.

GINNY: It's not going to be a problem. I promise.

TOM: Hey! I won't be the problem. I can get along with Vince when he isn't being a horse's ass.

MARY: *To Mike and Ginny:* Did I tell you that your father has a new play being produced in New York in the fall?

MIKE: That's great news.

GINNY: That's wonderful. What's the play?

TOM: It's called "Dave's Place." It's a play about two young gay men. Takes place during the pandemic. One owns a struggling neighborhood bar, and the other is a writer who comes in mostly just to be around people; he's had enough of the isolation thing. They get to talking and find they like each other a lot. They end up having to work together to deal with two different men who come into the bar. One of those men is your stereotypical drunk who happens to be a banker, the other is a right-wing Trumpster—both of them creating havoc. By the end, the two young men fall for one another and are likely to become a couple.

MIKE: You go, Dad! They don't die of AIDS or rot in hell.

TOM: No. Actually, nobody dies. Nobody rots in hell.

GINNY: So, is that the point? That gay is okay?

TOM: Gay is okay! But that's not the point. I was thinking of you, Mike, when I wrote it. Both men show a lot of intellect and courage. They don't play into the stereotypes at all. I tried to make the gay thing as normal as any male/female relationship. If I have to sum it up, I guess the point is that it's in human connections that we're saved! The rest of it—life, that is—is mostly bullshit. That's the message. Love and hope is what keeps us going. I hope you two and Alan will come see it!

GINNY: Any laughs?

TOM: I suppose in the strictest sense of the term, it's a comedy! It's funny, but it has ideas. It challenges assumptions. I feel real good about it.

MIKE: It sounds wonderful. Alan and I will definitely go see it. Maybe we'll drag old Ben here along with us too.

BEN: You won't have to drag me.

MIKE: You won't be embarrassed to hang out with two old gay guys?

BEN: You know I won't, Uncle Mike. Of course not. Anyway, the way I see it, I'll be hanging out with my uncles, who just happen to be gay!

MIKE: Well said, my boy! Get that from your grandfather?

BEN: Nope. Just pulled it out of my butt.

Mike laughs. There is a brief lull in the conversation.

MARY: Ginny, you haven't shared much about what's going on with you.

GINNY: I know. I'm just enjoying being with you all. You and I'll talk.

MARY: Of course, dear. Whenever you like.

TOM: This sounds serious! Are you pregnant?

GINNY: For God's sake, I hope not. No. Just would rather not get into it right now.

TOM: Meaning not in front of an audience of men. Especially your father.

GINNY: That would be a fairly accurate interpretation.

MARY: How about you and I go out to the kitchen for a cup of tea and let the men have some time to themselves.

GINNY: I would like some tea.

TOM: I think that's our cue to get lost.

MARY: Well said, Tom.

TOM: Come on, Boys. Let's go shoot some pool in the basement.

The men get up and exit. Mary and Ginny go into the kitchen. Lights fade out SL. Lights up on SR. Mary busies herself with the tea making, setting the cups, etc. Ginny goes to the table and sits down.

MARY: I think your father is really enjoying having time with you all.

GINNY: Yeah. I think so too.

MARY: I wish he and Vince could have hit it off.

GINNY: Well, they didn't. Not much can be done about that. And it just doesn't matter anymore.

MARY: Never give up hope, dear.

GINNY: No, Mom. It doesn't matter anymore. Vince and I are done!

MARY: What do you mean, done?

GINNY: I mean done! As in it's over.

MARY: You're divorcing him?

GINNY: Yes!

Mary comes to the table, puts an arm around her daughter, then sits down next to her.

MARY: Ginny, I am so sorry to hear it.

GINNY: Dad was right! Vinnie was just as awful as Dad thought he was. I just didn't want to accept it until . . . until . . . She starts to cry.

Mary quickly gets up, goes over to the counter, takes a box of tissues from the counter or a cupboard, and brings it back to the table.

MARY: *Trying to comfort Ginny:* It's alright, darling. You can tell me if you want.

GINNY: Mom, he was hitting me! He punched me a couple of weeks ago. I'd had enough and called the cops.

MARY: Oh, my God, Ginny. Are you all right? *Becoming a bit frenzied.* Are you out of there now? I mean, you're not still living with him, are you? I hope not. Oh, my God. *She starts to cry.*

GINNY: No. I left that same day. Haven't seen him since.

MARY: You did the right thing calling the police.

GINNY: They came and took him away. He was raging and scream-ing at me and the police, threatening to sue everybody on the planet. I had him charged with domestic violence. The bastard! He and all his attorney buddies will fight everything I say, make me the aggressor and him the victim if they can get away with it. I just don't care anymore.

MARY: They took pictures, didn't they? Somebody did, I hope. I mean of the marks where he hit you. I mean, did the cop? Did you? Why didn't you call me before this? That awful man. Oh, Ginny, I'm so sorry. I'm stumbling all over myself trying to think what to do.

GINNY: Mom, please! You don't have to do anything. I just needed to talk. I've done everything I can for the moment. I just need my Mom right now.

MARY: Of course, Honey. I am here for you. *She brushes Ginny's hair away from her face, attempting to soothe her.* How long has this been going on?

GINNY: Almost from the beginning. I just couldn't tell anybody.

MARY: I am so sorry. I wish I'd known. I could have helped you. You always spoke so positively about him. Now, I find out he's a monster. Why didn't you leave when it first started?

GINNY: All the usual stupid reasons people give! I wanted him to love me like I loved him. I wanted to believe I could change him. I lied to myself for the past five years thinking I could somehow make him not want to do those things to me. I was an idiot. I let it happen.

MARY: *Mary takes Ginny into her arms and tries to comfort her.* Oh, Darling. I hate that you had to deal with that all alone. I wish you had reached out to me sooner.

GINNY: I couldn't. I felt like such a failure. I knew Dad would blow up. I just didn't want to drag you into it. I thought I could work my way through it somehow. But I finally realized I had to get out, get away from him.

MARY: You're here now. You're safe. Are you afraid he'll come after you? Has he tried to contact you since he was arrested?

GINNY: He sent a couple of text messages saying he wants to talk. That's his usual way of dealing with our marriage. Get me to listen to his crap, watch him cry while he's telling me how sorry he is and that it won't happen again.

MARY: I hope you won't give in to him.

GINNY: I sent a message back telling him not to contact me again. I told him to call my lawyer.

MARY: Good for you! Isn't there anything I can do to help you?

GINNY: You're already doing it. I just needed to talk to my mom. Please don't tell, Dad.

MARY: How can I not tell him? He's going to find out. He's your father. He loves you. We can help you.

GINNY: You know how he's going to be.

MARY: You may be right. But he has a right to know. I can't keep this a secret from him. He's going to have questions about why you are divorcing. What am I supposed to say, "You were right, Tom, he was a half-wit and your daughter finally agreed"? He's believed for a long time Vince didn't treat you well. He read it in him somehow. Men know those things about one another.

GINNY: I'll leave it up to you then. But I don't want to get into any discussions about this with Craig or Carrie. I can't think of anything I'd hate worse than having to listen to them yap at me about how it wouldn't have gone this way if I'd been a better wife. I'd probably end up wanting to punch one of them in the nose. Then they could call the cops on me.

MARY: They are judgmental, I know! And I won't tell them anything. I'll leave that to you when the time is right. They don't need to know any details other than that you are divorcing. If they want to know more, they'll have to ask you or Vince. But all that aside, what are you going to do for a place to live? Are you going to keep the business?

GINNY: Mom, I haven't figured it all out yet. Right now, I have a protection order against him. I'm staying in a motel while I think it through. He'll do everything in his power to keep the house. Thank, God, I purchased the business on my own, and his name isn't attached. It will keep me going for a while. Right now, I just don't know what I want. I just want time to figure it out.

MARY: Of course, dear. You should take as long as you need. Oh! I forgot the tea. The kettle is going to boil dry!

Ginny sits at the table. Mary goes to the counter, pours water, brings teacups and saucers to the table.

MARY: Can I get you anything else? Sugar? Lemon?

GINNY: No. I like it plain.

MARY: I am so angry at that man. I have half a mind to go up there and tell Mr. Vincent Sardis exactly what I think of him. Wife beater! Of all the cowardly things a man can do!

GINNY: It would just make matters worse. I just want to be rid of him.

Tom has come into the living room. He knocks on the kitchen door and peeks in, sees that the women have been crying.

TOM: Sorry to interrupt, but . . . this doesn't look like it's going well. Anything I need to be worried about?

MARY: Later, Tom. What can I do for you, my dear?

TOM: I was just going to grab the bottle of cognac and some glasses and give the boys a nip. I guess it can wait.

MARY: No. Do what you need to do.

Tom looks concerned, but goes into pantry, grabs the bottle of cognac. Mary has arisen and goes to cupboard and pulls down three cognac glasses and hands them to Tom as he passes back through.

TOM: Ginny, Is everything all right? Anything I need to know?

MARY: *Speaking emphatically:* Later, Tom.

TOM: Okay, okay! *He starts to exit.*

BLACKOUT.

Act One: Scene Three

Still later Friday evening. Mike, Ginny and Ben are in the living room playing a game of Monopoly at the coffee table. Mike and Ginny are on the sofa. Ben is sitting on the floor. Ben is clearly winning and enjoying hitting his aunt and uncle for money every time they stop on one of his properties.

BEN: You hit Boardwalk with a hotel on it. You owe me two thousand dollars, Aunt Ginny.

GINNY: You old cheapskate. You're going to charge your dear old auntie all that money. Who do you think you are? Donald Trump?

BEN: God, no! Please don't put me in league with him. How about I put you on the auntie discount? I'll just charge you a thousand so you can stay in the game.

MIKE: Hold on there, pardner! You made me pay full rent. Why does she get special treatment?

BEN: You have more money than she does. But if you insist ... All right, Aunt Ginny, you have to pay two thousand dollars. Sorry!

GINNY: I have a better idea. How about you just give your Uncle Mike a thousand and I'll pay a thousand, and we'll call it even?

BEN: No can do! Treat everybody the same, I always say! No special rates for relatives. And by the way, you are now broke! Uncle Mike's all but bankrupt.

GINNY: Looks at Mike, smiles. What do you say, Mike?

MIKE: I say do it!

They both abruptly get off the couch, tackle Ben, and start tickling him. Lots of laughing. Ben keeps trying to hold them off, but they have overwhelmed him. He can't stop laughing until they finally get off him. During the tickling, Ben is trying to call for help. He says he is being robbed. He might say such things as "Help! Help! I'm being robbed! Call the cops!" When it ends, they all start picking up the pieces and putting the game away.

BEN: Not fair! Two against one!

MIKE: I don't want to hear it, Mr. Besos! Buy yourself some protection!

BEN: I'll tell Pops! He'll kick your butts. Worse yet, I'll tell Gram!

GINNY: Oh, no! Not the mother weapon! Please! Please! Don't tell my mommy!

BEN: Only if you declare me the game master.

MIKE: We bow to you, Oh-Mighty-One!

BEN: All right then. Seriously, that was fun. I've missed you guys so much.

GINNY: We've missed you too! We've been worried about you.

BEN: I guess I caused a lot of pain for a lot of people.

MIKE: Not pain, Ben! Concern! We love you. Always have and always will

BEN: When that all happened, I didn't feel like anybody could love me. I sure as hell didn't love myself.

GINNY: You don't have to talk about it if you don't want to.

BEN: I'm trying to get past being ashamed of myself. My shrink is helping me learn how to accept the day-to-day stuff for what it is. This has been nice seeing you. Laughing. God! I needed a laugh. I've needed it for a long time. I'm glad I came. Almost didn't. Wasn't sure I could deal with my parents for a whole weekend. Just in case you hadn't noticed, my mother can be a real pain.

GINNY: Never noticed that! Did you, Mike?

MIKE: A pain? No. Ben, what are you talking about?

All three of them start laughing.

GINNY: I'm sorry, Ben. We shouldn't be joking about your mom.

BEN: Why not? That's part of what's keeping me sane. You have no idea what it's like to have her on your case twenty-four/seven!

MIKE: She's still your mother.

BEN: Yes, she is. But that doesn't give her a free pass for making my life hell all those years when she chose my friends, interfered in everything I ever wanted to do, picked my college for me, controlled my every movement, and I let her. That's the part that pisses me off the most. I let her get away with it all.

MIKE: You couldn't control the situation then.

BEN: I get that up here *[pointing to his head]*. Right now, I have to get control here. *Touches his chest.* I still get angry at her. I hated my life for such a long time.

GINNY: Despite all that, Ben, you've turned out to be a really great young man. Somebody must have done something right.

BEN: Maybe. At any rate, you don't need to hear my crap.

MIKE: It's not crap. And you don't need to tell us anything you don't want to. But if you need someone to talk to, you can talk to us about anything. Any time! Anything! All you've got to do is say you need to talk. Anything we can do to help.

BEN: *Deflecting.* Will you find me a hot date?

MIKE: Well, yeah! I just didn't think you were into men!

BEN: Think I'll stick to women for right now. But thanks anyway.

GINNY: Don't ask me. All the women I know are as old as I am. Not only that, you'd have to have a long-distance romance. Any woman I know lives in Patterson! Who's going to pay the plane fares?

BEN: Good point. But! You said you wanted to help. I ask for one simple thing, and you both bomb out. Losers!

GINNY: We'll work on it. I don't know about you two, but I'm about ready to turn in. It's been a long day.

MIKE: *To Ginny:* You, okay, Kid?

GINNY: Life's a little tough right now. But it's good to be with you and the family. We'll talk some more when I'm not so tired. Okay?

MIKE: I'm here for you, you know?

GINNY: I know, Mike. You've always been there for me. I just haven't let people into my life much since I married Vince. I've got to change that. We'll talk, I promise.

MIKE: I'll be up soon. I'm going to hang out with the night owl here for a few more minutes.

GINNY: Good night. *Exits.*

MIKE: Looks like it's just you and me, Kid! It was fun, wasn't it?

BEN: Yes. First time I've laughed like that in a long time. Do you think something's going on with Aunt Ginny? I get the feeling things aren't . . .

Mary's voice is heard. She is speaking loudly from her bedroom and is following Tom who makes his way to the living room. When they arrive in the living room, she is trying to take his arm. He is pulling away. She is in a nightgown. He is fully dressed and is buttoning up his shirt and trying to tuck it into his pants as he comes into the room. They are both highly animated and shouting.

MARY: Tom. No. Please. That's not going to help anything.

TOM: You are not stopping me!
Mike and Ben are alarmed at Tom's agitation. Mary starts crying.

MARY: You damned stubborn old goat! What do you think you're going to accomplish?

TOM: I'm going to kill the son of a bitch!

Both Mike and Ben have stood up. Ginny comes running in just as Mike speaks.

MIKE: What in the hell is going on?

TOM: I'm going to kill that son of a bitch Vince!

GINNY: Dad, No! Please.

TOM: I knew the bastard was no goddamn good. I knew it.

Mike goes to his father, standing between him and the door.

TOM: Mike, don't try to stop me! I'm going and that's all there is to it.

MIKE: Dad. Please! What has he done? Can we just talk about this first?

Mike puts his hands on his father as if to slow him down rather than restrain him.

TOM: No need to talk. Get out of my way.

GINNY: *Goes to her mother.* I told you he would get like this. I told you. *To Tom:* Please, Dad, don't do this. For my sake!

TOM: *Growing more agitated.* For your sake? For your sake? It is for your sake. That prick was hurting you. It makes me sick.

Ben is stressed and emotionally charged by this experience.

MIKE: Wait! *Looks over at Ginny.* He was hurting you?

MARY: He punched her in the face a few weeks ago! Your father was right about him.

MIKE: Oh, my God! He was abusing you. And you never said a word. *To Tom angrily:* I'm going with you!

MARY: Mike, don't you start now! None of this is going to help. Now we all know. We've got to help Ginny. Confronting Vince isn't going to solve anything. *To Tom and Mike:* Let the police handle it.

TOM: Police aren't going to handle it the way I'm going to handle it! I'm going to punch his lights out!

Tom breaks free of Mike and heads toward the door. Ben runs over to his grandfather. He gets between Tom and the door.

BEN: Pops! Uncle Mike! No. Don't go! Please don't do this. *Emotionally charged and on the verge of tears.* Stay here. Gram is right.

TOM: What the hell am I supposed to do? Please don't get all upset, Ben. Please.

Tom realizes that this scene is upsetting. He is trying to get himself under control for Ben's sake.

TOM: I'm sorry. I didn't mean to put you through this. It'll be all right. I'm just being a stupid old man. Please don't let this hurt you. Everything will be all right. These things are stressful. Calm down now. Go comfort your Aunt Ginny.

MIKE: You're right, Ben. It's a bad idea.

Ben takes a step away.

TOM: *Speaking to the group:* I'm sorry. I let my anger get away from me. I'm okay now. You don't have to worry. I'm past it. *He goes to Ginny.* I'm so sorry he did that to you. *He takes her in his arms; she is still crying.*

MARY: *To Ginny.* Let me take you up to bed. It will be okay now. It's over. Come on now. *They exit.*

MIKE: *To Ben:* Are you going to be okay?

BEN: I think so. *To Tom:* Are you really okay?

TOM: Sure. Just needed to blow off some steam. That's all. I wish you hadn't seen that.

BEN: I'll survive. I just can't believe that Uncle Vince would do that stuff.

TOM: You don't have to call him "Uncle" anymore if you don't want to. Your Aunt Ginny is going to divorce the prick.

BEN: I don't think I ever heard you use that word before tonight, Pops.

TOM: Which one? "Divorce" or "prick"?

BEN: Heard a few words today I've never heard you use before.

TOM: Sorry. I should watch my mouth. *Chuckles. Deflects.* Words. Stupid stuff we say.

BEN: What do you mean?

TOM: Think about it: "I should WATCH my mouth!" Unless I have a mirror handy, I can't watch my mouth; and besides that, the phrase has nothing to do with watching anything. It's like calling Vince a prick. No self-respecting prick would have anything to do with him.

BEN: You're out of control, Pops.

Mike comes to Ben, puts his arm over his shoulder as he speaks to Tom.

MIKE: So, that confab in the kitchen between Ginny and Mom! That's when Ginny told about all of this stuff with Vince?

TOM: Yeah. Your mother told me just a little while ago when we were in the bedroom.

MIKE: So, what exactly were you going to do if and when you could get to Vince tonight?

TOM: I thought about killing him. But probably just flatten his fucking face.

BEN: Another one! My vocabulary's growing.

MIKE: Did you consider that Vince is twenty-five years younger than you, outweighs you, and works out regularly?

TOM: So, what am I supposed to do? Just let him get away with what he did to your sister?

MIKE: Dad, I get it! But did you really think you were going to accomplish anything?

TOM: I might've gotten off at least one punch.

MIKE: If he let you in the door. If he's home.

TOM: All right! You've made your point. I just had to do something. I'm over it. Why don't you guys go off to bed now? I'll be fine. You need some sleep. God knows we've all got to get ready for another attempt at playing big, happy family tomorrow.

BEN: Thanks for reminding me. Now, I'm depressed again.

MIKE: I'll protect you, Buddy. If they get on your nerves, just let me know. I'll run interference.

BEN: Thanks, Uncle Mike.

Mike and Ben start to leave just as Mary comes back into the room. They hug/ kiss her goodnight and leave. Tom has moved to the sofa. Mary looks at him with concern.

MARY: May I join you?

TOM: Of course. Come snuggle.

Mary sits beside him. He puts his arm around her. She lays her head on his chest.

MARY: This isn't working out so well is it?

TOM: What do you mean?

MARY: I thought I'd get them all together and it would somehow feel the way it used to feel.

TOM: How could it? They're grown-ups! They've been tainted by the world of adults. They welcomed people into their lives that I wish they hadn't. We can't control any of that. And if we had tried, we'd be more obnoxious than our daughter-in-law.

MARY: I know. I just wish we could go back to those old times even if for just a few minutes.

TOM: You heard Mike and Ginny and Ben in here laughing and fooling around. It was kind of like that wasn't it?

MARY: It was. But Craig wasn't part of it. He just isn't one of us anymore. I can't believe that it's all Carrie's doing. Our first-born, and he's like a stranger. He was such a beautiful child. Sensitive. Kind. What happened?

TOM: I have no idea. He never let me in. He was all about you when he was a kid. Didn't share with me. Wasn't much interested in being around me, no matter how hard I tried. Always kind of a loner. Then he met that awful woman. First woman who ever gave it up to him, I suspect. That was the end of him. She latched onto him, and he's become even more distant. What they did to that boy is unforgiveable. It's difficult to even look them in the eye.

MARY: At least, Craig let us have access to Ben. That's worth something. And Ben's turned out to be a fine young man. I see a lot of you in him.

TOM: Really? They didn't deserve him.

MARY: I have to admit I have never liked Carrie much. But, you never know what a person has gone through to be the way she is. I suspect there's a lot of hurt under that posturing she does.

TOM: You are always so kind, Mary. But believe me, she's the spawn of Satan.

MARY: Slaps him playfully. Oh, stop it now. Your son loves her for whatever reason he does, whether we approve or not. She produced your only grandchild. She can't be all bad. We just have to make the best of it and not invite them in too often. I wish there were a way to get Craig here without her attached.

TOM: Be careful, you might just find that there isn't much of Craig left. She's been eating his brain for years. Enough about them. Talking about her makes me nauseous.

MARY: What did you think of Mike's news? Wonderful, isn't it?

TOM: It is. I guess I'm a little disappointed that we haven't heard about this Alan guy in all this time. But I'm happy for Mike. He's had a lot of disappointments. But what I love about Mike is that he always comes through everything with a positive attitude. He refuses to let the bullshit of the world get him down. I'm proud of him. That's why I wrote the play. I just wanted to tell the world that it's okay to be who you are. I just hope Alan is different from Carrie and Vince. I'd like to like at least one of my children's spouses. That goddamned Vince ...

MARY: *Cutting him off.* You suspected Vince for a long time when none of the rest of us could see anything terribly wrong with him. You read people better than I do.

TOM: That son-of-a-bitch! I didn't know how bad he was or what he was doing to our daughter, or I would have killed him long ago.

MARY: You're going to have to let it go, Tom. This is beyond your control. Let the police and the law handle it. Why don't you come to bed now? Let's get some sleep. It's easier to think about things after a good night's sleep.

TOM: Yeah. Morning's a good time for thinking. Why don't you go to bed? I'll be in in just a few minutes. I'll take care of the lights. Go on now. I'll be right in.

Mary exits. Tom walks to the entrance door in subdued light, looks back on the room, turns, and steps out into the night, closing the door behind him. We hear an automobile start up. Mary comes quickly out of the bedroom.

MARY: Tom! Tom!

She gets to the door, pulls it open, but Tom has gone. And still she calls.

MARY: Tom! No!

BLACKOUT.

ACT TWO

Act Two: Scene One

Saturday morning. SR lights up on kitchen. Ginny, Mike and Mary are sitting at the dinette table talking. They are drinking coffee.

GINNY: I didn't hear him leave. That must have been awful for you when you heard the car start up!

MARY: I thought I was going to have a heart attack for certain. That man! Uggggh! He makes me so angry sometimes. Scaring us all to death like that!

GINNY: I wish I hadn't talked about Vince. He causes problems even when he's not around.

MIKE: Come on, Ginny! This isn't your fault. You needed to talk about what Vince did. We just all made assumptions about Dad that we shouldn't have made.

MARY: It's his own fault. All he had to do was come tell me, "I just need to go off for a drive and get out of the house for a while!" But No! He just slips out. I thought for sure he was going up to Patterson to confront Vince ... causes me to wake you all up, upsets Ben all over again . . . well, you know the rest of it. Damned old goat!

MIKE: After the show he put on, last night, how could he think we wouldn't be worried about him just taking off like that without letting somebody know what was going on?

GINNY: I would have liked to have seen Vince's face when he got Mike's call to tell him a madman may be coming for him. I hope he was scared. He deserves it ... the bastard.

MARY: It was all a big misunderstanding—your father's fault, but still a misunderstanding. You heard him when he came in. He knew he was in the doghouse.

MIKE: I can hardly wait until Craig and Carrie get here. None of us has had much sleep. Dad's cranky with them when he's at his best. Not that I blame him, but it's always tense when the three of them are together. I'd sure like it if we didn't end up in armed combat.

GINNY: It's not easy for any of us to relax around them. How did our brother become so judgmental? I mean, it's like he's becoming her. Have you noticed even the simple things are weird? He now calls Dad "Father" and Mom "Mother." That's okay, I guess, but it's just so formal. Not what we grew up with. It's just one example. He never jokes around anymore. He's like a robot instead of a person. I feel like we're talking to strangers.

MARY: You just never know what's going on behind the scenes. As you well know, Ginny, sometimes what we're seeing in others is a performance. Your brother is still under there somewhere. I won't give up on him, and I hope you won't either.

MIKE: He doesn't make it easy to hang on to that hope. Guess, I'd better go up and rouse old Ben out of his beauty sleep and get him moving. Lots of showers to be taken this morning.

MARY: I'm worried about him. All these stresses. He hasn't been out all that long. Did he calm down after the fiasco last night?

MIKE: You, know. I think he's doing okay. He was upset, but he got himself under control. By the time Dad got back, and the real story came out, he was laughing. He loves Dad so much and thinks Dad's hilarious.

MARY: He's hilarious all right. His hilarity is driving me to an early grave!

Mike snickers, gets up and exits through kitchen door and goes off to bedroom.

MARY: *To Ginny:* Did you sleep at all last night?

GINNY: Very little. You know, Mom? When I thought Dad was headed up there to kill Vince or do whatever it was that he thought he was going to do to him, there was a part of me that took pleasure in the notion of Vince suffering, and when I caught myself feeling that, I was ashamed. I really didn't like that about myself. Then I went the other direction and wanted to protect him from harm at the same time. That's why I had Mike call him. I wanted to protect Dad too. I don't know why I'm all over the place with my thoughts and feelings all of the time.

MARY: You've got a lot of your father in you, Ginny. You see that living is complex. You both think there should be a way to sort out what is wrong in the world and make sense of it, make it all work the way you wish it would. Sometimes, there just aren't ways to fix problems, just like you couldn't fix Vince. Sometimes the best we can do is to find ways to work around our problems or find the courage to walk away from them and know they weren't ours to fix.

GINNY: I wish I could be more like you, Mom.

MARY: Well, I wish I could be more like you. I own all the rights to this model. You own all the rights to yours. You'll have to make do with who you are, my dear!

BLACKOUT.

Act Two: Scene Two

Saturday, mid-afternoon. Mary and Ginny are in the kitchen putting snacks on a tray, preparing coffee and tea. Tom is sitting in the living room reading the newspaper. As lights come up, Mike and Ben come into the room from the basement/den area.

BEN: Hey, Pops! I just beat the crap out of Uncle Mike in pool.

MIKE: All right, Hot Shot! You don't have to humiliate me in front of my father.

TOM: *To Ben:* Michael needs to get knocked down to size once in a while. You've heard him gloat when he beats me.

BEN: So, what you're saying is if Uncle Mike can beat you and I can beat him, I'm the man! King of the Pool Sharks! Lord of the table!

MIKE: All right! All right! You won! This time! We'll see later if you can hold onto your title, Mr. Too-big-for-your pants!

TOM: What neither of you understands is that I've been letting both of you win for years. Maybe I'll just have to stop being so nice and show you both how the game is really played.

BEN: Yeah! Right.

TOM: You never know, Buddy. I might not be lying! But, then again . . .

Tom is cut off by the doorbell ringing.

MARY: *Calling out from the kitchen.* They're here! Tom, let them in, will you?

TOM: *Yelling back to Mary.* Do I have to?

MARY: Yes, you do!

The doorbell rings again.

TOM: *Yells:* Coming! *Aside:* Why the hell can't they just come in without knocking like normal kids do?

BEN: *To Tom:* I can already feel all of the air being sucked out of the room. Let me catch a breath before you open the door, Pops.

MIKE: Come on, Ben. You can do it. I'm here for you.

TOM: Can you back me too, Mike?

MIKE: We've got to open it sometime.

TOM: Why?

Mary comes out of the kitchen, followed by Ginny.

MARY: Stop it. All of you. Tom, open that door.

Tom opens the door to Craig and Carrie.

TOM: Craig! Carrie! *He shakes hands with each as he pulls them through the door.* How wonderful to see you! Come in. We've been looking forward to your getting here. What took you so long?

CRAIG: We just decided to enjoy a little time walking around the streets, looking at how things have changed over the years. We stopped for a pleasant lunch at a quaint little restaurant not too far from the hotel.

MARY: It's good to have you here at last. *She hugs each of them.* Do come in. Can I get you some tea or coffee?

CARRIE: No, not right now. As Craig said, we just came from lunch.

MARY: Of course, dear.

CARRIE: *To Ben:* Did you sleep well last night? You look a bit tired.

BEN: Yes, Mother. Thank you.

CARRIE: Ginny, Michael, it's good to see you, as always.

Craig goes to Ginny, gives her a brief hug and has said "Hello" to Mike and shaken hands with him. Carrie sits down on the sofa, and Craig sits next to her. The others find their places and sit, except for Mary.

MARY: Do any of the rest of you want coffee or tea or some snacks?

BEN: Snacks for sure.

Tom and Mike ask for coffee.

GINNY: *Getting up.* Let me help you, Mom.

CARRIE: Let me help you as well.

MARY: *Surprised.* Thank you, Carrie.

CRAIG: Mother, I would like a cup of coffee after all.

The women go off to the kitchen. They pour coffee for the men, tea or coffee for themselves, except for Carrie, put them on a tray. They mime some polite chatter amongst them.

TOM: Craig, how was the hotel? Did you like it there?

CRAIG: It was fine. I've certainly stayed in nicer places. Anything interesting happen here after we left?

TOM: Not much!

Craig notices Ben laughing at Tom's response.

CRAIG: What? What did I miss, Ben?

BEN: Nothing, Father.

CRAIG: Obviously, it's something.

TOM: Ben's laughing at his grandfather, Craig, I was stopped by the police last night, taken to headquarters, put under the lamp, and interrogated in a major crime investigation. For a while, I was afraid they'd get me to confess to being the don for the mafia. But I held firm. Didn't give them anything. The operation is safe.

CRAIG: What? *To Ben:* Why would any of that be funny, Ben?

TOM: I'm joking, Craig. I went out for a drive without telling your mother. She panicked and called the police. They found me and told me to go home. Ben and Mike have been teasing me all morn-ing about being a jailbird.

CRAIG: Sometimes, I think this whole family is caught up in one of your damned plays, and we'll all realize some day that we're just words on a page instead of real people ... if that makes any kind of sense.

TOM: I like that, Craig! Can I use it in a play? And what do you mean by "damned plays"? They've helped keep this family going for a long time.

CRAIG: I'm sorry I said it. I know you are right. My apologies. Seriously? That's all there was to the story?

The women have come through the door, Carrie leading with the tray of snacks. Ginny is carrying the tray with the coffee and teacups. The snacks, drinks, etc. are put on the coffee table and are distributed by the women as the discussion continues.

CARRIE: All there was to what story, Craig?

CRAIG: Father was arrested last night.

MIKE: He wasn't arrested. He was pulled over by the cops.

CARRIE: Whatever for?

MARY: I called them. Tom took off for a ride without telling me where he was going, and I thought he was going to do something really stupid, so I called the police and asked them to stop him.

CARRIE: What on earth did you suspect Tom of doing, Mary? Killing someone?

MARY: Oh, Lord. Now I've done it.

GINNY: Craig! Carrie! Sit down. I'll explain it.

TOM: Ginny, you don't have to do that.

GINNY: Might as well get it out in the open and over with,.

CRAIG: What are you talking about?

GINNY: Give me a minute, and I'll tell you. Let's just get this out in the open and be done with it. Last night, I told Mom the truth about what's been going on between Vince and me.

CARRIE: Ginny, dear. We've suspected for a long time that you haven't been happy in the marriage, that perhaps you'd lost interest in being the wife he expected you to be.

GINNY: Carrie, please don't pretend to understand. You don't! Vince has been abusive for a long time, and I kept it a secret.

CRAIG: What exactly do you mean by "abusive"?

GINNY: Physical and verbal. After an incident a couple of weeks ago, I couldn't take it anymore. I've left him and am getting a divorce. I told Mom. She told Dad, and next thing I know, the whole house knew about it. *She is crying but is holding herself together.*

CARRIE: He hurt you? I can't believe it. He was always such a sweet man. I don't believe it.

GINNY: *To Carrie:* It's true whether you believe it or not.

CRAIG: *Ignores Carrie.* The son-of-a-bitch hurt you? He hit you? *Others are nodding their heads yes. He leaps up.* I'll kill the bastard

CARRIE: Craig! There's no need . . .

Ben and Mike stand up and restrain him. Tom stands up as well.

MIKE: To Craig: Calm down, big boy! We've already done this routine. It's not going to get us anywhere. Might get you put in jail.

TOM: Craig, you're sounding like your father.

CARRIE: I certainly hope not!

TOM: I believe I was saying essentially the same words last night that Craig just used.

CARRIE: I don't like all of this talk of violence. It's unbecoming among civilized people. Craig, I am shocked by your crude talk!

Craig is calming down, breaks free of Mike and Ben and goes to Ginny and hugs her—ignoring his wife's words. Tom sits down again.
MIKE: Relax, Carrie, nobody's going to kill anybody.

CRAIG: I'm sorry, Ginny. I wish I'd known. You never said anything.

GINNY: There's nothing you could have done, Craig. And I was embarrassed and ashamed, kept thinking I could fix the problem. But I couldn't. But thank you for being my big brother just now. I've missed that—even the stupid male "go beat him up" part.

TOM: So, now that that part of the story's been told, let's get back to the story that Ginny started. Last night I went through what we just saw in Craig, I was angry, and my first thought was to go kill the son-of-a-bitch. *To Carrie:* Sorry for the crude language, Carrie ... just quoting your husband. *To Craig:* Later, I was still somewhat upset, so I went out for a drive. I just wanted to go down to the river and clear my head. I didn't tell Mary where I was going or why! So, when she found me gone, she assumed I'd run off to kill Vince. And though the idea of killing him still has merit, that wasn't why I left. It never crossed my mind that Mary would call the cops. But she did. They pulled me over, checked my car for weapons, talked to me for a few minutes and told me to go home. That's really all there is to it.

CRAIG: So, all of you knew about Ginny last night except Carrie and me.

MARY: You weren't here last night, Craig!

CRAIG: But you weren't going to tell me anything. You were all trying to keep me out of the loop.

GINNY: I intended to tell you today once you got here and settled in. I didn't want to start things off with a lot of drama.

CARRIE: What drama? Craig is your brother for crying out loud! There are always secrets in this family, everybody plotting and playing games, getting everybody all stirred up. Craig is the oldest and should know everything about what's going on for when ...

TOM: When what, Carrie? When I croak? What do you think this is? The Godfather movie? Craig's going to step in and take over the family business? Ginny has the right to tell whoever she wants to tell in the manner she wants to tell it and at the time she thinks it most appropriate.

GINNY: *Reacting to Carrie.* Like I said, Craig, I didn't want to start off with a lot of drama. But here we are.

TOM: Craig, it hasn't been easy to talk with you about family issues for a long time.

CRAIG: So, I'm not a part of the family anymore?

CARRIE: No. He means because I'm not part of the family, Craig. They don't like me.

MARY: That's not true, Carrie.

BEN: Stop it! All of you! Father, I'm sorry you feel left out. But let's face it, you are judgmental about all kinds of things.

CARRIE: Ben, you have no right to talk to your father that way.

BEN: Why not? He is judgmental. So are you! I have as much right as you do to tell him what I think?

CARRIE: How dare you? Who do you think you are talking to?

BEN: At the moment, I am talking to you. I was trying to talk to my father until you took over.

MARY: Let's all calm down and have our coffee and tea.

CRAIG: *Ignoring Mary.* Ben, what are you saying?

BEN: To you, or to Mother?

CRAIG: To me!

BEN: I am saying that you are judgmental about all kinds of things. You didn't approve of the way Aunt Ginny lives her life because you assumed she was the problem in her marriage. You treat Uncle Mike like less of a man because he's gay; you treat him like he somehow failed the family when no one else in the family has a problem with him but you and Mother. You've put Mother's needs ahead of mine my whole life and treated me like I am the family problem instead of your son. You've allowed her to control everything, including you! And I am saying you are not easy to talk to about much of anything, mostly because you don't speak for yourself. You parrot Mother.

CARRIE: Control everything? What are you talking about? I have given you the best years of my life. *Angry.* If I had had control of everything, you wouldn't be here! *Realizes she shouldn't have said it.*

BEN: I guess that just about says it all, doesn't it, Mother? You got knocked up well before your marriage and you didn't want a child, and I've been a pain in your ass ever since.

MARY: Oh, Dear Lord in heaven!

TOM: Ben, I thought that was between us!

CARRIE: *To Tom:* How dare you? How dare you tell my child intimate things about me.

BEN: Hey, folks! I'm not an idiot. I figured that one out all on my own long ago. I actually know my birthdate, and *[to Carrie]* I've seen your marriage license in the old album you keep on the library shelf. Unless I was a miracle birth, my birthday fell only four months after your wedding day. How about we not play stupid?

CARRIE: "Stupid"? You're calling me stupid?

BEN: I didn't call you stupid! I said you were playing stupid.

CARRIE: I have taken care of you your whole life. I've given you every opportunity to grow up in a far better life than I had as a child.

BEN: Better life? Whose life? You didn't give me opportunities to be me. I'm sorry you had a rotten childhood, but you made mine rotten too. You tried to make me into a male version of you. You manipulated me my whole life until I had nothing of myself. Why the hell do you think I overdosed? Because I like drugs? I overdosed because I had to escape your never-ending nagging and domination. I'm not doing it anymore, and, right now, that is pissing you off!

CARRIE: Don't you blame me for your cowardly, self-centered suicide performance. You made that decision all on your own. You did that to embarrass me. And now you are trying to humiliate me in front of your father's family. Calling me controlling! Stupid!

BEN: To embarrass you? Humiliate you? Why is it always about you? And I didn't call you stupid! Again, I said ...

TOM: *Cuts Ben off.* Carrie, you need to stop this. Ben has been through enough! *To Craig:* Craig, you can't let this continue!

Ben is shaking. Mike and Ginny go to Ben as a show of support.

CARRIE: Craig has no say in this! I can see you are ganging up on me. I'm going out for a walk. When I get back, either my son will apologize and be respectful to me, or I am leaving.

Carrie gets up abruptly and storms out of the house.

CRAIG: I have no say?

BEN: That's right, Father, you have no say about anything. You've just been blind to it longer than I was.

TOM: Ben, you don't need to do this. Maybe this is a conversation for another day.

BEN: Pops, this is the day. I'm saying what I've been afraid to say ever since I can remember. *To Craig:* I've wanted you to love me my whole damned life. And maybe you didn't mean to be so distant, but you have been! You've always been so caught up in Mother, you didn't even know I existed much of the time. When I was little, I prayed that you'd save me from her, but you never did. You let her dominate both of us. And I resent that I felt like the only way I could deal with my life was to take it away. And you weren't there even then. I went through hell and back, and you never even tried to understand what I went through. All you and Mother could think about was how I was upsetting your lives.

CRAIG: That's not true. I never meant to hurt you, Ben.

BEN: You may not have meant it, but you did. I hurt a lot for a long time. You weren't there for me. But you know what? I'm okay anyway! With Pops' and Gram's help and with some professional help, I started putting the pieces together for a life without you and Mother in it. I'm getting healthy. I am even happy sometimes.

CRAIG: So, you don't want me in your life? At all? Is that what you're saying?

BEN: You know what, Father? Despite all the crap, I wish you would be a part of my life, but not at the expense of my feeling the way I've felt for as long as I can remember, not at the expense of having Mother control my life. And I'm not willing to wait for you to find a backbone.

CRAIG: Is that how you see me? Spineless? You don't think I love you? That's not true. I do. And I want to be a part of your life.

BEN: Then give up all of the phony bullshit you've been putting out there while playing Mother's whipping boy and get real! I'm not playing the old games anymore. For your own sake, quit giving into Mother's control over you!

CRAIG: You think that ...

BEN: *Cutting off his father's words.* And if you're serious about loving me and wanting to be a part of my life, you can start recognizing that I'm a person, a grown up ... not your wife's project. You can talk to me about real stuff—like what's really going on in our lives— and let go of all that shit that's been filtered through her for you to talk about. All that shit about being a big player at work. You think that's going to make her any nicer to you? Talk to me about real stuff. Who you are. What you wish you could do. Not what she tells you to think and do.

CRAIG: Do you hate your mother that much, Ben?

BEN: I thought I hated her for a long time. I hate the way she acts sometimes. But I'm trying not to hate anyone. I'm just trying to learn to like me. And I am not going to let her take that away or control me. If you and Mother don't like me the way I am, that's your problem. I can't spend the rest of my life trying to make her happy. That's not my job. I'm open to the future, but I can't keep on doing what we're doing.

CRAIG: You've grown up on me, Ben. And I'm really sorry I haven't been everything you needed. And you are right. I have let your mother control you and me. I am sorry. More sorry than you'll ever know. I've been a damned fool. But I don't want to lose you. Give me a chance to do better.

BEN: Making a change would be a challenge for you with Mother in the picture.

CRAIG: You're right. But I'd still like to try if you're willing. I do love you.

Craig embraces Ben. They hug. Tom goes over and hugs both of them. Mary and Ginny are crying. Mike is fighting back tears.

TOM: If you two aren't careful, you're going to have everyone in the room crying, including me.

CRAIG: Thanks, Dad. *Calls attention to the word, "Dad" here. Hugs him. Kisses him on the cheek. It's been a long time.*

TOM: Glad to have this Craig back.

CRAIG: *To the whole group:* I need to go out for a walk. I think my wife and I need to talk for a while. If she comes back before I find her, tell her to wait down at the park bench on the corner. I'll be back.

Craig hugs Ben again, then exits. Ben is emotionally charged, has tears in his eyes. He is comforted by Tom. Ben is wiping his eyes with the back of his hand. Mary runs to the kitchen for a box of tissues and brings them in. Ben goes to the sofa and is flanked by his uncle and grandfather. The women sit in the lounge chair and the settee.

BEN: I'm sorry I'm such a big cry-baby.

Tom puts his arm around Ben and pulls him against him for a moment and then releases him.

TOM: There is nothing to be embarrassed about, Ben. What you said to your father has needed saying for a long time. And nobody but you could say it. He wasn't able to hear it until today. It took real courage to do what you just did.

BEN: Do you really think so?

MIKE: It was powerful. You asserted yourself; you didn't back down. You told the truth about what you've held in for a long time. I admire you.

MARY: We're all proud of you!

BEN: I'm afraid it's going to get ugly when Mother gets back here.

GINNY: You know what, Ben? I suspect she's going to be less dominating from now on. I think she got the message that you aren't going to allow her to bully you.

BEN: She'll probably hate me now. Mother doesn't deal well with people fighting back.

GINNY: You might be right. She might be angry for a while, maybe even nasty for a while. But I think she'll get over it. And if she doesn't, are you really any worse off with her than you've been?

BEN: Good point.

BLACKOUT.

Act Two: Scene Three

Saturday evening. Lights up SR. Craig and Mike are at the dinette table in the kitchen, sipping at drinks. There is a bottle of whiskey between them.

MIKE: So, do you think she's going to get over it?

CRAIG: I don't know. She doesn't deal well with anybody standing up to her. Ben and I pushed all her buttons today. It might take a while.

MIKE: I think Ben needed to get that stuff out. He's been holding it in for a long time.

CRAIG: You probably think I'm a real horse's ass right now.

MIKE: I don't think that. But, for whatever it's worth, I've never understood what happened to you or Ben. Your son, my nephew, is a really great guy! He's smart, sensitive, loving, good looking . . . he could have the world by the tail. Why did it have to be so hard for him?

CRAIG: You mean, why didn't I do something about the way Carrie is with him?

MIKE: Well, yes. I guess that's what I really want to understand.

CRAIG: I didn't want to marry her, you know. But by the time I figured that out, she was pregnant. I just tried to make the best of it, do the "right" thing. She didn't want to be married either, but she had no means of support. So, there we were. And once we got married, she made it clear that I'd be punished daily for putting her in the position she was in. I just shut down after a while. Did whatever she wanted just to keep the peace. Ben was right. I let her control everything. I just gave up trying. I gave her my son; I gave her whatever I had left of me.

MIKE: It's not too late, Craig. He wants to love you.

CRAIG: He was pretty damned good today, wasn't he?

MIKE: He's tougher than even he knows. He's going to be all right.

CRAIG: He's a better man than I am already. More courage, for sure. I've been a total "wuss" as Ben would say.

MIKE: Ease up on yourself. Have another drink.

Mike pours a small amount of whiskey into Craig's glass.

CRAIG: God! I hate to think of going back to that hotel tonight. When I dropped her off and told her I was coming back here, she flew into a rage, accused me of not supporting her, preferring the family over her. It felt good to just drive off and let her fume. Women!

MIKE: Men are the same way, brother. It's people! There's plenty of stupid out there floating around. And I hate to tell you this, but it's in us too! I think she did a good thing not coming back to the house after her walk. What she said to Ben was pretty tough. Probably best they didn't go right back at it. Gave everybody a chance to cool down.

CRAIG: Believe me, it's not "cooled down." It's still plenty hot, maybe not full boil. But simmer can still burn the hell out of you!

MIKE: You think she'll try to see him again this weekend?

CRAIG: At this point I don't know what she'll do. I'm glad to be here right now and not there with her. *Tries to change the subject.* You got anybody in your life right now, Mike?

MIKE: You sure you really want to know?

CRAIG: Yeah, I think I do.

MIKE: I'm still into men, you know.

CRAIG: I guess I kind of knew that. You know I hated that about you, right?

MIKE: No. Really, Craig? I never guessed that in all the years we've known each other.

CRAIG: All right. I deserve that. You want to know the real reason I hated that about you?

MIKE: Yeah. Actually I would.

CRAIG: I was afraid. Maybe I thought somehow your being gay was a reflection on me, on the family. Maybe if you had those gay genes, maybe I do too. It sounds kind of dumb when I hear the words coming out of my mouth.

MIKE: I get it, Craig, but you need to get it through your thick head that my being gay is about me, not you. It's who I am. I didn't stop being your brother when I learned I was gay. To me, I was just your brother. Can't I be both gay and your brother.

CRAIG: I guess I've got a whole lot I need to be working on.

MIKE: In response to your question, "Yes!" I have someone in my life, and he and I are going to get married this fall.

CRAIG: I guess I should have known it would happen sometime. I just didn't really think about gay guys settling down. Being mo-nogamous. Stupid, huh? Does he make you happy?

MIKE: Yes, very much so.

CRAIG: Will I be invited to the wedding?

MIKE: Do you think you can handle it? We might kiss at the end of the ceremony. And what will you do about Carrie?

CRAIG: She can either come and keep her thoughts to herself, or I'll come alone. And you know what? If I'm uncomfortable with a kiss, I'll keep that to myself and try to just be happy for you.

MIKE: Then, yes. You're invited.

Lights go down on SR and come up on SL where Mary and Ginny are sitting.

GINNY: I was just thinking about how, just before the blow-up, Carrie came out to the kitchen with us. She's never offered to do that before. And she was even pleasant. I hadn't known she was capable of a smile until then. I always figured her face would crack if she ever tried one.

MARY: I've never completely understood her. Lord knows I've tried.

GINNY: Do you think we'll ever get it together as a family?

MARY: I continue to hope. Craig dropped Carrie at the hotel and came back. That's a first! I don't remember the last time I saw just him without her. He and Mike are out in the kitchen talking. That hasn't happened for a long time. All three of you are under one roof and there isn't any fighting anywhere in the house. Ben seems to be doing well.

GINNY: All we've got to do now is make it through the night, right?

MARY: Don't be glib, dear. All families have issues.

GINNY: I think we have enough for any two families.

MARY: Oh, come now, Ginny. We're all fine. I like to think of it as having some interesting challenges. It's the bickering that gets to me more than the actual problems. You're all good at bickering. I'm not. I guess I've always thought we should be able to sit down, discuss a problem, try some possible solutions and move on. We used to do that. Then Vince and Carrie came into the family, and everything changed. I'm not blaming them for that. I guess it just comes with the package. You all had to grow up and move on.

GINNY: We probably could have made some better choices there.

MARY: You made the choices you made. You can also make different choices. You've done that. Who knows where this thing with Craig and Carrie will go? We don't know anything about Alan. I want Mike's husband to be a wonderful guy that I can call a son, but I won't know about that until I get to know him. Someday, Ben's going to find someone. That's life. It goes on. But I do so want to have you all in my life for as long as I have one. And I will do my best to love who you love for as long as I can.

GINNY: I love you, Mom.

MARY: I love you too, dear.

Tom and Ben come from the basement area where they've been playing pool. Tom is in the lead; Ben is taunting him.

BEN: So tell everybody! Come on, you promised.

TOM: You're a tyrant! Do you know that?

BEN: I learned it from you! Tell them.

TOM: *Yelling.* Craig? Mike? Where are you? Come in here.

Craig and Mike come into the living room from the kitchen.

TOM: I have an important announcement to make. Everyone gets quiet. My grandson is a pain in the ass!

Laughter.

BEN: Nice try, Pops! Now tell them what you agreed to say.

TOM: *To the group:* See what I mean? Okay! A bet's a bet. I must now confess to you all and to the world that I did my best to beat my grandson at billiards! I tried every trick I knew, including cheating, and he still won! I hereby set aside my crown as the best pool shark in the world and concede that title to Benjamin Harold Grayson who is hereinafter to be referred to as God of the Table.

All applaud. Ben takes a bow.

MIKE: Wait a minute. I beat you three or four times yesterday, Dad. As I recall, you didn't win even one game! Didn't that mean I held the title that Ben had to win?

TOM: Nah. I let you win. I really tried to beat the kid here.

MIKE: Right!

TOM: *To Ben:* Does that meet the requirements of the bet, your highness?

BEN: It will do for now.

TOM: Don't go getting too cocky, boy, or I'll have to show you who's still king of the household.

BEN: I've already met Gram!

TOM: Smart-Ass! We've created a monster! Craig, get your kid under control!

CRAIG: No can do, Dad. He's made it obvious that he won't be controlled.

The doorbell rings.

TOM: Who's ringing the doorbell at 10 o'clock? Hope it's not the cops.

MARY: Why on earth would it be the police?

TOM: Maybe they still think I'm a potential murderer, thanks to you, Mary.

MARY: Stop it, you old goat. Answer the door!

TOM: Yes, dear.

Tom opens the door. Carrie appears. She is clearly on a mission and is commanding in her speech and in her demeanor initially. As she becomes more frustrated throughout the scene, her anger grows until she melts down.

CARRIE: Thomas.

TOM: Carrion.

CARRIE: I wish to speak with my son!

TOM: *To Ben:* Your mother is here, Ben, and she wants to speak to you. *He gestures for her to come in.*

CRAIG: How did you get here?

CARRIE: I took a cab. I'm not helpless, you know? *Speaks as if scolding a child:* And you and I have some issues to resolve later.

Others look at one another in surprise at her comment to Craig.

CRAIG: *He has found his backbone:* Yes! We do.

CARRIE: Benjamin, I want to talk to you in private.

BEN: No, Mother. Whatever you have to say can be said in front of the family.

CARRIE: I am your family.

BEN: Mother, you are a part of my family. But this is my family too. *He gestures to the others in the room.*

CARRIE: Very well. I'm not the one who needs to speak. It's you. I want an apology from you, and I want it right now.

Tom moves to Ben's side, places his hand on Ben's back as a show of support.

BEN: What would I be apologizing for, Mother?

CARRIE: Don't you play your grandfather's games with me. I hear his voice in that question. You know exactly why you need to apologize. You will not behave like him with me.

TOM: What's wrong with me?

CARRIE: Thomas, please! Stay out of this. Don't you think you've done enough damage teaching him to be disrespectful to his mother?

TOM: I don't recall teaching him that. And I don't really appreciate you treating my grandson the way that you do.

MARY: Carrie, you're being unfair!

CARRIE: Mary, I don't care about fairness or Tom's feelings, or yours for that matter. My son is going to apologize to me here and now. Why don't you just go make some tea or something?

MARY: Why don't I just come over there and wring your neck, young lady?

BEN: Gram, please don't let her get to you. *To Carrie:* I honestly don't know what it is you want me to apologize for.

CRAIG: I think Ben was very honest with you. It took a lot of courage for him to tell you how he feels. I didn't hear anything that was mean-spirited. And I think you should be embarrassed by the way you are acting. Leave Ben alone!

CARRIE: Oh, you too! They've turned you against me too? *To Ben:* Now, I have a husband undermining me in addition to a son. Are you going to apologize for the way you talked to me earlier? You called me "controlling" and stupid. You had the audacity and crudeness to refer to my error as a young woman as getting "knocked up."

BEN: I'm sorry . . .

MIKE: Ben, you don't need to apologize . . .

BEN: I was going to say, I am sorry that I can't give an apology when I did nothing wrong! I won't take back anything I said. I said what has needed saying for a long time, and I'm glad I said it.

CARRIE: You've become a beast! You've never appreciated anything I've ever done for you. Take! Take! Take! That's all you know how to do. And now you are an ingrate as well. How dare you?

TOM: How like a serpent's tooth is an ungrateful child!

CARRIE: Tom. Shut up! For once! Stop meddling in my son's life! Stay out of this!

TOM: Have you ever looked in a mirror when you are on a rant like this? Not a pretty sight.

Carrie storms toward Tom and slaps his face. The room goes dead silent briefly until Mary speaks.

MARY: Oh, my God! How dare you hit my husband?

Mary starts toward Carrie in attack mode, but Tom puts his hand up in a motion for Mary to stop.

TOM: It's all right, Mary. *To Carrie:* Have you said everything you want to say to Ben? Because when you're done, I'm going to throw you out of this house bodily. I've had enough of your bullshit.

CARRIE: I haven't even begun. *To Ben:* If you don't apologize to me right now, I am walking out of your life, and you'll never see me again.

GINNY: Carrie, think about what you are saying here. That's emotional blackmail. You don't mean that!

CARRIE: Don't I? I know exactly what I mean. And you have no business telling anybody how to take care of a child or a husband. Obviously, you failed on both counts. Now shut up. *To Mike:* And before you stick your nose in, don't! Nothing you say is of any consequence to me whatever. I've had enough of this whole brood and your meddling.

MIKE: *To Craig:* She's definitely not invited to the wedding.

CARRIE: Wedding. You? To a man? I am sick being in the same room with you.

BEN: Mother, stop!

MIKE: It's all right, Ben. Your mother is right. I've already coughed my gay disease onto you and your father. You're both doomed. It's too late for anyone here to survive. I think I got some on her too. It'll take us all in the end. Oooh, poor choice of words ... taking it in the end.

CARRIE: You disgust me.

MIKE: That may be, but you are not going to harm my nephew ever again. We've stood back too long. No more!

CRAIG: Carrie, get yourself under control. You're making a fool of yourself.

CARRIE: A fool? Here you are in a family of lunatics. And I'm the fool? You're a pathetic excuse for a human being. But what chance did you have coming out of this asylum?

CRAIG: So that's what I get for putting up with you for all these years?

MARY: Carrie, what have we ever done to you?

CARRIE: You took my son from me. He's always loved you more than he has loved me. You have plotted against me.

MARY: No one has plotted. We've tried to welcome you.

CARRIE: Hah! Welcomed me? Never. I have never been welcomed here! You've hated me from the beginning. It doesn't matter any-more. This will be the last time I ever step foot into this house. I want what I came for, and I'll have it, or else!

TOM: Or else what, Carrie?

CARRIE: You stupid old man. Stay out of my affairs. Go write some stupid play that no one with any breeding would want to see.

TOM: You going to hit me again, Carrie?

CARRIE: *Ignoring Tom.* Ben! Now!

BEN: You have been horrible here tonight. You've said things that I'm not going to forget for the rest of my life. I am apologizing for nothing! You're the one who needs to apologize. You're a miser-able, unhappy woman who's taken it out on me and Father my whole life. You've pushed aside anybody and everybody who could ever love you. You suck the joy out of a room merely by entering into it. You owe everybody here an apology for your hatefulness, for your backstabbing, for your disregard of their lives. You know what? You can take your threat of never seeing me again and keep it. I don't want to see this person who's standing here in front of me. I don't like this person. If and when you ever get around to being the decent person you are capable of being, you look me up. Otherwise, go and don't look back.

CARRIE: You miserable . . .

Carrie lunges at Ben. Ben pulls back. Craig steps in front of Ben to stop her. She attacks him with everything she has. This should feel like a rough and tumble mess with her not pulling her punches. *Mike, Tom, and Ginny struggle with her in an attempt to subdue her without hurting her. She fights through to the end of the scene.*

BEN: *Yelling over the chaos.* Mother, please stop! Please. *Yelling to his grandmother:* Gram, call the cops. She needs to go to the hospital. *Mary runs off stage to make the phone call as Ben tries to shout over the struggle between his mother and the others.* Mother, please stop! Please. Let us help you!

BLACKOUT.

Act Two: Scene Four

Sunday Afternoon. Tom, Mary, Craig, Mike, Ginny, and Ben are gathered in the living room. Craig is saying his goodbyes to Ginny and Mike. Tom and Mary are standing off to one side DS from the door. Bags that came with Ginny, Ben, and Mike are beside the front door to be picked up as they leave.

CRAIG: Well, all, Mr. Ben here has a flight to catch. I'm going to drive him to the airport. Ginny, Mike, it's been wonderful seeing you. I mean it. I feel like I've finally come home, like when I was a boy, like I belong here. *To Ben:* Why don't you say your goodbyes while I go out and get the car warmed up.

BEN: It's summer, the car doesn't need warming up.

CRAIG: Okay! You're right. I'm going out anyway. You come out when you're ready. Mom! Dad! I'll be back after I see Ben off. You're sure you don't mind me staying with you?

MARY: Of course not, darling. I am thrilled to have you for as long as you need to stay.

TOM: I am happy to have you stay if you let me win at pool once in a while.

CRAIG: No problem there. I'm horrible at the game. I'll be back in a couple of hours. Mike! Ginny! Be safe. See you at the wedding, if not before. *Exits.*

BEN: *Hugs his grandmother.* Gram, I love you so much. Thank you for everything.

MARY: You come back soon!

Ben turns to Tom and hugs him, whispers in his grandfather's ear. Tom pats him on the shoulder.

BEN: I love you! Thanks for everything.

TOM: You've got it!

MARY: Secrets?

TOM: Never mind, Mary. You'll find out soon enough. *To Ben:* You call if you need me or if you get in a pinch. Anytime!

BEN: Thanks, Pops! Bye, Aunt Ginny, Uncle Mike! *Exits.*

MIKE: *To Tom and Mary:* I'm glad I came this weekend. I'll be back in a couple of weeks with Alan. I want him to meet you both. *To Ginny:* I hope you'll come visit and meet him. *To his parents:* Thanks for everything.

They hug. Mike waits for Ginny. Ginny hugs her parents.

GINNY: I know you're worried about me. But I'm going to be fine. I realized this weekend that there's a lot of toughness in us Graysons. All of us. I'll see you in a couple of weeks. And I'll keep you up-to-date about what's happening. I love you.

They exit. Tom closes the door behind them. Mary goes about the room straightening up. She picks up the Sunday paper that is lying somewhere about the room and brings it to Tom.

TOM: *Facetious.* Well. That was fun. We should all get together every weekend.

MARY: Why don't you sit down and read the paper? Relax for a bit.

TOM: Relax? It's going to take me a month to calm down after this weekend. I hurt all over. And now Craig's going to be here dealing with what's her face. I should sue her for assault and battery.

MARY: What's-her-face is your daughter-in-law. And no matter what, for as long as she is, we will find a way to get along. And you are not going to sue her either.

TOM: Well, she's not coming here when she gets out of the hospital.

MARY: I doubt she will want to, dear.

TOM: What did I do to deserve you, my darling?

MARY: Nothing. And you don't deserve me. I'm here because I love you in spite of yourself.

TOM: You've cut me to the quick, dearest!

MARY: Just read the paper and relax.

TOM: Yes, my sweet!

Tom sits down and is looking at the paper while Mary continues straightening the room.

MARY: Tom?

TOM: Mary?

MARY: What was Ben whispering to you about?

TOM: A caper. He and I are planning to rob a bank. But don't worry. We'll tell you when we do it, so you don't call the cops on us.

MARY: I'm serious!

Tom lowers the paper and looks directly at Mary.

TOM: So am I. The children think they're getting an inheritance when we die. Only way that's going to happen is if we rob a bank.

MARY: Will you please stop?

TOM: He asked if I would write a play about this crazy family.

MARY: So, are you going to do it?
TOM: I already have! Just finished it!

BLACKOUT.

Jar in the Rain

ONE

Fall fomenting anarchy.
Glops of rain everywhere splattering eight and ten
inches and eternities outward from impact upon
metal car hood, and concrete sidewalk and drive-
way . . . "way too
hard" . . . say those
who grow mad chained by the universe
for reasons myriad, unstated, all their own,
as they hang on their walls alone
like bad art bemoaning their fate.

TWO

A fractured fascination I have found in this
day that fades fast like thought of Nirvana
in a filthy and festering soul.

Once again, I have swooped and scooped with a holy net
at words that flee from me all directions
at lightspeed,
but I foolishly try again
and again to catch them, pretend they could be held
in jars like bugs with grass.
Yet I know I have captured so little in one lifetime,
lost so many might-have-beens,

what I would-have/could-have-written as
poems had I been fast and agile
enough to have captured things like slippery rain drops
with a bigger net with smaller holes.

Yet . . . as my little life moves
relentlessly to its ultimate conclusion
I have accepted
watched hopelessly, helplessly
as wonderous things still unknown slither
irretrievably away
into a soaked ground's arrogant mouth
slurping and swallowing them whole,
teasing with momentary traces of their having been
upon mud and shards of grass
(from which, even a forensic poet
could make no sense
after such a clue-cleansing deluge).

Here I am without witness to bear me out. I saw them, I say!
. . . those wiry, little, no-good bastard beasts . . .
that would be such good eating. I know . . .

But I could not snag them for myself or us,
and they have slipped through even
the porous skin of my hands that grasped wildly, unhappily
at their disappearing act.

And, . . . ah, foolish me, deluding myself
That for a fraction of time I could hold . . .
to think I could hold heavens in my hand, taste
them, when worlds of knowing even greater
escape me and us all . . .
even better hunters than I.
And had it been possible . . .
even had I held "them" in my jar for seconds
or, for that matter, even for
millennia from now, would I have dared partake?
Would they (Could they?)—the "them"—have lived in space

upon a shelf with dusty books and framed pictures of people
little known and soon to be lost
like corpses of lizards in mud ponds?

THREE

Still . . . for all the loss that has been
and will be, I find myself
grateful for this chance
among cattle-classes—civilization
where we waddle in sludge already up to our ankles
and rising—
to see beyond comprehension
to say little things about great things I cannot hold.

But why must we humans be so, hapless?
. . . like clingers to the Titanic
while sea spray pounds our fingers
desperately grasping at slippery rails,
laughs at us—at our wild eyes looking into forever
and distorted voiceless mouths hanging
wide open and spilling
prayers like spittle into an ice-cold sea.

FOUR

Perhaps I am but a poor impersonation of a poet,
have what are thought but second-rate words
with which to trudge
through mud, perhaps, another would avoid . . .
in which case, I leave her
or him
to happy obliteration
and toss my own frustration upward toward
whatever gods will see
my arms wildly flinging muck
over my head and back like an elephant
suddenly lost in whimsy
on this drizzling day in the valley of bones waiting.

Notes From a Life Now Fleeting

ONE

Having been born into a poor family wasn't a "problem" until I was forced into the sorting shed called "school." There, I was taught to become a shadow, a tangential figure in the lives of my classmates and teachers—a Dickensian waif deserving of punishment for my sin of living in poverty and bearing the reputation attached to my family name, my ignorance of the culture owned by the middle class, not wearing the right clothes, not knowing how to throw a ball or catch, not having the charisma for making friends.

In order to survive the thirteen-year ordeal that is American public education, I dreamed, imagined my way into a life I might someday have where fathers are not alcoholic and mothers don't lie, where even people born poor do worthwhile things that make a difference in the world, a world where a person can outrun his feelings of inadequacy and shame.

How I picked up on it, I don't know, but my mantra became, "work hard, hope you're lucky, and pray—just in case you're not lucky. The working hard part was something I understood, but luck and faith rarely came to my aid, and my accumulating experience over those years played on my fears that my chances for becoming "worthy"—whatever that meant to me at the time—were slim to zilch.

What I couldn't understand then was that I was spending my time hoping others would tell me when I was worthy. I couldn't conjure the notion that I should have been worthy from the start whether other people treated me that way or not. I couldn't know back then that it would take most of the years I would live on this planet to finally acquire the belief that many others claim as soon as they can think.

TWO

A s a child, I wanted to believe in God. I wanted to believe there was magic for changing my life, something that would make me into someone else, someone self-confident, someone other people liked to spend time with, someone like the boys and men I wished I could be. I had it in my head that God was a granter of wishes, and all I had to do was to be good, to chat with Jesus every once in a while, and to try to read the Bible my grandmother had given me. I tried for a while. When nothing came of it, I tucked the whole concept of a loving God into a nook of my brain alongside the debris of other disappointments. I was done with religion, and spent considerable time as a young man throwing stones at the sky (literally and figuratively) and telling the God who was supposed to be there to go fuck himself ... wishing that same God would knock me on my ass for saying such a thing ... knowing nothing was going to happen, and I was on my own, alone in this shell of a body given me through the careless mixing of genes from my parents' bodies in a moment of passion.

THREE

In winter, our house and my uncle John's house (just down the road from ours) were heated by wood ... wood that no one ever seemed to anticipate needing until winter crawled up on somebody's lap and kneaded its cat-like claws through the fabric of their existence and demanded attention.

"Goddamn it," was the thought I wasn't allowed to say as I tried to extract myself from the needle-sharp lacerations of cold and accept the yearly ritual of spending nearly every weekend working with my father and uncle in the woods felling trees and cutting them up for firewood for the two households.

I dreaded the task, not so much for the work involved, but for the inevitable fights that would occur between the warring parties of fathers and sons: my father and uncle vs. my brother and cousin, whose concepts of work were radically different from what my dad and Uncle John expected of them. Their ideas about "helping" were to be as unhelpful as possible, enrage their fathers, and hopefully get dismissed for being more of a pain to manage than they were worth. They were masterful in their ability to disappear from the worksite when they weren't being monitored. Many times, my father or my uncle had to go in search of them (sometimes finding them further off in the woods running around, playing games; other times finding them in one of the two houses watching TV). Early in the yearly process, the men would drag the two boys back to the worksite, demand that they engage in helping ... that they learn responsibility. Inevitably, the boys would continue to do as little as possible and stay only long enough to find another opportunity to escape. The war of wills was fought for two winters that I can remember.

Ultimately, they escaped for good. My brother, Sam—twelve or thirteen-years-old at the time—was first. On the day it happened for him, he was standing around with his hands in his pockets while the rest of us worked. Angry, my father let his finger off the chainsaw's trigger and yelled at him to help. My brother refused. After several demands were ignored, my father, on the verge of resorting to physical force, yelled, "Get the hell over there and help, or I'm going to kill you, Goddamn it!" My brother, always defiant, sneered at him, didn't move, just stared at him, daring him to act. (The threat of "I'm going to kill you," was something said so often it was meaningless, or so Sam had assumed.) On this occasion, my father became more furious than usual at my brother's failure to do anything other than stare. He revved the chainsaw, and ran toward Sam, yelling once again, "I'll kill you," but this time adding, "you son of a bitch." Fortunately for Sam, there was enough distance between our father and him that Sam had time to get a head start on running. He left our father in his wake and made it safely to the house where he knew our mother was likely to protect him. I watched it all, trying to believe that my father would have stopped short of using the chainsaw to carve my brother up, maybe set the chainsaw down and go at him with his fists. But he stopped at the house, ranted just outside the door as if it could somehow convey his anger better than the chainsaw had, and then he returned to the worksite. Sam had won. When it was over, and my father made it back to where the rest of us stood, there was nothing to say. We worked until the work was done. I anticipated the inevitable end-of-the-workday showdown between the warriors, my brother accepting the accusations of being worthless, maybe taking a couple of blows ... and then taking pleasure in watching his father give up on him and leaving him alone. Obstinance was the one weapon he had. He used it well ... and I envied him for it.

My cousin, on the other hand, wasn't chased by a madman with a chainsaw; he just stopped coming out to "help," and my uncle didn't explain it or speak of it again. Thereafter, there were three of us—two men and a boy—harvesting green trees that did not burn well, the ever-present blue smoke of the chainsaw hovering above us like despair.

FOUR

Schooled largely in plowing, harrowing, disking, and harvesting behind a team of horses on his father's farm, my father was ill-prepared for the world beyond his youth, new-fangled products and ways of thinking, confusing ideas about the way things were supposed to work. He liked black and white much more than gray, or at least, that's what he tried to believe. I often wondered what kept him locked into the past, a life that couldn't sustain a single man, let alone a man with a wife and children. I wanted to understand him but didn't know the right questions to ask, wasn't mature enough to have framed the real questions I wanted answered like, "Who are you under all that façade of ignorance?" "What happened to feed the seething anger you obviously have."

His life—his part of my family history—came to me in fragments—a small handful of jigsaw puzzle pieces long-since separated from the others and from the box where the completed picture might have been printed. They were abstract images that became soggy in the sweat-soaked pockets of my efforts to understand him and who he had been before I knew him: hints of carousing and tomcatting, obsession with "coon hunting" and "coon dogs," and work ... always work, ball- breaking hard work ... the war that did not call him to service when it took three of his brothers—one younger than him—all of whom spent their tours retrieving bodies from battlefields in places my father couldn't pronounce ... how he met my mother and what made them think they loved, when they so obviously did not ... had he ever had courage?

Farm hand, construction worker, trash hauler, odd-jobs worker, and finally factory worker running a mill press for dental chair parts ... my father always found work of one kind or another and yet never seemed to be able to make enough money for my mother to buy groceries and pay bills. I remember well being at the Welfare Department where my mother and I waited to pick up blocks of processed cheese, pounds of butter, and boxes of powdered milk. Though I was a small boy at the time, I have never forgotten the shame that swept over me like a high wind and threat of rain that causes oak leaves to curl. Thereafter, corn-meal mush firmed up in the refrigerator to be cut into thin slices—the remnant in an otherwise empty refrigerator—that could be thin-coated with jelly was better food somehow, to my way of thinking, than ever going to the Welfare Department for hand-outs again. My mother went alone thereafter.

Being poor didn't seem to bother my father. He made the money. Paying bills and buying groceries were my mother's problems. He took whatever he got in the way of food, accepted whatever she told him about bills and the paying of them. "Rob Peter to pay Paul" was the money management technique my mother adhered to. That she tried to stretch money my father made was the incessant lie she told. "Wish Books" from Sears and Montgomery Ward and others called to her like a song of heartfelt love not to be refused. The charge card she got in my father's name forging his signature ravished her like the men in her endless supply of romance novels who made passionate love to the women there. She always said that if my father ever signed his own name, he'd be arrested for forgery, but it was him they came after when payment was due. When phone and electric services ceased, my father, whose name was on the bills, was the cause according to my mother. He was a drunk. Worthless.

FIVE

I don't remember how old I was when I first started keeping a hard, glass, quart-size "pop"[15] bottle beside my bed, carefully placed within easy grabbing distance to fend off my father if he were to come at me in a drunken rage. Strange how it all comes back to me after all these years, the fear, the sounds of furniture harshly scraping the floor in the kitchen below my upstairs bedroom, the crashing and smashing of whatever was at hand for my parents to use in their battles ... I can still hear their voices: My father's slurred, degrading words and threats; my mother's ceaseless knife-like and twisting regurgitations of his inadequacies and failures as a husband and provider piercing his body before a sugar bowl slammed against his head, while I cried into my pillow.

In my kinder moments, when my father had stopped drinking for a while, I consciously tried to think of him as a man doing the best he could do to provide for us and that my mother was unnecessarily cold to him, unnecessarily vindictive and unforgiving. I tried to reconcile that he was liked by his friends and neighbors. He worked hard. He didn't speak ill of my mother when he was sober; he wasn't mean to my brothers or me unless we openly defied him, refused to do our assigned chores, or my mother sicced him on us for our misdeeds and said we needed a lesson with the belt ... but then he'd drink, and my noble thoughts vanished into the clouds of danger that filled our home.

And yet, I liked being with him sometimes. He and I spent many weekends working on construction projects that brought in extra money. He treated me well because I knew how to work.

I had learned quickly how to anticipate his moves, and put the right tools, nails or screws in his hand at the right time. He took pleasure in that. I never received any payment for my time. It didn't occur to me that I should. The compensation for the pains in my back from lifting items too heavy for my age and my long, skinny body was that I had time to heal before the next project if I could work the healing in around doing daily chores and school-work. Back then, it was enough for me that he told his friends I was "a hell of a good worker."

But then he would drink again. One drunken rampage after another added to my mother's commentaries about him. Her unhappiness was his fault, and therefore, I should hate him ... and I did at times. It hadn't occurred to me that he might have hated me as well for taking her side. I was around fifteen or six-teen-years of age when in one of his drunken tirades, I became a "fucking faggot." In those two words he destroyed me, forced me to face feelings I had never defined and now knew were the equiv-alent of a death sentence; in that moment I was changed forever. I was a fucking faggot—everybody could see it, knew it, but me.

At first I was angry: I was a fucking faggot, the same fucking faggot who had once saved him from the knife blade my mother wielded against him ... stepped between them, took it from her before she brought it down against his chest ... my father cowering behind me like a frightened little boy; a fucking faggot adolescent who continued to do the work of a man whenever needed and keeping his own anger in check as he waited to be eighteen—a fucking faggot who lost himself in the struggle to avoid becoming like his father. When I was done being angry, I settled into accep-tance of his verdict like accepting a diagnosis of terminal cancer.

SIX

I paid for college degrees with loans, paid for the failures of two marriages with holes in my heart and estrangement from two of my four children and their children, and arrived on the precipice of old age still trying to determine what parts of my existence were real and which were the creations of my imagination. I was a college professor, a husband, a father, a writer, an artist, an actor … I had all the credentials of acceptance within the middle class … everything but the belief I was worthy of any of it.

There is a saying, "A man is not a man until his father dies." It's not true, of course, but it seemed to matter when I last saw my father and knew he was on the verge of death. As I stood in the nursing home in Brockport, New York, my father asked me if I was his doctor. Still feeling the resentment I had allowed myself to feel about him and my upbringing, I thought about saying, "Yes, I am your doctor, your son with the PhD who broke the familial chains of poverty and made it into the middleclass with no support from you whatsoever." There would have been no point; I would have felt guilty for saying it out loud to an old and dying man; even without the dementia, he would not have grasped the irony. I lied to myself that it didn't matter anymore and said confidently, quietly, sadly, "I am your son: Ron!"

"You're my son?" my father asked? "Ronnie. I know you!"

"Actually, you don't know me at all," I thought, but wouldn't say. I made small talk about driving from Ohio because I wanted to see him. I reminded him of things we had done together while he looked beyond me and then started talking as if he hadn't heard a word I had said. He talked about how we were going to fix "that hole in the wall"—the one that he could see, and I could not; how we were going to go hunting later with two long-dead hounds he had named "Rex" and "Queen," but first he needed a nap. He talked in bursts and then nodded off for a while. I watched him sleep, studied the characteristics of the face that I saw in my own. When he awakened again, he had forgotten who I was. I reminded him. At one point, he remembered he had other sons though he couldn't recall their names. When I named them, he wanted to know where they were, why they didn't visit. I made the mistake of reminding him that my brother, Andy, had died five years earlier. Shocked and weeping, the old man wanted to know why no one told him ... and then he forgot again and restarted telling stories I had heard my whole life, asking, "Did I tell you about ...?" And I would say "yes," though I knew it meant nothing. He tried to tell whatever he was wanting to tell again, forgot the details and then trailed off into talk of fixing the broken wall, working, hunting, asking me who I was ... an endless loop until he finally slept for the night and I kissed the whiskered cheek and whispered, "I forgive you, old man" and walked out into the loneliness that comes in the dark.

SEVEN

I am old now and sometimes think about all the living I've done as I have traipsed across the landscape of a world so different from my father's—a world better at explaining the "who" "what," "when," "where," "how," and "why" of it all, a world better at at converting violence into other forms of abuse and control. A world made wider with possibilities my father never dreamed. And yet, not so different in terms of the human heart. Early on, I too, like my father, had taken to alcohol—the model I knew for dealing with pain. I took it when I was down and then when I was up and needed it more than wanted it ... then stopped to save a failing marriage. It failed anyway, then another ... two failed marriages ... two of my four children hating me for not being enough, as their mother had taught them (the other two from a mother who had not) ... while I gained acclaim from students I taught and loved as my own ... received honors ... shared disappointment.

I have traversed two worlds and found them both wanting in one way or another, and what have I learned? Only that in the end there is love and loss, success and failure, a longing to give what wasn't wanted, and *hope*, the eternal hope, that as part of humanity, my life will have had some meaning even though there are no rewards beyond its end.

These days, I often think about how that end will come—all the potential scenarios. Most often, I imagine myself saying my last words to some fool who attempts to pray over me: "Pie in the sky? No, thanks, I've eaten plenty," and then I hope I die before anyone can say another goddamned word.

Endnotes

1 Also known as "Pie in the Sky," "Long-Haired Preachers," and "You'll Get Pie in the Sky When You Die." It was first published in the 1911 edition of the Industrial Workers of the World's Little Red Songbook. The words are set to the tune of "In the Sweet By and By." The song was originally written as a counter to the Salvation Army's opposition to the IWW's "leftist goals" of fairness.

2 Action against the Un-German Spirit. This phrase refers to the 1933 book burnings initiated by the German Student Union. The point of these burnings was to destroy books that didn't conform to Nazi ideology and books by leftist-leaning authors, particularly Jewish writers and people promoting communism and/or socialism.

3 Das Vierte Reich: The Fourth Reich. Pronunciation: Das Veer·teh Ri·shh [long "i" as in "rise"].

4 Pronunciation: Mai·daa·nuhk.

5 Pronunciation: Bel·ghick.

6 Soon, such people will be silenced." Pronunciation: Baallt ver·den zol·cha Loy·ta schtoom ge·makt.

7 "In-bys and out-bys, pillars and rooms": Terms used in coal mining. Essentially, An "in-by" is part of an underground tunnel path that leads deeper into a mine, and an "out-by" is the means for returning to the exit; "pillars and rooms" refers to areas of the mine (rooms) where coal is cut out and pillars refer to the stone and coal left in place to keep the mine from collapsing.

8 "Four squares" refers to the box shaped houses (4-equal sides) miners lived in. "Shotguns" were houses that were long and narrow; the entrance (front of the house) was usually one of the narrow sides. Both were rented to miners by the mining company. When the mines shut down, the houses were sold on the open market.

9 This narrative is loosely based on events that took place in West Virginia in 1903 combined with another reported story (date unknown) of a man who was hanged three times. Newspaper clippings are adaptations of actual news articles of the period. Names of characters and places are fictitious.

10 Scabs: People brought in to replace union workers on strike. They were often brought in without being told they would be displacing other workers and being used for "union busting." Sometimes they were just people desperate for work regardless of the impact on others.

11 The Baldwin–Felts Detective Agency (1890s - 1937) became a resource for companies battling labor unions. They played a major role in the violence against striking miners in the Battle of Stanaford on which this short story is based. They continued to do such work for many years thereafter and played a major role in the notorious Battle of Blair Mountain in 1921. The Pinkerton Detective Agency worked similarly.

12 Powerhouse: Building containing the machinery for lowering and raising the elevator through the mine shaft. The elevator is used for moving men, supplies, and equipment into and out of the mine and used for lifting loaded coal cars up to the tipple.

13 Tipple: a specific tall structure where coal was dumped ("tipped" out of coal cars) in preparation for loading train cars that would haul the coal to market. In a shaft mine, the tipple is uses an elevator system for lifting the coal out of the tunnel and taking it up to the "sorting" areas above. Trains pulled their empty coal cars under the tipple and were then filled from above.

14 Truck System: This refers to the practice of employers paying workers in scrip (company-manufactured tokens) rather than cash. Scrip was only of value in the company's store where prices were much more expensive than stores in nearby towns. Company stores extended credit to miners who quickly ran up

debts and found themselves working only to pay off the company store's bills. The practice was eventually stopped due, in part, to union influence, but continued in some places up until 1938 when it was finally outlawed.

15 A "pop" bottle both physically and metaphorically.